THE DARKEST HOUR

The Surrender Series - Book 4

LAUREN SMITH

For Terri and Craig. I'm so honored that you named your son after Royce Devereaux. I'm blessed to have you in my life.

Cover design by Cover Couture

Stock Photography © Shutterstock and DepositPhotos

ISBN: 978-1-947206-53-3 (ebook)

ISBN: 978-1-947206-54-0 (Trade paperback)

1

Long Island, The Gold Coast

MacKenzie Martin rubbed her eyes, which were blurred from staring too long at her computer screen. The antique clock hanging behind her desk ticked away, and she could see the numbers reflected on the monitor. Ten minutes before eleven. It had been a really long day and she just wanted to be done with her work.

Rain tapped softly against the window. Kenzie couldn't see any of Hampstead University's campus through the darkened pane. It was unusually warm for the middle of December, warm enough that she'd trudged through icy rain rather than snow to get to the campus offices. Usually the campus would be buried in snowdrifts which was typical for Long Island this time of year. All she wanted to do now was get home, take a hot bath, listen to some music, and fall into bed. But she had to finish what she'd come to do.

She focused on the screen and entered the final grades into the university's online grading software. As a graduate student and teaching assistant to Dr. Devereaux in the paleontology department, she had the "lucky" job of inputting his grades for the semester. Dr. Devereaux despised logging grades into the university system, and whenever she mentioned it he went rigid before rattling off a dozen excuses of things he had to do instead before he vanished from the office so quickly papers were still ruffling.

She shouldn't have been surprised. He was not the sort of man to sit idly behind a desk and read through hundreds of essays.

Kenzie smiled. Royce Devereaux was *anything* but idle. He was a tall, dark-haired, brown-eyed walking sex-god. With muscles that made her stomach flip whenever she saw them and an ass made for gripping during hot, wild sex, Royce was like catnip mixed with ecstasy. During the in-person job interview, she'd had to relearn how to speak because he'd fried all of her circuits when he'd flashed that sexy *I'll-fuck-you-good-baby* grin at her.

He hadn't made a move on her during the interview, of course. He'd been a perfect, but all-too-tempting gentleman as they discussed her duties as a teacher's assistant and the possible research projects they'd work on together.

Protoceratops were her specialty, and she'd focused on that over and over in her head rather than the thought of her future boss sliding everything off his desk so he could bend her over it and take her until she screamed. She bit her lip, trying to erase that particular fantasy. It had been a recurring dream she had every night whenever she and Royce worked late into the evenings.

Saturday nights were off-limits, though. He never worked that day of the week, and she knew why. When he wasn't deep into a dig in the Badlands of South Dakota, he was usually paired with the latest flavor of the month. Not that she knew that for certain—she'd only overheard the whispered chuckles and agreement to meet for drinks at some club here on Long Island.

More than once she'd imagined herself as the lucky woman on Royce's arm. There was something about the feral intensity of his eyes when he looked at her that made her certain he would be explosive in bed. She was almost afraid to look him in the eye because she feared he'd see her darkest desires reflected back, that he'd see what she wanted a man to do to her.

Would he tie her up with those rough hands? Lay a strong hand on her ass to punish her? His tanned skin sliding over paler, softer skin as he fucked his woman into oblivion... A shiver of forbidden excitement ran through her like quicksilver.

I should not be fantasizing about my professor.

She felt guilty that she even had such thoughts. It was far from the professionalism she wanted to project. But she wanted a taste of that darkness so bad that it made her body ache and throb to the point of pain.

I'm screwed up. I should be happy with the guys I've dated and the nice sex I've had.

Nice. That was how she categorized her past sex life. And it more than anything else described the problem.

It was a battle she fought every day. Her little desk faced his across a large office. More than once she had glanced up and seen him leaning back in his chair, wearing faded blue jeans, his biker boots propped up on the corner of his desk as he sketched out lecture notes, a pen cap hanging from his lips. He would tap a light, unrecognizable rhythm on his desk with two fingers, and his rich chocolate-brown hair would fall across his eyes. Royce would eventually get bored and toy with the tyrannosaur claw he had on his desk, a small trophy from a dig in Montana.

He never noticed her watching him. It would be embarrassing if he ever found out she was crushing on him in such a big way. Besides, she couldn't be in a relationship with the professor she worked directly under. If she wanted to date any other professor she'd have to file paperwork with the department, but if she dated Royce she'd have to stop working with him.

Even knowing how off-limits he was, she clung to her fantasies. Despite the fact that they were both adults—she was twenty-eight and he was thirty-three—there was a professional code of conduct that professors and grad students had to maintain. In just five months she'd be done with her program and have her own doctorate. Then they'd be equals, at least in their profession.

Kenzie had worked with him for an entire year, often late into the night, and she had gotten to know a lot about the infamous Dr. Royce Devereaux. As an undergrad she had been spellbound by the sexy professor who rode a million-dollar one of a kind Harley Davidson Cosmic Starship motorcycle and looked like an Armani model. Now she was working alongside him and was even more fascinated by him.

Maybe it was totally normal to fantasize about a man she spent most of her time with. Maybe she was just bored. Her sex life thus far had been average at best. The only time she ever got hot and bothered was when she thought of Dr. Devereaux. Sometimes just thinking about Dr. Sexy got a little too real for Kenzie, and she had to force herself to take a step back.

"God, if I don't leave now I'm never going to get home." She knew she shouldn't be talking to herself, but she often did when she worked late on her own. Sometimes the campus creeped her out late at night.

She exited the program on her computer and had just shut it down when she heard a distant crash, like the shattering of glass. Kenzie froze, her ears straining to pick up any sound.

There was an eerie silence before a hiss of low whispers rippled up from the hall toward Dr. Devereaux's office. A janitor wouldn't be whispering or talking to anyone, right? Kenzie tried to ease out of the desk chair, but it creaked and she winced at the loud sound. The lamp on the corner of her desk was still on, calling out like a beacon to whoever was down the hall.

Shit.

Footsteps echoed against the stone floor outside, and Kenzie had no choice but to hide and pray they weren't interested in breaking into *this* office. She pushed her chair back and ducked under her desk, hiding in the space beneath. An instant later she heard voices directly outside.

"It's locked," a voice growled. "I thought you said you saw someone in here."

"Of course it's locked, you moron. Just break the glass, Monte."

"We're supposed to be using code names. So shut the fuck up, *Gary*," the second man snapped.

"Oh for fuck's sake, just do it!"

Oh shit...oh shit...

She held her breath, but her heart was beating like a drum.

The office window shattered. The frosted glass scattered across the floor, stopping right at the edge of the desk she hid under. Kenzie stared at the pieces, inches from her hands, fragments of Royce's name scattered in wild disarray. She closed her eyes, panting as her heart raced.

There were more muffled curses, the click of a deadbolt unlocking, and then a creak as the office door opened.

"He's in here. I know he is. I saw the light from outside," Gary said.

"I don't see anyone," Monte muttered.

Black boots appeared by the edge of her desk. Kenzie swallowed the sudden lump in her throat and tried to hold her breath.

"Light's still on." The man leaned over her desk. "Computer's warm too."

Kenzie couldn't think. Every instinct told her to run, but she couldn't.

Maybe they'll leave if I'm quiet.

One man jumped down to the other side of her desk and crouched, like a cat leaping in front of its prey. She jumped up, hitting her head on the underside of the desk. His face held an evil grin.

"Well, well, who do we have here?" He snagged her by the arm, dragging her out into the open.

"Let go of me!" She balled a fist and smacked the man in the jaw.

"You little bitch!" he bellowed, and backhanded her across the face. She crumpled against her desk, clutching her face. The man still held her by the arm, his grip now bruising.

"Who the fuck is that?" Gary demanded.

Monte shook Kenzie roughly by the arm. "How the fuck should I know?"

Gary stepping closer to her. "Who are you, and where is Devereaux?"

They're looking for Royce, here, in the middle the night? What the hell had her professor gotten himself into?

"I'm his TA. I don't know where he is. I swear."

Monte's eyes swept up and down her body. The predatory gaze made her skin crawl.

"If you lie to us, we'll cut you into little pieces and throw you into the sea, you got me? After we've had some fun, of course." He laughed, and his friend sneered.

Kenzie tried to think fast. What was someone supposed to do in a hostage situation? Negotiate? Comply? Resist? Right now she felt like throwing up and crying—but that wasn't going to save her life.

"Please, I don't know where he is. Just let me go. I won't tell anyone you're here."

"Where's your phone?" Gary demanded.

She didn't answer, but she couldn't stop her gaze from darting to the brown leather purse on the couch by the door. Monte jerked his head, and Gary picked up her purse and emptied the contents onto the floor. When he saw her phone, he picked it up and turned it on.

"What's his number?" Gary asked.

Kenzie stared at him, lips pursed in silence as she held her breath. He scrolled through her contacts until he found Royce's number. Then he pulled out a gun and pointed it at Kenzie's head. She stared down the barrel, fixated on the tiny black hole that could end her life in an instant.

"Tell him you need him to meet you here," said Gary. "Make up some excuse. If he doesn't come, we'll shoot you and find him another way."

"And if he comes?" she whispered.

"Then we get him to help us. We have no intention of hurting him. Once we have him, we'll be on our way."

"Help you with what?" She couldn't imagine Royce would have any connection to men like this. He was rich and had the world was at his fingertips. The only thing he indulged in was that club. Thugs like these weren't a part of the Gilded Cuff crowd, though. So who were they?

"Devereaux has expertise in an area of our boss's latest business venture," Gary explained.

Smugglers? It was the only thing that came to mind.

Kenzie swallowed hard. Why would smugglers want Royce? It also occurred to her that when bad guys told someone their plans, they didn't typically leave that person alive to talk about it.

Monte was still gripping her arm when his phone rang. He glanced between her and Gary as he answered. "Yeah? Stay downstairs by the van. We have a plan to bring him to us. Keep an eye out and call if you see him." Then he hung up.

Kenzie focused on the details, trying to calm down. Three men. Monte, Gary, and an unknown third. Gary was short, muscled, and bald, with cold black eyes. Monte was tall and lean with hard lips and icy blue eyes. She tried to memorize their faces and their voices so that she could identify them later.

Assuming they didn't kill her.

Gary hit the dial on her phone and the speaker button. Then they all waited, listening to it ring. The room was so silent that she swore everyone could hear her pounding heart.

Finally the voicemail cut in.

"This is Royce. Leave a message."

Gary nodded at her.

Kenzie licked her lips. "Hey, Dr. Devereaux. It's Kenzie. I'm at the office. I know it's late, but you need to come here right away. It's really important and can't wait till tomorrow."

When she was finished, Gary ended the call and lowered his gun.

"Fuck. He might not check his phone. We should have our guy in the PD put a BOLO on his car." He turned back to her. "Seems like we might not need you after all." He set the gun down and looked at Monte, who suddenly grinned. A wave of terror rolled through Kenzie, and she tried to think fast.

"H-he could be in the teachers' lounge. They have a couch

he sleeps on when he works late. It's just down the hall. I'm sorry I didn't think of it earlier."

Monte narrowed his eyes. "Why didn't you say that before?"

"Because you have a gun on me and I'm fucking scared."

A cold draft seeped in from the cracked window between her desk and Royce's. Although it was shut for the winter, there was always a sliver of a chill that got in. It gave her a wild and completely insane idea. If she could get Monte and Gary to leave her alone for one second, she could climb out that window. There was a drainpipe she could shinny down, and it was just one story. If she fell it might not hurt that bad, and her car was only fifty feet away in the student lot. If she could escape, she might not die tonight.

"Gary, go check it out."

"It's the fifth door on the left. He might have locked himself inside." If he broke the window, she'd hear it and know he was busy checking the lounge. That would leave her alone with Monte, giving her one quick chance to try to escape.

Monte's fingers loosened on her arm as he leaned back against the desk. There was a phone there, an old nineties-style one that was big and hefty. She could use it to knock him out, at least long enough to get to the window.

She reached her free hand for the phone while Monte watched the door. The moment she heard the glass shatter down the hall, she snatched the phone from the desk and swung it, haymaker style, right at Monte's head. He started to turn around, but it was too late. The phone smacked into his temple with a loud crack.

He released her arm, and she grabbed her phone and keys from the floor, shoving them into her pockets. Then she ran for the window. It groaned as she forced it halfway up.

Monte clutched his head as he staggered toward her. "You fucking piece of shit!"

Fuck, fuck, fuck! She kicked out the still open window. The glass shattered and the windowsill fell down, but it left a space big enough for her to get through. She scrambled through the window, but just as her hands closed around the drainpipe, Monte grabbed her feet and began to tug her back inside.

"No!" She screamed and kicked wildly, every instinct sending her into flight mode. Her boots connected with something that crunched, and Monte howled in pain. Her grip on the drainpipe slackened. Cold metal scraped her palms as she slipped and fell fifteen feet to the ground. The bushes crunched as she landed on them, and their branches jabbed her as her breath rushed out of her lungs.

It took every ounce of willpower for her to get up and run. Everything hurt, and she was shaking bad enough that she could barely walk, let alone run. One of her knees stung, and she felt something warm run down her leg. *Blood.*

Kenzie raced for her gray Mazda in the student lot around the corner. She scrambled to dig her keys out of her pocket as she reached the car. She expected Monte or Gary to stop her at any moment, but less than a minute later she was speeding out of the lot. Glancing in the rearview mirror, she sagged in relief at the empty road behind her. No one was following her.

Her hand reached for her cell phone to call the police. It took her two tries before she got 911 dialed.

"Nine-one-one, what is your emergency?" a cool feminine voice asked.

"My name is Kenzie Martin and..." She froze, remembering what one of the men had said about their man in the local police department. "There's been a disturbance at the university. Someone broke into the campus offices."

She hung up the phone, cursing. Then she called Royce again. This time he answered, and his gruff voice made her want to cry with relief.

"Kenzie, you know my policy on Saturdays. This had better be an emergency."

"It is," she gasped, her eyes blurring with tears. "Please, I'm so scared, I—"

Royce's tone changed completely. "What's wrong? Tell me what happened and where you are."

"I'm driving. Where are you?"

"Kenzie, pull over to the side of the road and take a deep breath."

"I can't," she gasped. "Some men broke into your office, Royce. I barely got away. I can't stop."

There was a heartbeat of silence, and then Royce was back in control.

"Follow these directions exactly, do you understand me? It's a safe location. You're going to drive to the Gilded Cuff. It's a nightclub in an old warehouse. Ask for me at the front desk."

Kenzie took note of the directions as she drove, and when she felt she could handle it, she hung up. Her hands were shaking, but she gripped the steering wheel tight, refusing to let herself panic more than she already was. She was going to Royce and to a safe place. It was going to be okay. Soon her breathing calmed and she was able to think a little more clearly.

She kept the car lights off as she drove, only turning them back on when she reached the turn in the road Royce had directed her to. She knew the cops weren't likely to be out on this particular road. She'd never thought she'd be afraid of cops, but if one of them was involved with Gary and Monte, who could she actually trust?

The nightclub was hidden just off a little road, and the

club itself occupied a huge old warehouse. He had described exactly how to get there over the phone.

No doubt he'll be pissed for ruining his Saturday night.

But she didn't care. She'd had a gun shoved in her face, and two men had threatened to kill her. Because of him. Kenzie knew at some point she was going to come to a grinding halt and the shock of what she'd survived was going to set in. But she had to fight that off for now and focus on the next step, then the next, and however many more it took to feel somewhat safe again. She almost missed the sign for the road that led to the nightclub. She parked right in front, not caring that the sign in the spot she'd taken said "Reserved."

Her body stung and ached as she walked to the door of the club. The rain drenched her clothes, making her shiver. The club's front door was made of heavy oak, and she used the last bit of her strength to pull it open. Her breathing echoed harshly off the craggy stone walls and floors of the lobby. For a second Kenzie simply stood there, listening the sound of her own breath bouncing back at her from every angle.

You got this far—you can keep going. She wasn't a fan of nightclubs in general, but she wasn't going to let a strange new setting scare her, not after everything she'd been through tonight. If anything, she'd feel safer in a crowd.

A fancy antique desk was toward the back of the lobby, close to another door. The woman behind the desk was studying the screen of a sleek computer monitor. She wore a pencil skirt and fitted jacket, and her hair was pulled up in a fashionable chignon, like some kind of sexy librarian. A man in a black suit stood behind her, and his grim expression showed a brief flicker of surprise at Kenzie's disheveled state.

"Mistress Aria." The sound was a low murmur, but Kenzie heard it due to the acoustics in the room.

The woman at the desk looked up at Kenzie, now standing in front of the expensive antique desk.

"Excuse me, could you tell Royce Devereaux someone is here to see him?" she asked, shivering.

"I received no instructions that he was expecting any guests, which means you are not permitted inside to see him." Aria glanced at the man behind her before meeting Kenzie's gaze. There was some sense of controlled power about the woman.

Mistress Aria. Why had the man called her "Mistress"? That was such an old-world sounding word that didn't fit with a nightclub. Aria reminded her of Royce, with that cool, bossy attitude. She'd never admit to anyone that it turned her on a little when he got that way.

Sometimes he'd tease her, saying little things that set fire to her body, like *"Little Mac, you better get that lecture ready or I'll remind you who's in charge."* He'd smile at her like he was thinking something particularly wicked and wonderful. Yet he'd never said anything bad enough to get either of them in trouble. He knew how to walk the line between acceptable and not. And God, she wanted so badly for him to just cross that line and do what his eyes seemed to promise.

"I know all the members of the club, which means I know that you are not one. I cannot give away any information regarding our members to nonmembers, and I will not allow you to enter the club to speak to them. We are also not open to new memberships at this time, so please don't pretend to ask for a tour."

Kenzie shook her head. "I don't care about that. I *need* to speak with Royce Devereaux. It's an emergency. I'm his teaching assistant at the college. He said I should come here. Just go ask him. *Please*."

She paused, remembering how the man behind the desk had addressed this woman. Maybe it would curry more favor if she did the same. "*Mistress* Aria." She lowered her head, doing her best to look pitiful, which wasn't hard considering how much pain she was in and how scared she was. If Aria didn't let her speak to Royce, she was going to call him again.

The woman was silent for a moment. Kenzie didn't dare look up to see if her behavior was having any effect.

"Very well. What is your name, little one?" Aria asked.

"MacKenzie Martin."

Aria arose with a nod to the man behind her. "Stay here with her, Bruce." She walked over to the door at the back and disappeared behind it.

"Please, take a seat, Ms. Martin." Bruce escorted Kenzie over to a bench against the wall. She sat down and curled her arms around her chest, shaking from the cold. Water dripped from her hair onto the bench and pooled at her feet. Her heart was still pounding heavily. The door opened, and she lifted her eyes.

When she saw Royce Devereaux, her heart stopped. He wore jeans and a black T-shirt that hugged his torso tight enough to fill her stomach with butterflies.

"Dr. Devereaux?"

He strode over and knelt down on one knee, cupping her cheek, turning her face to his. "Kenzie, what happened?"

She suddenly realized how she must look right now, and she closed her eyes, blinking as tears flowed down her face. Royce brushed a tear away with the pad of his thumb.

She felt safe now that she was close to him. He had that effect on her. Royce projected strength, and he had a way of making her feel that he would stand between her and the world if she needed him to.

"Can I speak with you privately?" she whispered. Bruce and Aria were still there, watching them.

Royce's eyes narrowed. "Okay, sure. There's a room in the club where we can have some privacy. But I have to warn you, this isn't just a regular nightclub. The Gilded Cuff is...well, it's a BDSM club. Just stay close to me. You might feel a bit startled by what you see. No one will harm you."

He held out a hand, and she didn't hesitate in grasping it. She needed him to touch her, to ground her so she didn't feel like she was going to fall apart. It was the only way she could stop shaking.

But a BDSM club? Was he serious? She knew what the letters stood for: bondage, discipline, sadism, and masochism. But she'd never thought she'd get to see a real-life club where people participated in an alternative lifestyle. She was going to have to trust him to keep her safe. She followed Royce toward the door leading to the club's interior, hugging his side.

She drew in a deep breath as she stepped into the Gilded Cuff and saw Royce's private world for the first time.

2

The scents and sounds of sex surrounded Kenzie like a dark erotic haze. She clenched Royce's hand tightly as they wove through the maze of brocaded couches and past the imposing yet elegant drink bar. Kenzie stumbled as she noticed a woman clad only in expensive-looking lingerie who lay stretched lengthwise down the bar on her back. The bartender placed a row of shot glasses on the woman's torso, then retrieved a bottle of whiskey from the back of the bar and began to pour into the glasses. Men in expensive suits watched the alcohol drip over the tops of the glasses and trickle down the woman's skin.

Oh God... Kenzie pictured herself as that woman, every man's gaze on her bare body as she lay there exposed, whiskey dripping down her body. Would one of the men lick it off? Taste the alcohol on her skin and lose himself in her body? A shiver rolled through Kenzie, but it wasn't one of disgust. It intrigued her in ways she didn't have words to express. She wanted to experience that. Wanted it so bad it hurt.

The overwhelming decadence and carnality of the room was intense. Whispered sighs and the slap of leather on flesh were punctuated by the occasional gasp and shout of pain and pleasure blurring together. Men and women were bent over leather benches while Doms stood behind them, wielding paddles. A man was strapped to a Saint Andrew's cross, while a female dominant stroked the strands of a flogger along the corded muscles of one of his biceps. Submissives sat beside couches, leather collars tied with silver chains around their throats, keeping them close to their masters. It was everything Kenzie had read about in her romance novels, an erotic playground that was too decadent to be real. Yet here it was.

So this was Royce's dark paradise. She never would have imagined he'd be into something like this, but now that she was here, seeing it for herself, she could picture him here every Saturday night.

Women in sexy lingerie walked with smooth confidence throughout the room. They were nothing like her. She'd never felt so out of place in her life, and that scared the shit of out her. Her heartbeat pounded up against her eardrums. As freaked out as she was by everything she was seeing—the whips, the chains, the sexual indulgence—one thing at the back of her mind scared her more than anything: this place was turning her on.

Her body hummed at being in a place where her own fantasies could come true. She thought of the small leather cuffs she'd hidden in a box beneath her bed and what Royce might do with her if she gave them to him.

The one time she'd asked her last boyfriend to use them, he'd flipped out and dumped her the next day via text message. She'd felt like a freak, and he'd call her a girl whose "weird needs" he couldn't satisfy. The words had burned. She had gone into a funk and hadn't dated anyone since.

That had been four months ago. Since then, she'd buried herself in her work and shoved the leather cuffs deeper into the recesses of her bed, trying to forget they were there. She wished she could embrace this dark world tonight, lose herself in this land of sexual fantasy, but she couldn't. She had to talk to Royce.

He led her into a hallway with a series of heavy wood doors that each had a silver letter to identify them. She had only a few moments to appreciate the beautiful hallway with its gilt sconces and elegant artwork between the doors before Royce pulled her into the first door on the left. She halted when she saw massive black wood bed in the center. The fantasies she'd been indulging in seconds ago ground to a halt as she the reality of this moment hit her.

She'd followed her professor into a sex club and was now alone with him in a secluded room with a bed. He was staring at her, that all too sexy man, with his jeans just tight enough and a shirt that looked like it had been painted onto his body. Concern darkened his brown eyes. In that moment, all she wanted was him, and that was dangerous.

"What—" She swallowed hard. She hadn't come here to break her vow of staying away from him. No, she couldn't. *They* couldn't.

"Relax, Kenzie, it's just a bed. We needed some privacy, and the rooms here are as private as they get. Sit down and tell me what happened."

His hands touched her shoulders, gently easing her toward the bed. She collapsed onto the black velvet coverlet and saw him go to a dresser. She stared at Royce's nice tight ass in his jeans as he opened the top drawer. She sighed. What she wouldn't give in that moment to be just a girl and not his TA. They could have been on this bed together, exploring every desire she'd kept bottled up inside for years. Trying to distract herself, she focused on the room and not him.

So this is a sex room. She looked around at the walls. There were metal rings and hooks, half hidden by the expensive decor. Like a medieval torture chamber designed by Hugo Boss. Kenzie was fascinated, not afraid.

When Royce turned around, he had a small first-aid kit in his hands. He sat on the bed beside her and dug through the kit for antiseptic pads and Band-Aids. He tore open a package and lifted her injured leg on the bed. Blood oozed from a cut on her knee where her jeans had been torn during the fall from the office window.

"This may sting," he warned.

The cloth did sting as he wiped away the blood and dirt. Kenzie bit her lip, holding the hiss of pain inside. The last thing she wanted was for him to see how much pain she was in. He applied a Band-Aid to her cut, then cupped her chin and tilted her head back so she had to look up into his warm brown eyes.

How could a man who had such a dark side be so... compassionate? But then, wasn't that how true Doms were? In the romance novels she'd read, they were strong, sexy as hell. Men who fucked a woman until she couldn't walk. But then they also cared for her as if she were the most precious thing on earth.

Kenzie wanted that, wanted it so damn much. *And he can't give it to me, even if I wanted him to.* She'd worked too hard to let one mind-blowing night of sex cost her everything. It could put her doctoral candidacy at risk. All the work she'd done with Royce would be tainted by an inappropriate relationship, and the committee in the paleontology department could refuse to grant her PhD. Ten years' worth of work would go up in smoke. It wasn't as though she could start over. An inappropriate relationship with her mentoring professor would follow her to any other university. It was a *career ender*. It could also create chauvinistic and sexist expectations from men she might work with in future jobs.

"Tell me what happened." His tone was soft, but there was a strength of command in it that she couldn't ignore.

She swallowed and nodded. "I was in your office, uploading the exam scores to your database." She licked her lips, wincing at the sting of a cut she hadn't realized was there. "Two men broke into your office while I was there."

Shadows flashed across his eyes, and a strange intensity masked his features, shocking her. She was used to the calm and cool professor, the demeanor he carried through the working day, interacting with her and the students. She had even glimpsed that playboy charmer side of his—when he picked up calls from various women as she worked, unseen, next to him. But this? This was something altogether new and a little scary. He looked as though he would burn the world to ash in vengeance, and more importantly, that he had the power to do it.

"And?"

"They were looking for you, Dr. Devereaux. They grabbed me before I could get away. One hit me a few times." She reached up to touch the aching spot on her cheek and winced. That was going to leave a nasty bruise.

Royce continued to watch her, so she went on. "I tricked one into looking for you in the teachers' lounge. When the second guy wasn't looking, I climbed out the window behind your desk."

"What? That's a second-story window."

Remembering that fall made her cringe all over. "Yeah. One hell of a drop. It's how I got so banged up. I'm just glad I had my car keys in my jeans and not my purse. I drove straight here."

"Why didn't you go to the police? Or go home?"

A flush of heat infused her cheeks. "I thought they might have checked my wallet. It has my driver's license in there, with my apartment address on it."

A frown marred his beautiful face. "You should've gone to the police." He disposed of the cleansing wipes and Band-Aid wrappings. She bit her lip to keep from snapping at him.

"They said something about having an inside connection in the police department. I didn't want them finding me. And they seemed to want to talk to you about illegal trafficking. I didn't want to get you into the middle of something..." She let the words die as he faced her.

He leaned back against the dresser, his palms curved over the edge of the wood by his hips. His shirt hugged his abs, hinting at the six-pack beneath. It was a good thing he only dressed like that on Fridays and weekends. Most days he rocked a three-piece suit, which was sexy in a completely different way. More than once she'd imagined going into his office and asking to be bent over his desk for a spanking. It didn't matter what he wore in her fantasies, but somehow the T-shirt and jeans made him feel more real, like she could really lose control and beg him to take her.

Man, I have some serious issues.

"Illegal trafficking?" he mused. "I have no idea what they're talking about."

"Dr. Devereaux, I'm afraid to go back to my apartment."

His gaze softened, and he smiled reassuringly. "Don't worry. I'll take you somewhere safe tonight."

Kenzie lowered her bandaged leg over the side of the bed, wondering if he was referring to a safehouse or something. "Where?"

"My home."

She opened her mouth to protest, but that fierce look was in his eyes again, the one that made her all fluttery and a little scared at the same time. It was a commanding look, but it didn't frighten her.

"Until I figure out what's going on, I want you near me. You'll have to trust me when I say that I've been in situations like this before. Allow me to protect you. Understood?"

What could she say besides yes? Guns, trafficking, and bad guys were way out of her depth. She nodded at him.

"Good. Now, let's get you out of here. The quicker we figure this out, the better." He held out his hand again. Part of Kenzie felt she should keep her distance, but she wasn't sure she could walk through a sex club without holding on to him. It would be like Alice tumbling through the rabbit hole.

They left the bedroom and walked back through the club. The woman on the bar was still lying there, but her lingerie was gone and a man now had a hand between her thighs as he drank directly from a bottle of scotch. His fingers were playing with the woman, inserting slowly, withdrawing, toying with her, and she moaned on the counter until he set the bottle down and gave her thigh a little smack. She gasped and attempted to hold still as he resumed his teasing touches.

"Jesus." Kenzie clenched her fingers around Royce's hand as they walked by. Royce slowed and glanced down at her, then at the woman on the counter. He didn't say a word—then again, he didn't have to. She knew her face had to be fire-truck red, and she kept licking her lips. She was intrigued and a little aroused. She couldn't stop looking. And the devilish grin growing on Royce's lips told her he knew exactly what she was thinking and feeling.

"Can we go?" she begged him in a whisper.

He chuckled as they reached the door. "Kenzie, you are a delight. Just when I think I have you figured out, you manage to surprise me."

A delight? What the hell did that mean?

They left the club. Royce nodded at Mistress Aria and the serious-looking bouncer beside her before they walked out to the parking lot.

"My car," she said as they passed by the Mazda.

"Leave it. I'll send someone to collect it. Tonight we're taking mine." He nodded to the red-and-black Lamborghini Aventador parked in a reserved spot. Royce opened her door, and it lifted up rather than out. *Wow*. He'd never driven this to campus before. He noticed her eyeing him and then the car before he shut her door. The man looked far too smug at her open appreciation.

Royce walked around and got into his seat to start the car. The engine had a throaty purr, like a big jungle cat.

"Where's your motorcycle?" she asked as she buckled herself in.

Royce chuckled. "Sometimes I don't go home alone, and the women here are dressed for straddling me, not a motorcycle."

The thought of straddling him made her insides quiver. *Stop it. Don't think about him or sex.* She'd managed to be his TA for a whole year—she would not blow it now by letting herself get carried away. She changed her focus to something much safer.

"So what's the plan?" she asked.

Royce didn't speak for a long moment as he drove them down the winding New York's Gold Coast roads back to Devereaux House. She'd never been there, but she'd seen pictures on the internet. The Gold Coast was famous for sweeping American castles and 1920s era oil baron mansions. Royce's home was part of that historical legacy. The sweeping lawn, the lavish gardens, the white ashlar stone a sunny beacon amid the green foliage on summer days. Of course it would be different by night, but she felt safe now that she was with Royce. She smiled as she let the anticipation build inside of her. Would it look more like an antebellum-era ghost in a pale white gown drifting from the dark woods?

"We'll go to my office tomorrow morning and check things out, but I don't want you going home. Not until we learn more. I know a guy who has some connections with the police. He can do some digging to see what's going on there. I also want to make a few calls to some friends and colleagues."

Kenzie angled herself in the passenger seat to look at him. "Oh?"

"Yeah. There's only one kind of trafficking anyone could try to connect to me."

"What kind?" She held her breath, but she couldn't stop her heart from pounding wildly.

"Fossil smuggling."

The answer caught her off guard. "Fossil smuggling?" She knew about it, of course, but she'd never really given it much thought since it didn't relate to her work directly.

"It's a bad business. Easy to get into, and it pays well for those involved. Big finds go for hundreds of thousands in legitimate auction houses. Some steal fossils from museums and sell them on the black market. Sadly, it happens quite often, and the public never knows. Museums rarely ever publicly acknowledge the thefts. I've consulted for the New York Natural History Museum in the past to assure them that their collections are indeed legitimate and not replicas. Occasionally during that process I find out a fossil isn't from where the paperwork says it's from. Fossil smugglers lie about the country of origin if that country doesn't allow fossils to be sold." He turned the car down a narrow gravel road. Two white stone pillars marked an entrance to an estate. Iron *D*s in cursive script were carved in the stone.

"Wow." Kenzie had never really focused on the dark side of her chosen field. She'd focused on the joy of discovery and the research of the animals' lives, not how much you could sell it for at an auction block.

Rain was coming down hard on the front windshield, making it hard to see as Royce pulled the car into a circular drive in front of a large house.

"You're shaking like a leaf," Royce said.

Kenzie's body was shaking, but she pushed aside her discomfort. There was too much at stake right now. He exited the car and came around to open her door. She had never wanted a guy to open a door for her before, but there was something sweet about the gesture. She couldn't help but wonder if that was part of Royce's charm. He was the guy who'd open your door, hold an umbrella over your head, protect you, but once you were in his bed, he would be wild, uncompromising, and rough during sex. Like a god delivering pleasure to his devoted worshipers. A man like that could own the world, could own *her*.

She got out of the car walked up to the house, blinking away the rain that still fell. The house was lovely, the stones almost pearly white in the dim light. It was built in the style of one of the chateau mansions in Newport, with a mansard roof and eaves with decorated brackets below. Simple, elegant, and old-world. Her father had a thing for architecture and was always talking about the East Coast mansions.

Royce started up the steps and unlocked the front door. "My butler, Mr. Lansdown, will be asleep. I'll get you a room and something to wear to bed. You hungry?"

Kenzie shook her head. After the scare she'd been through, she wouldn't be hungry for a *long* time.

She brushed her feet on the entry mat and then gasped when she looked up. Ahead of her was a massive staircase of walnut wood. The wall cloth bordering the stairs resembled a tapestry made to look like a forest. The ends of the banister were lit with bronze lamps nestled into the wood. The soft gold glow make Kenzie feel like she was passing between worlds, leaving reality behind as she entered a wooden glen lit by midsummer fairy lights. Dark-green carpets rippled up the stairs, adding to the effect of a forest floor. She took in the entryway and staircase, her breath caught by its beauty.

A gentle hand touched her shoulder. She turned to see Royce standing there, watching her. Raindrops clung to the tips of his dark hair, glistening like diamonds before they dripped onto his shirt. He looked so...

Irresistible, like a god of storms who'd taken mortal form to seduce an unsuspecting maiden.

For the hundredth time Kenzie cursed her libido and how she longed for things, for a man, she could never have.

"Let me make you some hot cocoa at least," he offered.

If there were two things that tempted her most in the world it was hot cocoa and a hot man. Put them together and...

I'm so screwed.

Royce took her to the kitchen. It could have produced enough food for a hundred people, but it had been redesigned for more modern-day uses, including an open-concept eating area. A small table was tucked in a cozy nook next to a large walk-in pantry. Kenzie sat down in one of the chairs and watched Royce as he turned the stove on. The blue gas flames lit up, and he placed a pan on the stove. He retrieved milk, sugar, and a tin of cocoa.

Homemade cocoa? This man really was the devil.

He opened the fridge again, giving her a chance to study his profile in its sharp light. His features seemed to be cut from marble. His patrician nose and full, kissable lips were a siren's call to her. Every part of him she could see was well defined, and Kenzie tried not to fantasize about nibbling him in more than one place. He had a body made for love bites. With a slight frown, he closed the door and turned back to her.

"I hoped I had a steak or cold pack for your cheek. Some ice will have to do." He put some cubes in a bag and wrapped a tea towel around it while the milk heated. He placed the makeshift ice pack against her cheek. Their hands met when she tried to hold the bag. For a long moment he didn't move his hand away. The connection made her skin burn deliciously.

"I'm so sorry, Little Mac. You must have gone through hell tonight." He let go of the pack, but he didn't move away. Instead, he brushed a wet lock of her hair behind her ear. His fingertip lingered against her skin as she shivered, but it wasn't from the cold.

Little Mac. Mac for MacKenzie. The affectionate nickname he used when they were working in his office that drove her insane and made her feel special at the same time.

He cleared his throat and stepped back. "I better check on the cocoa," he muttered, and resumed his preparations.

When it was ready, he offered her a mug, which she gratefully accepted.

"I can't believe you made homemade cocoa." She let the heat from the mug seep into her fingers before she took a sip. Taste exploded on her tongue, and a hint of nutmeg gave it an extra kick.

"My father taught me two things: to seduce a woman you need to know how to dance and how to make homemade cocoa." As he spoke, his smile was bittersweet.

Kenzie held her breath as she hurt with him. Everyone knew the story. The Devereauxs had died in a plane crash. Royce had been nineteen and an only child. She couldn't imagine how lonely he had to have felt in this house with no one but him and the servants to keep him company.

She smiled, hoping he'd smile back. "Your dad sounds like a smart man." She was rewarded with a slow grin.

"He was. Best man I've ever known. He was an architect. He wanted to make things. Create dreams, he used to say." Royce sipped from his mug, a thoughtful expression on his face. A lock of damp hair fell across his eyes, and Kenzie fought off the urge to stand and brush it away for him.

"My dad is big into architecture too, as a hobby. And your mom?"

"She was a doctor. They didn't need the money, but she loved helping people." His head dropped a little, lost in thought. She'd never known a deep loss like that. She was lucky. Her parents were a dentist and a paralegal, both still alive. Nothing world-changing had ever happened to Kenzie or her family, but they also had never suffered a loss. She was fortunate. Yet she had a feeling she'd never truly lived either.

Royce suddenly straightened and pulled a cell phone out of his pocket.

"I need to make a call. Be right back." He slipped out of the kitchen, leaving Kenzie alone. She stood at the closed door, wishing she knew what to do next. She shouldn't stay here at his house, but she didn't want to go home either.

Please let no one find out about this. It could ruin his career and kill hers before it even had a chance to start.

That was assuming those men who'd hurt her didn't get to them first.

3

Royce slipped into the hall and leaned against the banister by the stairs as he struggled to get control. Tonight was going to be a huge test of his strength. Letting his sweet, innocent and incredibly smart teaching assistant sleep under his roof was going to damn near kill him, because he wanted her.

There were reasons he preferred visiting the Gilded Cuff. The safety and security of a place where everyone understood the rules, and everyone was a temporary player. MacKenzie Martin was not that type of girl. She was the kind a man fell in love with and married, and he wasn't the marrying kind.

Having her under his roof was like waving an expensive glass of scotch in front of an alcoholic. Just the scent of her, the feel of her hair beneath his fingers, and seeing those wide brown eyes begging for his help... She was a temptation he would do almost anything to possess.

He hadn't hired her based on her looks, even though she was sexy as hell. He'd chosen to hire her after a stellar phone interview followed by an in-person follow-up. But the moment she'd walked into his office two years ago as a twenty-six-year-old graduate student wearing nothing but jeans, a Hendrix concert T-shirt, and black Converse shoes, he had taken one look at her and known she was going to be trouble. She had that girl-next-door sweetness and vulnerability but also a touch of sass that drew him in and made him a little crazy with lust. Yet there was so much more to her than just the physical temptation.

She was funny and so smart he sometimes wondered how he'd gotten lucky that she'd wanted to work for him. When she looked at fossils, it was like she could see the past, see the ancient creatures roaming a very different landscape than the one where the bones had been found. Kenzie had a gift for reading the dirt, reading the fossils and the rocks in a way he'd never seen before. And when she talked to him about their work, her eyes lit up and her face was so full of animation, and he was fascinated. He wanted to watch her and listen to her for hours. And that was when he'd realized he wanted more than just her body. He wanted her—*all of her*.

He hadn't known he'd want a woman like that, but he did. Fuck, he *really* did. So he'd hired her on the spot. That meant he had to ignore every instinct in him to cross the professional lines that kept him on his best behavior.

It was the curse of every good dominant involved in the BDSM lifestyle; they were drawn to protect those who needed it. Kenzie was strong as hell—most submissives were—but when it came to responding to commands, they were delightfully obedient in the bedroom. He sensed Kenzie was a natural sub. Smart, feisty, and naturally equal to him, she likely had no idea that she needed a bit of kink in her bed, kink he wanted to provide over and over again until she was exhausted or overwhelmed with ecstasy.

Her reactions tonight at the club had suggested that she was a submissive in nature. The woman stretched out on the bar being handled by Jaxon, the club owner, seemed to have aroused Kenzie. Her cheeks had flushed, and she'd been unable to look away. More than just idle curiosity there. It would be such a treat to show Kenzie how fun his world could be. He was tempted to lean down and whisper in her ear, "Come over to the dark side. We have cookies and hot sex."

But dating students was off-limits, and for good reason. A BDSM relationship involved a power exchange, and someone who wasn't familiar with the lifestyle would mistake his domination as an abuse of his power as a professor and not see his being a Dom for what it was.

If he wanted to date Kenzie, she'd have to leave her position as his TA and then sign a ton of relationship forms with the paleontology department and the school. If he didn't, his reputation would be ruined. It would be a fucking nightmare. He knew he shouldn't be thinking about that right now. He and Kenzie had bigger problems, like the men who'd hurt her tonight trying to get to him.

Guilt dug into him. He should have been there working with her on the grades tonight, not enjoying himself at the Cuff. He had no way of knowing those bastards would show up, but still, he should have been there.

I just have to figure out what these men want, then I can keep Kenzie safe. He lifted his phone up and called someone he knew who could help. It rang only twice before someone answered.

"Brummer here," a deep voice said.

"Hans, buddy...I need some help." Royce grinned as he heard a dramatic sigh on the other end of the line.

Hans Brummer was a professional bodyguard. He had been employed by the family of Royce's closest friends, Emery and Fenn Lockwood, since they were eight years old. Hans had been Emery's protective shadow ever since Emery had recovered from being kidnapped as a child, along with his twin brother.

The danger to Emery was over, and his long-lost brother was home again. Now Hans was bored. For the last couple of months, Royce had taken to hiring Hans to teach them things like lockpicking, safecracking, and tactical firearms. He'd always been a fine shot at a target range, but he'd never had to shoot like his life depended upon it. Now he was glad he had improved his marksmanship.

"What did you have in mind?" Hans asked.

"Can you come over to my place tonight? My TA was attacked while working late at my office. She said they were looking for me. They roughed her up pretty bad, but she got away. I need someone I can trust to help me protect her and get to the bottom of this."

Hans chuckled. "Sounds like you need someone to watch your ass as well, Devereaux."

"Probably. You up for it?"

Hans sighed. "This is serious shit, isn't it?"

"Could be. They shoved a gun in Kenzie's face. Hit her too. She jumped from a second-story window to escape the bastards. I want to find them and make them pay." He couldn't keep the growl out of his voice as his anger built up like a storm.

"No cops?"

"Kenzie said they might be compromised. Best to keep them at arm's length."

"Understood," Hans said. "I'll be over in ten minutes. I'll bring my gear and some other fun toys. Make sure you turn on your security system. If they know where your offices are, they know where you live."

Royce wanted to hit himself. He'd been so focused on Kenzie that he'd forgotten the first rule Hans had taught him.

Make your home a safe place. He usually didn't worry about security. He'd never had a reason to, until tonight.

He pocketed the phone and went over to the small gray panel by the front door, activating the window and door sensors. Then he returned to the kitchen. Kenzie was perched on a chair, her mug of cocoa still in her hands. God, she was as cute as fuck. And every time he saw the bruise on her cheek and her split lip, he wanted to beat the shit out of the men who'd done it.

"Come on, Little Mac, let's find you a spare bedroom."

She rolled her eyes at being called Little Mac. He couldn't resist, though. It's what he usually called her at work, a way of keeping a level of deeper intimacy from forming, yet it also gave him a chance to connect with her because he *did* care, all too much.

Kenzie followed him out of the kitchen, and he led her upstairs. The Devereaux mansion seemed to impress her, judging from the way she took in the paintings and Edwardian-era furniture. His mother had loved decorating this house. It'd become a shrine to her fine taste after she died. In a way, the ghost of his happier days lingered here so long as the house remained just as it had been before his parents died. When the sunlight hit the library in the middle of the afternoon, he could almost see his mother curled up in her favorite leather armchair, a Mary Stewart book in her hands. She'd fostered his love of learning, and reading in particular.

"How many rooms does this place have?" Kenzie asked when they reached the top of the stairs.

"Ten bedrooms. Fairly small compared to the other houses on the Gold Coast. The Old Westbury Gardens, for one, is huge." He escorted her to a spare bedroom that was kept ready for guests. More often than not, Emery or Royce's other best friend, Wes Thorne, would crash there after a late night. But they hadn't been by that much lately, too busy getting married and running off on extended honeymoons. Royce felt decidedly alone in a way he hadn't since his parents died more than fourteen years ago.

"Here we are." Royce gripped the brass knob of the spare bedroom and opened the door. "My bedroom's at the end of the hall if you need anything."

Kenzie slipped past him into the room and turned, her eyes wide and soft.

"Do you have some pajamas or..." She rubbed her arms, and Royce nodded as he noticed her sweater was still damp.

"Sure, wait here." He left her and went down to his room. He didn't have any clothes for women there, but he had something that would do for tonight. He pulled out a pair of button-up striped blue-and-white pajamas with pants and walked back to the guest room. He found Kenzie standing by the tall window, arms hugging her chest.

The rain was still coming down outside, and the warmth of Kenzie's body fogged up the glass. It created an eerie ghost of her form, and the sight made him shiver. The fact that he could have lost her tonight was starting to sink in. His Kenzie. His Little Mac. Royce didn't let these thoughts continue. It wouldn't be smart to admit she meant more to him than just being his student. Over the last year he'd grown to think of her as a friend first and foremost.

He came up behind her. "Try these."

She spun and almost bumped into him. "Oh! Sorry."

Too close... She was too close to him with that vulnerable look in her eyes. Every instinct inside him demanded that he rush in and slay her dragons for her.

"I need to see to a few things. Change and take a hot shower if you need to. Try to get some rest. The security is on, and I have someone I trust coming over to help." He gave her shoulder a gentle squeeze, even though he wanted to do so much more than that. As long as she was this close he'd be tempted, over and over again.

God, I'm so screwed.

KENZIE TOOK A MINUTE TO ENJOY THIS MOMENT, EVEN though she felt some guilt that she did. She was in Royce Devereaux's mansion in a bedroom just down the hall from him. She was staying the night in an American castle with a man who starred almost nightly in her fantasies.

Keep calm, girl! She tried to remind herself not to get carried away. She was here because he wanted to protect her, not because he wanted to sleep with her.

She set the pajamas down on the bed and was starting to undress when she heard the strains of an old song drift down the hallway. It was a song she recognized—Dinah Washington's "This Bitter Earth." A beautiful, crooning song that was half a century old. Typical Royce. The man could wear a leather jacket, a Van Halen concert shirt, and ride a motorcycle to work yet listen to Dinah Washington. He was a complete mystery to her sometimes. It was as though he was trapped in the past and yet streaking toward the future. It confused and intrigued her, knowing that she'd never be able to predict what he'd do or say next.

She changed into the pajamas and padded on bare feet down the hallway. She paused at the top of the stairs, listening to the song and watching the gilded wall sconces cast gold blossoms of light on the forest wall cloth.

How wonderful it had to be to live in such a house. It wasn't like her tiny apartment a block from the school's campus. This house was a like an old-world dream, a place where princes lived and magic whispered from the walls. Kenzie placed a hand upon the polished gleaming banister and followed the song's notes down the carpeted steps and through another corridor until she saw a door ajar. Pausing at the entrance, she peered inside.

A large wooden desk sat at the back of a beautiful room with pale butter-colored walls painted with creeping vines and blossoming flowers. Floor-to-ceiling bookshelves loomed behind the desk, filled with hundreds of books. Various curious objects were used as bookends, such as a saber-tooth tiger's skull, a hadrosaur's leg bone, and a cast model nest of oviraptor eggs. The nest would have been the most valuable piece in his collection if it hadn't been a replica. She'd heard real nest fossils went for a several million dollars at auctions. Everyone loved the idea of baby dinosaurs. And finding intact eggs was rare. Eggs were fragile and rarely survived the harsh conditions that led to fossilization.

Royce was seated at his desk, boots popped up on the edge as he leaned back in his chair. He was brooding, turning a large brown fossilized claw over and over beneath the light of his desk lamp. But Kenzie knew from his expression that he was thinking about something else. This was the way he tackled difficult problems at the university. Beside his desk was an old turntable, which was the source of the haunting and beautiful song.

Royce paused spinning the claw and looked up at her. His eyes darkened as he lowered his legs from his desk and got to his feet.

"Feeling better?" he asked. His voice was soft, a rich rumble that sent delicious shivers through her. She'd never thought a man's voice could sound like liquid sin, but his did, like a glass of bourbon aged to perfection.

"I guess," she replied. "I'm still not sure all this has really set in yet. I'm not used to jumping out of windows or running from psychopaths." *I'll probably have nightmares.* That part she didn't tell him. It made her feel weak, and she knew he already blamed himself. For a man who had wicked desires in bed, he had an amazingly soft heart at times.

A frown tugged his kissable lips down. "Don't joke."

"I'm afraid I'm going to just break down if I don't."

"It's okay. I'm here, Little Mac. You should try to get some sleep." He came over and cupped her chin, tilting her head back. His warm breath fanned her face, and she trembled. They'd hardly ever touched before, just friendly pats on the shoulder or arm. Always safe. Never intimate. Kenzie thought she could keep herself distanced from him and hide her attraction. Before tonight, she'd done a good job of rebuffing his occasional teasing, but now she was too vulnerable, too exposed, and it would be so easy to get lost in him.

The light from his desk lamp cast a silhouette of their bodies against the wall, and she shivered, her heart racing. Royce's masculine aroma with hints of pine enveloped her. She wanted to rub herself against him to trap the scent on her clothes, let it envelop her completely.

Royce leaned his head down ever so slightly as she rocked up on her toes, their lips just inches apart...

A distant door chimed, and Royce blinked, pulling back. He cleared his throat. "That will be Hans." He stepped around her to get to the study door.

"Who's Hans?" Kenzie asked as she trailed after him, her body deflated with disappointment. They had been so close only to be saved by an actual bell.

"Hans is a friend. A bodyguard. He's here to help us with our little problem."

Little problem? Kenzie snorted. *I had a gun shoved in my face. I wouldn't call that a "little" problem.*

When Royce opened the door, Kenzie saw a tall muscled man in his early fifties standing there, rain dripping off his coat. A black duffel bag hung from his shoulder. He was handsome, with dark brown eyes and dark hair with a threading of silver near the temples.

Royce grinned and welcomed the man inside. “Hans.”

Kenzie couldn’t take her eyes off the bodyguard. There was a lethal grace to him that made her pause. All her instincts were telling her this was a dangerous man. With a polite and warm smile, Hans came inside and set his bag down.

“Hans, this is MacKenzie Martin, my TA.”

“Just call me Kenzie.” She blushed as Hans shook her hand while glancing curiously between her and Royce.

“Nice to meet you, Kenzie.” Hans set his bag down with a heavy thump. Whatever was in there was definitely not clothes. “So, are you ready to fill me in?” Hans asked as he wiped his boots on the mat and slipped his coat off.

“Why don’t we make some coffee first, then we’ll tell you everything.” Royce nodded toward the kitchen.

Soon the three of them sat at the table. Kenzie shared her story, and Hans interrupted a few times with questions.

“Three men?” he asked.

She nodded. “Yeah, plus whoever they have in the police force, but I’m pretty sure they were all working for someone else.”

Hans stroked his chin. “Makes sense. Usually it’s hired muscle who do the smash-and-grab jobs.” He looked at Royce, his face solemn. “She’s lucky to be alive. People like that don’t have qualms about silencing whoever isn’t crucial to their plan.”

A shiver racked Kenzie’s body. She’d known those men intended to kill her. The evil in Gary’s eyes when he’d pointed the gun at her head was something she’d never forget. She buried the memory in the back of her mind and focused on Royce and Hans.

“So what do we do?” she asked them.

"I'd suggest having the police dust for prints at your office. Even if they have someone on the take, the department still has to follow protocol. You said they weren't wearing gloves. It might give us a match for aliases. If we can figure out who hired Monte and Gary or who they have ties to, it might give us some answers. We'll have to be careful about whoever they have on the inside helping them, but I suspect the most they'll be able to do is let the perps keep tabs on what the police are up to. Tonight we should secure the house and try to get some rest."

As exhausted as Kenzie was, she couldn't imagine sleeping, not when she knew three men were out there looking for her and Royce.

"Are you okay?" Hans asked.

The bodyguard was too perceptive. "Probably," she muttered, embarrassed that she'd revealed her fears so openly without realizing it.

"I've got a Jacuzzi if you want to warm up and relax," Royce suggested. "Hans and I will be busy securing the house. You will be safe. I promise."

A hot bath did sound nice. "Okay."

Hans and Royce headed for the hall, but then they both suddenly halted, their large bodies blocking her view of what was ahead.

"Did you...?" Royce whispered softly.

Hans shook his head. "Those aren't mine. I wiped my boots on the mat."

"Shit." Royce stepped back and turned to Kenzie.

"What is it?" she whispered. Every hair on her body was standing at attention.

"Wet footprints. *Someone else* is in the house." Royce's lips formed a hard line as he gave a nod to Hans before looking at her again. "I need you to stay right here. Hide in the walk-in pantry. Don't come out, no matter what. I'll come back for you. You hear me?"

His eyes burned straight through her, and the command in his tone was undeniable. She couldn't disobey, not when he used that deep dominant voice. She shivered, half from her reaction to him and half from fear of what might happen in the next few minutes.

Someone else is in the house? Oh God, oh God...

Kenzie struggled to calm her panic and nodded to show Royce she would do as she was told. She backed up, her gaze seeking the doors of the walk-in pantry by the fridge. Her heart was hammering so hard it felt as though it was bruising her ribs.

Everything became quiet. Silent. She closed the pantry doors, her breath shallow and harsh in the confined space, a rasping whisper that grated on her ears.

Moments later, gunfire erupted somewhere in the house. Glass shattered. A scream ripped from her lips before she could stop. Kenzie clapped her hands over her mouth. An animal instinct to hide drove her to her knees and then to her stomach as she flattened herself completely on the floor.

More silence, then the crunch of glass beneath booted feet. She heard shouts, low and guttural, followed by another deafening round of gunfire. The noises were drawing closer, the crashing, the guns, all of it. She covered her ears and prayed silently for it all to stop.

Jars and cans exploded above her, food raining on her along with shards of glass. Splinters of wood showered down as pinholes of light broke through the thick pantry doors. The handle fell to the floor. Kenzie stared in horror as the doors slowly creaked open. Straight ahead lay a man on his back. Monte. His face was turned up as he snarled at the man who stood over him, his booted foot pressed into Monte's chest. An automatic pistol was aimed at Monte's forehead, and the man holding the gun was Royce.

"Your one partner is dead, and the other just drove off in your ride. You're all alone, you piece of shit." Royce leaned heavily over the man, pressing more weight on his chest.

"I don't give a fuck. I'm not talking." Monte spat, and blood painted his teeth as he smiled coldly.

"You will," Royce promised and jerked his head toward Hans, who had just entered the room. "Or my buddy here will start cutting off your fingers in creative ways. He's trained in half a dozen forms of torture. Did you know that? He's one badass motherfucker." Royce's smile was dark and frightening. "But hey, if you do talk, I won't shoot your nuts off for hitting Little Mac, you get me? No one touches her." He pressed his boot harder until Monte wheezed.

"Fuck you," Monte said. "If I talk, my boss will kill me."

Royce exchanged glances with Hans. "Maybe. But we would give you a head start. Sounds like your boss won't."

Monte gasped for breath a moment longer before he nodded. "Fine. I'll talk."

"Good. Who is your boss, and what does he want with me?"

"Vadym Andreikiv. He lives in Moscow. He hired me and Gary. Sent along one of his own men for backup, Jov Tomenko. He wants to bring something out of Mongolia. He said you're the man to help him get it out. All he said was that we have to get you and bring you to Ulaanbaatar."

"Ulaanbaatar? Why there?"

"I don't know. Something about smuggling fossils," Monte said.

"Nice. This fucker sounds like a Bond villain," Hans muttered. "What does he do, twirl his mustache in his fucking yurt?"

"That's all I know, I swear." Monte started to lower his

hands, but Royce cold-cocked the bastard with his gun. Monte's head hit the floor, and he lay unconscious at Royce's feet.

"At least I didn't shoot your nuts off. Hans, would you take out the trash? I need to check on Little Mac."

"Sure." Hans bent and grabbed Monte's legs and started to drag him out of the kitchen.

Kenzie was lying flat on her stomach, staring up at him. Her body was locked in place, every muscle frozen. Royce slowly set his pistol down on the table before he approached her.

"Kenzie, it's okay, honey." He knelt down and gently helped her get to her feet. She swayed a little, and he caught her by the waist. Her heart was sprinting inside her chest, and she was having trouble breathing.

"Easy there," he said.

She stared up at him, confused by his separate personalities. The man who joked about torturing someone and pistol-whipped a man was not the same man who held her now and called her Kenzie in that husky and gentle voice. She knew she had to be in shock again. But she just couldn't seem to snap out of it.

"Why don't you sit down?" Royce's eyes were laden with concern. "You're really pale."

She looked back to the pantry, where splintered wood and shattered glass showed her just how close she'd come to dying.

"Dr. Devereaux... I don't feel so good..."

It was all she got out before she collapsed in his arms.

4

Kenzie had fucking fainted.

Royce cursed as he caught Little Mac in his arms and lifted her up. He should have known that would have been too much for her. Hell, it had been scary as hell for him too, and he'd had training for moments like this for almost a decade. Glass crunched beneath his boots as he carried her out of the kitchen. It had been a thankfully short battle, but violent. The three men had been in the room across the hall, waiting for them to come out. He and Hans had taken positions behind the walls and managed to put one man down. Another had shot his way through the large window and escaped. The third they'd captured, but not before he had riddled the pantry with bullets.

And almost killed Kenzie.

Royce would never forget the moment he'd run in after that man had started spraying metal death along his kitchen wall. Knowing he'd been the one to tell Kenzie to hide there. It would be his fault if she was hurt. His fault if she was killed.

But the door swung open and there she was, alive and safe on the floor. Her eyes had been wide with terror. It'd taken every bit of his training to resist the urge to run to her, not while the third man was still a threat in the room.

He had dealt with that piece of shit and now had Kenzie in his arms. Safe—for now. But how long would she really be *safe* while she was around him?

Everyone I love gets hurt. It was a thought that haunted him, ever since the policeman had shown up on his doorstep and he'd learned of the plane crash. Before that, he'd lost one of his best friends at age eight to a child abduction, the infamous Lockwood twins kidnapping. That had screwed with his head too.

Fortunately in Fenn's case, he turned out to be alive, but it still convinced Royce of one thing: loving someone meant losing them. Whatever sunny memories of boys playing in the woods he may have carried with him, he could not forget the memories that came next. The endless searches for a body, the baying of bloodhounds, the faces of his best friends on every paper and TV screen for nearly two months, the hushed conversations he heard his parents have about protecting him.

It was all dark, all bad.

Royce shook his head to clear the murky thoughts of the past. He needed to focus on Kenzie and turn his thoughts to the man behind their current mess, Vadym Andreikiv. Kenzie was in danger as long as she was connected to him. If Royce had learned anything from Hans it was that in a situation like this you had to take the fight to the other side. Sitting and waiting for axe to fall was no way to live, and it gave the enemy all the advantages.

No, I'm a fighter. If Vadym wanted Royce that badly, he was going to get far more than he'd bargained for. He was going to go to Moscow and take him down.

Royce reached the spare bedroom he'd chosen for Kenzie and sat down on the bed. Tucking one pillow under her head, he lost himself in the sweet scent of her, a sexy, tempting woman who would always be off-limits. He stroked her cheek with the backs of his knuckles. Then, with a heavy sigh, he took the thick soft throw from the foot of the bed and covered her up to her chin to keep her warm.

"Rest easy, Little Mac," he murmured as he left the room.

Hans stood in the hallway, hands on his hips. "She okay? I saw you carry her upstairs."

Royce nodded. "She fainted. I think it was a little much for her."

Hans snorted. "You think? She just got dropped headfirst into your world without any warning or preparation. It's a little much for me too, and I should be used to it by now." Hans's smile didn't reach his eyes. "I called the local 5-0. They'll be here. We'll have to wake her up for them to take her statement. And then we have to call in flights to Moscow."

"You really want to fly to Russia with me? I'm touched," Royce teased.

The usually stoic bodyguard chuckled. "You forget, I *know* you, Devereaux. You are too damned cocky for your own good. You need someone to watch your back. Emery would be pissed off if I let you get yourself killed by some Ruskies."

Royce smirked. "Fair enough." He followed Hans back downstairs to wait. He didn't pick up or touch anything. The cops would treat this as a crime scene, so he went back to his office to wait and think.

His office had always been a place of refuge. No matter what happened in his life, he could always go there, shut out the present, and lose himself in the distant past.

He walked over to his bookshelves and lifted up a small fossil. It was only two and a half inches long. An *Archimediella* shell, white and rounded like a narwhal horn, with whorls overhanging the sutures that wound around the shell from base to tip. It was an ancient, primeval snail shell, yet it was also a thing of beauty, even though it was the kind of fossil one could find almost anywhere in the world.

This one had been found on a lonely stretch of New York's Gold Coast by a dark-haired woman with laughing gray eyes.

"Royce, come here, darling!" his mother shouted. She stood in ankle-deep water that rushed up the beach before it was pulled back out to sea. Royce ran across the cold sand to reach her, taking the slender object she held out in her hands. A white hornlike shell.

He wrinkled his nose and studied the object, wiping the sand off it. "What is it?"

"It's a shell, a very old one," his mother said. "A fossil."

"Like the dinosaurs?" Royce was immediately obsessed with the shell now. His room was full of dinosaur books.

"Yes, like the dinosaurs." His mother bent over and kissed his forehead, making him squirm and jump out of reach so he could wipe the offending kiss away.

"Ugh, Mom, please. I'm too old for that."

"Too old for what?" a voice asked behind him. Royce jumped at the sound. His father was a tall, handsome man with warm brown eyes that crinkled when he smiled.

"Mom's kisses. I'm too old for that, Dad." He returned his attention to the shell.

"Too old for your mother's kisses? What a pity. I never tire of them." His father rushed into the shallows and scooped his mother out by the waist, kissing her soundly. He twirled, letting his wife spin in the air before setting her down and kissing her again.

Royce watched them, smiling. Normally he would have shouted for them to stop, that it was gross, but not today. It was okay for Dad to kiss Mom. That's what a good dad did. And his dad was the best.

The memory caught Royce off guard. It was like a beacon of light cutting through the heavy shroud of darkness around his heart. The brightness made him flinch. Thinking about them, two good people dead and gone, two people who'd been his whole world—it fucking hurt like hell.

They had also set him on his course to be one of the world's most renowned paleontology experts. Every time he dug into the earth and found a new fossil, somewhere deep inside he became that boy again, seeing that shell for the first time. And for a brief moment, his parents were still alive.

Setting the shell down, he glanced out his window to see two police cars and an ambulance racing down the drive toward the house. Damn, this part was going to suck. He didn't have time to explain to the cops why he and Hans had shot a man, and he hadn't forgotten what Kenzie had said, that the men involved claimed to have a man planted in the local PD.

"Royce," Hans called out from the hallway. "The 5-0s are here. I'll wake Ms. Martin."

Royce wiped the blood off his hands before he left his office and met the officers at the door.

Half an hour later, the ambulance took the body to the morgue, and the asshole they had captured was hauled away in a cop car. Kenzie had barely spoken except to answer the questions the police asked. Royce had told her to tell the truth, even about the smuggling. He was not connected to anything bad, so it didn't matter what the cops heard. What mattered was the police finding that the fatality was in self-defense and that Royce was not required to stay for further questioning.

Fortunately, that's exactly what happened. He was sure part of that had to do with who he was. There were some perks to being the sole heir to a vast fortune on the New

England Gold Coast. He didn't usually like that he was treated differently, but in this case having the cops off his back was a good thing.

Hans escorted the officers to the door, and Royce focused on Kenzie, who was still in shock. Hell, he would be too if he'd been normal, but normal had died in him a long time ago.

"Hey, Little Mac, why don't you take a shower?" He would have suggested a bath, but he could see the look in her eyes—a glassy, almost frozen look. A shower was better for clearing a person's head after crazy shit went down.

"Okay." She bit her bottom lip. He cursed inside as the sight of her teeth sinking into the soft, pale-pink flesh of her lips made him hard. It was probably all the adrenaline from the firefight. He normally had better control.

"Come on." He held out a hand and she took it, trusting and sweet like a child, but there was nothing childish about the full curves of her womanly body. The tall, model-thin blondes he usually slept with at the club didn't feel real, and he couldn't fall in love with something fake. But Kenzie? She was the sort of woman men would fight to the death over, not just to make love to, but to keep and treasure *forever*. That was the last thing Royce needed. He knew he needed to keep his distance from Kenzie, for both their sakes. He tightened his fingers around hers, squeezing in a silent show of support.

"Come to my room. The shower is better in there," he said as they climbed back up the stairs. She looked so small and vulnerable in his large button-up pajamas. *Fucking adorable. And I'm the idiot who's telling her to use my shower.*

If anyone needed a shower, it was him. A cold one.

"Thanks, Dr. Devereaux," she said as they reached his room.

"You can call me Royce, Little Mac. We're not on

campus." He smiled at her look of startled hesitation. "Seriously, Royce is fine." After everything they'd been through together, he did not want a reminder of the big fucking elephant in the room between them.

"Royce." She smiled a little, and it warmed him inside. The smile was a good sign. She was coming out of the shock if she was showing more emotions.

As they entered his bedroom, he nodded toward the shower in the bathroom. "Go and take care of yourself. I'll have Hans make a run to your apartment for some clothes and anything else you need."

She wrinkled her nose and blushed. "He doesn't mind? I mean..."

"He won't mind, and don't be shy, not unless you've got something to hide. Do you have something to hide, Little Mac?" He was teasing, but given how wide her eyes grew, he wondered if there might be. He reached out, catching her hips in his hands so she couldn't retreat.

"I can leave a list of all the things I need," she said, avoiding the question. He could feel her trembling in his hold, and her pupils were a little dilated. So she was hiding something. Rather than pry for details, he decided he'd have Hans find out whatever it was.

"There's a notepad in the drawer by my bed. Make a list before you shower, and I'll get it to him."

He let go of her, forcing himself to remember this kind of contact was wrong. He needed to go downstairs and figure out what the hell to do about all the damage to his place while he was in Russia. He went back downstairs and found Hans in the hall with a broom, sweeping up the glass. Mr. Lansdown, the butler, stood next to him in his dressing gown, eyes wide and solemn.

"Dr. Devereaux, I can arrange to have someone out here

tomorrow morning to give us a quote on the glass and other repairs."

"Thanks. I'll be leaving for Moscow sometime tomorrow. I'll leave you to handle it. Call me if anything urgent arises."

"Will do, sir." Mr. Lansdown was used to running Devereaux House whenever Royce left for a dig or a conference.

"Hans," Royce said. "Would you mind running to Kenzie's place and grabbing a few of her things from her apartment?"

"No problem. It will give me a chance to see if her place is being watched."

"Oh..." Royce paused. "It's probably nothing, but let me know if you turn up anything interesting. I think Kenzie might have a few secrets she's hiding."

Hans raised a brow. "Anything I should be worried about?"

Royce grinned a little. "Probably nothing serious. My guess is just something that embarrasses her." Royce tucked his hands in his jeans pockets and watched the bodyguard shake his head. "Still, better safe than sorry."

Hans rolled his eyes. "You boys, your women and your secrets."

Royce laughed. No doubt the bodyguard had thoroughly searched more than a few women's homes over the years.

"I'll just go grab her list." Royce went back upstairs and heard the water running. The door to the bathroom was ajar. Kenzie's curvy body was beneath the spray, but she wasn't standing. She was huddled in a tight ball in the center, her head bowed as water rained down around her. Royce grabbed the list and ran to give it to Hans, then raced back to the bathroom. His Little Mac needed him.

KENZIE KEPT HER EYES SHUT TIGHT, BUT SHE COULDN'T

keep out the violent flashes of memory of everything that had happened tonight. The gun barrel aimed at her head back at the office, which already felt like a lifetime ago. The escape through dark and wet streets to the Gilded Cuff, uncertain if anywhere would be safe. And then the shots, the shattering glass and wood of the pantry door exploding above her.

I could have died. The panic filled her with an unexpected rage, and she shook all the harder beneath the hot water.

"Kenzie, honey..." Royce's rough voice drew her slowly out of the depths of her thoughts. She didn't look up, not at first. She was too ashamed, too mortified he was seeing her like this.

"Honey, please." The shower door opened, and Royce stepped in, still in his clothes, but without his boots. He knelt beside her, then eased onto the tile floor, his arm touching her bare shoulder. He reached his arm around her shoulders, holding her close to him.

Kenzie watched his other hand settle on one of her knees. Small cuts on his hand caused thin red rivulets of blood to trickle down from his skin to hers. She raised her head. Her nose brushed his cheek, feeling the slightly rough stubble along his jaw.

"You're hurt," she said, gazing at him. A pain hung there in his eyes, burning like a setting sun upon a distant horizon, but she didn't think it was because of the minor cuts.

"This is nothing," he said. She could almost hear the unspoken words flashing in his eyes. He'd hurt so much more than she'd ever know. She could feel the pieces splintering inside her chest.

She brought his hand to her lips, pressing a light kiss on the back of it, wishing she could take the pain from his eyes. From the moment she'd met him, she'd noticed this pain inside him, especially when he thought no one was watching. There had been a part of her that wanted to hold him close and promise she would not let him suffer any other hurts the world would bring. Yet here she was in a fetal position in the shower, unable to help herself, let alone him.

Royce's lips parted and he cupped her face, turning her toward him as he leaned down. Their mouths were inches apart, and Kenzie felt an overwhelming need to feel those lips upon hers.

Please kiss me.

"What you went through tonight was hell, I know. It's not easy to shake off the memories or the thoughts of 'What if?' But you can do this. You're safe now. You can get through this, you got me?" He stared at her lips, and she leaned into him, wanting to close the last inch between them.

He pulled away before they would have kissed. A half-hidden smile twisted his lips. "I always knew you'd be the death of me, Little Mac." The words cut but the tone was tender, which only confused her.

"You don't want...?" She swallowed her humiliation. *He doesn't want me. All this time he was just teasing me for fun, not because he was interested.*

His dark eyes were full of honeyed fire. "I do...*want*. But you've been through a nightmare tonight. No good wolf touches his kitten when she's hurt and scared, except to comfort and protect her."

"Wolf? Kitten?" she asked, not understanding the comparison.

Royce traced her lips with a fingertip. "It's sort of BDSM lingo. A Dom is like a wolf, fierce and rough but loyal and protective. The sub is like a kitten, quick, smart, with sharp claws, but she needs to be handled with care. It's a common analogy for my lifestyle. Do you know about BDSM?" he asked, still stroking her lips.

She nodded. "A little." Her body was no longer shivering.

A new heat spread through her at his close proximity and his touch.

"Never think I don't want you." He was frowning now. "But we both know that we can't. It's not wise." He growled the words as though he were as frustrated as she was with their situation.

"But you *do* want me?" If he did it would only make this harder, but she needed to know she wasn't alone in her desire. She was so tired of feeling alone and shut out from a world that was full of passion. Her friends were all in great, loving relationships. She was the only one left out in the cold because she yearned for something more, something darker.

He smiled again, a playful grin. "Yes, Little Mac. I do. Someday, when you're not so full of adrenaline and crashing from shock, I'll tell you all the things I've imagined doing to you."

She sighed, and her shoulders dropped. The hot water was burning her skin into his, almost melting them together.

"We need to get you to bed so you can rest. Hans has your list and will be back soon."

She didn't want to leave the shower or give up this rare, unusual intimacy they were sharing.

"Royce?" She watched him stand, his clothes dripping as he got out of the shower.

"Yeah?" He retrieved a large fluffy white towel and held it up for her, his face turned away. Ever the gentleman.

She paused, trying to figure out how to ask what she needed. "Can I stay with you tonight?"

"Stay with me?" He waited as she stood and took the towel, wrapping it around her body. He nudged gently for her to dry off.

"In your room...with you? I don't know if I can sleep alone right now. I keep seeing those men." She shuddered.

He watched her, his keen eyes not missing her body's

reactions to the memories. "Sure." He then smiled at her. "Guess that means no more sleeping naked. Damn."

And just like that, one little tease from him and she felt safe.

He left her alone in the bathroom, and she watched him through a crack in the door. He peeled off his soaking T-shirt, revealing a beautiful back with rippling muscles. A few cuts marred his tan skin, but he didn't seem to notice. When his hands went to the fly of his jeans, she turned away, her face flushing. She knew better than to torture herself with visions of a naked Royce. She was already going to have trouble sleeping.

Once she was dressed and her hair dried, she entered the bedroom. Royce had fresh jeans and a shirt on, and though his hair was damp he looked a little drier, as if he'd bent over and tousled it dry with his hands. He nodded at the bed.

"Get some sleep. I'll stay with you." It was a promise, but she sensed his thoughts had gone somewhere far away.

"Are you not sleeping?" she asked.

"I will, once Hans gets back. We'll take turns watching the house."

Kenzie's muscles went rigid. "You think the other man will come back?"

"I don't." His reply was confident, no sense he was hiding any worries from her. "We're just taking precautions, that's all."

Kenzie walked over to the large king-size bed. She almost had to get a running jump just to get on top of it. She pulled the covers back and climbed inside. The pillow smelled of Royce, like a rich aftershave. It was an addictive scent and so very male. She nuzzled the pillow and closed her eyes. She heard him chuckle in the darkness.

"You're deliberately rubbing in how comfy you are, aren't you?"

"Hmm," she purred softly, biting her lip to hide a smile. It was fun to tease him back for once. She'd never had the chance to before.

"Rest," he said, firmly but gently.

It was so easy to obey that voice and just drift away.

5

Royce stood beside his bed, quietly watching Kenzie as she slipped into sleep. Her breathing slowed and became deeper, and her hands unclenched for the first time in hours. The worry lines that framed her eyes smoothed as she slipped into dreams.

Damn, he had to be careful. She was his, but she could never *truly* be his. And not just because protecting her meant not letting her ruin her career for him. No, it was because life was a cruel bitch.

Whenever he thought of loving someone, he was overwhelmed with thoughts of the loss of his parents. The night they died and what had happened to them became a recurring nightmare as his imagination played out what their final moments must have been like. He was watching the runway through a small plane window. The blinking lights of the plane flashing and fading in the thick fog. The white dashes of the runway vanishing...the sudden flash before everything went dark.

After the accident, waking up became a routine: His chest constricted until he could barely breathe, and his eyes stung with tears. Then he would slowly remember where he was and regain control of his body. He couldn't take another trauma like that. He couldn't lose a loved one if there was no one to love. This was why he only took home women who knew their time together was casual.

Yet Kenzie was still his. Could a man claim a woman without ever kissing her?

Sounds from below came to his attention. A door shutting. He pulled the covers tight up to Kenzie's chin and turned off the bedroom lights before he left to check who it was.

Hans shook off the rain and glanced up the stairs as Royce appeared. He wasn't alone.

"Cody still falls asleep listening to his police scanner." Hans chuckled, and the two men behind him came into the light - Emery and Fenn Lockwood. His childhood friends. Emery had lived the life of a recluse for twenty-five years, until Fenn had been found in Colorado and brought home. Before that, Emery only had his bodyguard Hans and his resident tech geek Cody to keep him company. Not that Royce would ever call Cody a geek to his face. The kid was built like a surfer who spent as much time on the weights as the waves.

"Emery. Fenn," Royce replied slowly, sending Hans an annoyed look. He loved his friends deeply, and they were brothers in all ways but blood. That was why he didn't want either of them here right now. Because of the danger he was in, he'd never forgive himself if they got hurt because of him.

"You didn't think you'd keep this a secret, did you, Royce?" Emery grinned as he slipped off his black peacoat and hung it on the coat rack.

"Hans says you're having a bit of trouble?" Fenn shrugged off a black duster, looking every inch the Colorado cowboy he'd been until he was reunited with his brother and parents.

"It's not trouble," Royce argued, shooting Hans another

look. He did not want his friends getting caught up in all this. They'd only just survived some seriously fucked-up shit of their own. Their own cousin tried to have them killed so he could inherit the family fortune. After everything they had gone through, they deserved to be on a beach somewhere, drinking imported beer and sexing up their gorgeous wives.

"You know us better than that," Fenn said. "So what's this I hear about a grad student sleeping in your bedroom?"

Royce narrowed his eyes. "I never said she was sleeping in there."

The bodyguard shrugged. "If she isn't in your bed now, I bet she'll be there tonight. She won't sleep well alone after what happened."

Was Hans a psychic or something?

"I thought you didn't *sleep* with students?" Emery pointed out.

Royce came down the rest of the stairs to meet them. "I don't and I haven't. It's my TA, Kenzie Martin. And she's in shock. I'm just trying to keep her comfortable."

Fenn whistled, a mischievous glint in his eyes. "*The* Kenzie?"

Royce crossed his arms over his chest. "What's that supposed to mean?"

The Lockwood twins exchanged glances. Emery grinned. "Royce, you *always* talk about her. Kenzie this, Kenzie that. She's the only woman you ever talk about."

Royce huffed, ignoring whatever his friends were trying to imply. "She's my teaching assistant. I work with her. I don't spend enough time with other women to have a reason to talk about them."

"Uh-huh." Fenn was still smiling, but he quickly sobered. "So what happened? Cody woke us up shouting about shots fired at Devereaux House and a fatality."

"Hans here won't say a damn thing, despite the fact that I

sign his paychecks," said Emery. "Said it's up to you to fill us in if you want to."

He had to give Hans credit for not letting anything slip, but he'd have felt better if he'd also told the brothers to go home. He sighed. It seemed the only way out was through. "It's a long story. Come into the billiard room. I'll pour us some drinks."

Hans and the Lockwood twins followed him into the billiard room, where brandy was poured and the balls were set for a game. As they played, Royce and Hans relayed the night's events, including all that had happened to Kenzie.

"Jesus," Fenn muttered. "That's fucked up."

"So you intend to leave for Russia tomorrow?" Emery asked as he bent over the billiard table and took a shot.

"Yes."

"And you want us to look after your TA while you're gone?"

Royce took a sip of the brandy. The liquor smoothed away some of his worries, but not all of them. "Could you? I need to know she's safe."

"Of course," Emery and Fenn replied in unison. He nearly laughed. They used to do that all the time as kids. God, he'd missed that.

"So we keep an eye on your student. Should be easy," Fenn said.

Easy? There was nothing easy about Kenzie. She was a temptation no man could resist. Lucky for him they were both married.

The door suddenly burst open. Kenzie stood there in his PJs. Who knew a woman in oversize PJs could look so damned cute. She had rolled up the legs and the sleeves. *Fuck.* How much trouble would he be in if he just ripped them down and

"I'm going with you to Moscow," she said.

Royce held back the growl that started to rumble in his chest. "No, honey, you're staying right here where it's safe."

Fire lit Kenzie's dark-brown eyes. "I almost *died* tonight," she reminded him. Not that he needed that awful reminder of how close he'd come to losing her.

"Exactly. Which is why you're staying here where my friends can watch over you." He set his cue down on the billiard table and started toward her.

Kenzie stepped back but then seemed to reconsider and advanced again, her chin lifted.

"I'm involved in this now, and I'm not going to let you run off without me when I can help. I'm your TA. The *A* stands for *assistant*, so let me assist."

Emery and Fenn snickered behind him.

"You assist with grades and lectures, *not* fighting Russian fossil smugglers." Royce now stood directly in front of her, palms itching to smack her ass for disagreeing with him when it came to her safety. Was she completely ignoring him when he told her about the wolves and kittens?

"If you don't let me go, I'll just show up on my own. I have your phone LoJacked, and I can track you down in Moscow. Don't think I won't."

Royce's jaw dropped. Fenn started to chuckle. Behind him, Emery picked up his pool cue and poked Royce in the back with the tip.

"Didn't you say something about spanking the sass out of her the last time you mentioned her? Don't tell me you're getting soft now, Devereaux."

Kenzie glared at him, then she glanced toward his friends behind her, and she went very still, like a rabbit sensing wolves were sniffing her out. Smart little kitten.

"Maybe I should." He was definitely growling now. Kenzie moved away from him but didn't leave the room. Instead, she ran smack-dab into Emery, who caught her firmly by the arm.

"Easy, little one," Emery said with a chuckle. Royce glared at his friend. Earlier this year he and Emery would have laughed over the idea of catching a runaway sub. But Kenzie didn't know what she was doing to the men in the room. A sassy-mouthed woman with a natural submissive nature was every Dom's fantasy.

"Should you do the honors, or should I?" Emery asked.

Fenn and Hans were both hiding grins. Kenzie let out a strangled little sound of shock when Royce held out a hand and Emery nudged her toward him.

"Don't scare her, Emery. She's not used to our lifestyle."

"What?" Emery blinked. "But I thought... Why else would she...? Oh." He backed off a little, raising his hands.

Kenzie turned her focus on Royce, seemingly unafraid but definitely on edge.

"If you hit me..." She growled like a puppy snapping her teeth. Fuck if that didn't make him hot.

He had here a chance to live out a fantasy with her, assuming she was willing. He wouldn't go too far and take her to bed, of course, but if it turned out she was into it... Royce curled his fingers around her arm and turned her so she was pinned between the pool table and his body. He knew *exactly* how to deal with her now *and* keep her safe.

"So, you want to go to Moscow?" he asked, using his most seductive voice, the one he used right before he punished a submissive.

"Yes." He saw a hint of suspicion lurking in those brown eyes he adored. She was smart enough to know he was up to something but brave enough to stick to her guns and see what he would do next.

"If you want to go with me, you have to take a punishment for arguing with me just now. We aren't on campus. You're in my world. So I offer you a choice: If you don't take the punishment, there's no harm done. You can go back upstairs and sleep and let my friends protect you until I get back, but you won't go to Russia." He watched her face as comprehension dawned in her eyes. She took a long moment to think it over, just like he knew she would. What he did not expect was her response.

"And I get to go to Russia if I let you do whatever it is you want to do?"

He nodded slowly.

"Then do it."

He had to be sure she knew what he meant to do. "Do you understand what you're saying? You were at the Gilded Cuff..."

"I am going to Russia."

Emery and Fenn laughed. Hans rolled his eyes. "I'm going to secure the perimeter. I do not want to see whatever you're going to do that poor girl. But considering I found leather cuffs under her bed, I'm guessing she'll be into it." He left the billiard room.

"Cuffs, huh?" Royce grinned.

Kenzie glanced at Fenn, Emery, and finally at Royce. She gulped and didn't respond to his question about the cuffs. Royce nodded at his friend. Emery reached under the pool table and flipped a switch. Two panels by the end of the table opened on the felt surface and two silver rings appeared with handcuffs attached. Perfect restraints to keep a woman bent over the pool table.

She stared at the rings, her eyes wide. "What are those?"

"It's not too late to back out, Little Mac. No hard feelings." Royce prayed she would give in and go back upstairs. Who knew where this would eventually go? "That's part of the deal. You get cuffed and take ten slaps to the ass or the deal is off."

Kenzie stared at the handcuffs, biting her lip. He wished he knew what was going on inside her head.

"Okay." She said the word so softly that all three men leaned in to hear it.

"Holy shit," Fenn said with a laugh. Emery shook his head, smiling. Royce simply stood there, his finger still curled around her arm. She had actually agreed to take a spanking just to go to Russia? He wasn't sure if he should be impressed or concerned. But he knew Kenzie, and she was willing to put herself in danger to see this through…and to help him.

"Can we just get this over with?" Kenzie asked, her voice a little shaky.

He cupped her chin with his other hand. "You're serious?" He had to make sure. There was fear in her gaze, but also trust and no hesitation. She would make an excellent sub.

If only she could be my sub.

"I told you, I'm going to Russia," she said. The delightful spark of defiance in her eyes was marvelous.

"Very well." He released her arm and pointed at the restraints. "Bend over and place your hands by the cuffs."

Kenzie obeyed slowly, tremors running through her as she bent over the pool table. Royce nodded at his friends, who both stepped forward to click the cuffs around her wrists. If he'd dared to restrain her himself, it might have been too much to resist.

"Last chance, Kenzie. We can free you and you can still go upstairs." He dared not touch her, not until she was sure. The picture of her bent over the pool table, even wearing his large pajama shirt and damn pajama bottoms, was erotic as hell. He'd had a completely naked woman lie there before, but nothing excited him the way Kenzie had.

"Quit stalling, Royce," Fenn said. "The girl's made up her mind."

Royce walked to the side of the pool table so Kenzie could see him. He braced his hands on the table and leaned down so she didn't have to strain see his face.

"Ten blows. That's all. I want you to count each one and say, 'Thank you, sir.' If you fail to do this, we start all over again. If the pain is too much, just say *yellow*. I'll pause and we'll discuss. If you become too scared, can't breathe, or genuinely fear me or the situation, you say *red*. Red stops the game and I let you go back upstairs, but you won't go to Russia. Yellow means you can still stay and we keep going until we reach ten. Do you understand the rules?"

She met his gaze. "I do." Her fingers clenched, and the cuffs rattled shut. Damn, that was a wonderful sound. He could never truly hurt a woman, of course. That wasn't the point of such roleplay. It was all about being safe, sane, and consensual. But he liked it when a consenting woman showed a hint of apprehension, which was not the same as fear.

The real pleasure for him as a Dom was being with a woman who trusted him completely but didn't necessarily trust herself to give in to the pleasure right away. The woman's inner struggle to finally let go was the most erotic thing he had ever experienced. If Little Mac wanted to go to Russia, she had to prove she could take anything and surrender to the feelings she hid within herself.

Fenn and Emery settled in at the end of the pool table opposite Kenzie, which was good. She would need some space if she was going to handle the embarrassment of being spanked in front of two men she didn't know. Royce came back around behind Kenzie and trailed a fingertip down her spine. She started to shake, but didn't say a word. He stopped when he reached her lower back just above the waistband of her pajama bottoms. Normally he would lay a hand to bare flesh, but this was Kenzie, not a sub from the Gilded Cuff.

"Ready?" he asked as he cupped one ass cheek, squeezing lightly.

She tensed, her breath catching.

"Remember to count and thank me each time," he

reminded her. Her short nod was enough. He lifted his hand and smacked her ass hard enough to startle her, but not enough to hurt.

"One..." Her words seem to tremble upon the air. "Thank you, sir."

"Good girl," he praised and stroked her cheek, then brought his hand down again, lighter this time.

"Two. Thank you, sir." He smiled at the obvious relief in her words. That was best—let a sub believe that they knew what to expect, and then you surprised them. The surprise would flood them with adrenaline and arousal.

The third smack he made hard, with his open palm connecting in an almost whiplike strike.

That got a little yelp out of her and she jerked, the cuffs clinking as her whole body reacted. He had mastered delivering little blows that stung but did not do a sub any harm. He would never hurt Little Mac.

"Kenzie..." he warned as he pressed his palm against the tender spot, knowing it had to burn a little.

"Th—three. Thank you, sir."

Now he was getting somewhere. Punishment could serve two purposes in his world: sexual punishment, or genuine punishment. Sometimes light pain would be used to bring a sub into the subspace where they let go of inhibitions and fears and existed on a higher sexual plane. With Kenzie his goal was strictly punishment, however. If he was going to take her to Russia, where danger would surround them, he *needed* her to trust and listen to him.

He waited until her breathing calmed, and then he struck a new spot, closer to the back of her thighs.

"*Four*. Thank you, sir." The words came out through gritted teeth, and he smiled. She was fighting him again. While he wanted that fire and sass to stay, it did not belong in her punishment.

He glanced up from Kenzie and saw his friends were watching him, not her. Fenn held a half smile, and Emery had an odd expression on his face, one of bemused puzzlement.

Frowning, Royce delivered three successive blows to Kenzie, and she hissed out a sharp breath for each.

"Five, six, *seven*... Thank you, sir." This time he could tell she was close to breaking down. It was her first time being spanked in this fashion, he could tell. But she was taking it like a true submissive, in front of two men she didn't know. God, the woman was brave, and he would reward her for it later.

"Three more," Emery said to Kenzie in gentle encouragement.

Royce didn't let up. The last three were just as sharp, and he knew it would leave her bottom burning all night. She counted the last three, one at a time, her words almost a whisper, and by the last her muscles went lax and she lay panting on the pool table.

Royce glanced at his friends, who were still watching him.

"Take care of her," said Emery. "We'll have Hans update us." The twins slipped from the room together.

Royce unfastened Kenzie's handcuffs and tried to help her stand. She jerked away from him, her face stained with tears.

Fuck. He had gotten to her. Too much too fast. For a submissive who didn't know she was submissive, her only reactions to punishment could be frightening and humiliating. *But to me, her tears are beautiful.* They were a sign of trust, a sign of strength. Everyone thought subs were weak, but it was the opposite. It took strength and courage to give yourself over to another's control and let them own you in that vulnerable moment. Kenzie had done so beautifully, but he knew she had to feel raw and exposed.

He caught her up in his arms, even though she kicked and struggled.

"Hush, Little Mac. It's over now. You did very well, and I'm so pleased." He carried her to his room, where he planned to hold her until she calmed and fell asleep again. He passed by Hans on the stairs.

"We'll need three tickets to Moscow," he said. Hans nodded and continued his silent watch over Devereaux House.

"HUSH, LITTLE MAC. IT'S OVER NOW. YOU DID VERY WELL, and I'm so pleased."

The words seem to come through a fog. Kenzie was cuddled in Royce's arms, unable to move and barely able to think. Her bottom burned, and she knew she had been crying. But she had no energy left to care. She was exhausted. *But he is pleased with me.* Feelings of self-loathing swept through her, because she was happy that he was happy...for letting him hit her.

That can't be right. I am so messed up. And the worst part was that it had hurt, yes, but that edge of pain from the softer blows... It made her flush with heat, and wetness had pooled between her thighs. She had been aroused by him spanking her. Just like in her fantasies. Only she hadn't known that the pain would be that acute.

She wasn't *really* hurt. Royce had known just the right amount of pain to give her, and that terrified her. Yet *he* didn't. She burrowed into him now, inhaling his scent and wanting to imprint it on herself. There was nothing beyond this moment for her, the quiet breaths and her trembling, exhausted body wrapped against his.

I won't think about tomorrow or how I'll have to face him. I'll just enjoy this moment. After that, she surrendered to sleep in Royce's arms.

6

M*y ass hurts.*

That was the first thought that crept into Kenzie's head when she woke up. Bright sunlight shone through the windowpanes where the curtains had been pulled to the sides. She winced as she sat up and pushed the covers back. The sheets were heavy and soft—too soft—and the room she was in was lavishly decorated with antique furniture, not the cheap IKEA stuff from her apartment. A trickle, then a flood of embarrassing memories came back to her. She covered her face in her hands.

Oh my God, I let my professor spank me last night. In front of his friends.

She peeked between her fingers, checking to make sure the room was in fact empty. It was. Then she slipped out of bed and dashed to the bathroom. Her toiletry bag sat on the counter. Hans had been really thorough when he'd retrieved her stuff. She hastily brushed her teeth before she had the courage to tug down the pajama pants and look at her ass in the mirror.

It was a light-pink shade and still incredibly sensitive.

Every time she sat down today she was going to remember being bent over that pool table, cuffed, and spanked. How humiliating. And yet...

And I'm going to Russia. It'd been worth it for that. She knew last night that she had to go. She was wrapped up in this thing now and couldn't let Royce face this alone. She couldn't stay here when she knew what he would be facing. It didn't seem right to just sit back like some idiot damsel in distress when she could help him somehow. She'd find a way to justify going, but at least for now, she was relying on her instincts, and her instincts told her she had to go with him.

You only live once, right?

She stared at the mirror and took a brush out of her bag, running it through the tangled brown strands of her hair before she pulled it up into a ponytail. She needed to shower and change, but first she needed to call her parents and let them know she was leaving for Russia. She pulled her laptop from her backpack and turned it on. Her mom would be making coffee right now in the kitchen, checking her emails on the computer. When she called them via her webcam, she watched the little green phone icon vibrate on the screen.

Her mother's face appeared on the screen, a coffee mug in her hands. "Hello?"

"Hey, Mom! I'm glad I caught you. Is Dad around?"

"Andrew? Come in here, honey. Kenzie wants to see you." Kenzie smiled at the sight of her parents hunched together as they watched her through the screen. Her dad smiled broadly.

"Morning, kiddo. What's up?"

She braced herself, not knowing how they would take it. "I have some big news."

"Yes?" her mother asked.

"Dr. Devereaux is taking me to Russia today. It's a last-minute decision, but we're flying to Moscow."

"Russia?" Her dad's brows rose. "This for some paleontology thing?"

"Yes. We're going to visit some universities over there." She wanted to tell them they would be digging, but it would be frozen in Moscow and there would be no way to dig this time of year.

"Wow," her mom said. "Russia. You'll be safe, won't you? I hear it can be a little dangerous."

Kenzie nodded. "Dr. Devereaux is bringing a bodyguard. We'll be perfectly safe." The lie felt a bit acidic on her tongue, but there was no way she could tell her parents the truth about why she and Royce were going to Moscow. Telling them about a Russian fossil smuggler and the goons who tried to kill her sounded like a terrible idea.

Her dad pushed his glasses up on the bridge of his nose. "When will you be home?"

"I'm not sure. Probably a week?" That sounded reasonable.

"Good, we don't want to miss you coming home for Christmas."

"I won't." She smiled at them, feeling instantly better until Royce walked into the bedroom.

"Up and at 'em, Little Mac," he announced, and then paused. He'd noticed her sitting in bed with her laptop.

"Who's that?" her dad asked, his eyes narrowing.

"Oh, that's..." She glanced at Royce in terror. This she could not explain.

"Is there a man at your apartment?" her mother asked, then frowned. "Wait...that doesn't look like your apartment."

"I'm staying at Dr. Devereaux's." She knew this was one truth she couldn't avoid. "We had to be ready to leave for the airport together, so I stayed here overnight in the guest room."

"Oh, okay," her mom said, still frowning. "Can we meet him? Is he still there?"

Royce made a polite cough. Kenzie turned his way. He gave her a little nod, and she turned the laptop his way. Royce came over and bent to peer at the screen, flashing that charming smile of his.

"Hello, Mr. and Mrs. Martin. I'm glad to finally meet you."

Kenzie's mother all but swooned, and her father grinned. That was the thing about Royce Devereaux. He could charm snakes—and even overprotective fathers.

"So nice to meet you too! Kenzie's told us all about you. So, Russia? What a treat that will be." Her mother was beaming now, and Kenzie wanted to crawl into a hole and die. She loved her parents, but they were sometimes a little too eager to help further her career, and right now they were embarrassing her.

"Hey—" She cut into the flurry of questions her parents were currently directing at Royce. "We have to go now, okay? I'll call you when I get home." She slapped the laptop lid closed and once again covered her face with her hands.

"They seem nice," Royce said as he pried her hands away from her face.

"They are," she agreed, still not looking at him. They weren't going to talk about last night, were they? She wasn't ready for that. Hell, she'd *never* be ready for that discussion.

"You don't need to hide from me, sweetheart. Last night was intense for both of us. But you have nothing to be ashamed of." He gave her ponytail a gentle tug.

So they *were* going to talk about it. She finally looked at him, expecting *what* she didn't know. But she a saw fierce tenderness in his eyes, and he was smiling.

"Most subs are emotionally vulnerable after their first punishment. It's because you opened up to me, and that made you feel vulnerable. And I liked that you were open with me."

"You did?" She wanted to know what else he liked, but they were already treading in dangerous waters. He should not have touched her last night, and she sure as hell shouldn't have let him. But she had to know more about him and the dark world he lived in that seemed to fill a void inside of her.

"Yeah, I liked it a hell of a lot. If you and I weren't..." Royce's smile faded. "If we didn't work together like we do, let's just say I'd have done *everything* to you last night."

Her mouth was dry and she struggle to swallow. "What do you mean by everything?" *I'm only going to torture myself asking him to tell me what I want to hear, like looking at a pair of Jimmy Choos when all I can afford are sneakers.*

Royce leaned over her on the bed, one hand fisted in her ponytail, and he pulled her head back as he gazed into her eyes.

"I'd only scare you if I told you."

"Tell me," she begged. Her heart pounded against her ribs, and a hunger lurked deep within, wanting to know what he defined as *everything.*

He shook his head. "No sense in speaking aloud that which I cannot do." He said it like a kingly proclamation and was smiling again. "Get up and get showered. Our flight leaves in three hours." He released her hair after one more playful tug.

Half an hour later, Kenzie was showered and packed, her bag by the front door. Hans and Royce were there waiting for her.

Hans handed her a slim black phone. "Here. This is your personal satellite phone. It has a tiny tracker wired in that I can trace at a distance of five thousand miles."

"Whoa," she whispered as she accepted the phone.

"Five thousand? Emery must've extended the range of the

Black Widow." Royce was checking out his own phone with new appreciation.

"What's a Black Widow?" Kenzie asked.

"It's a tracking device. Emery's company makes them. Powerful little bug. Handy as hell." Royce pocketed his phone and focused on Hans. "We taking any protection?"

Hans shook his head. "Too risky, even with permits. Dimitri Razin will meet us in Moscow and see that we receive any necessary firepower."

Guns? They were talking about guns? The room spun a little as Kenzie recalled the shooting from last night. How she'd managed to forget it in the first place she didn't know.

"Kenzie, it's okay," Royce said, touching her shoulder. "We won't let you get anywhere near the dangerous stuff. I promise."

She nodded, wanting to trust him. But she certainly didn't trust whoever that man Vadym was. She knew in her gut that whatever they faced in Russia would not be easy or safe, and she'd made a vow to herself to face that danger and follow through on helping Royce. But if Royce wanted to pretend for a little while longer that he could keep her safe, she would let him. Her eyes would stay open, and she would stay alert.

"Everyone ready?" Hans looked at her, as though trying to make sure that she was truly set on coming.

She tightened her grip on her suitcase handle. "Ready."

This is crazy. Flying off to Russia with my professor and his scary-ass bodyguard to stop fossil smugglers? God, I hope I know what I'm doing.

❧ 7 ❧

Royce hated planes. He didn't used to, but since he lost his parents, he'd viewed them as giant death-traps. The pilot announced their flight time and the weather conditions on the way to Moscow, and Royce's stomach knotted. He'd flown often over the years but had never gotten over the ache of his memories of that tragic night.

He would sit frozen in his first-class seat of the Boeing 747 and not be able to breathe. The engines would come to life and the flight attendant would walk the length of the cabin, calm and casual, but nothing could distract him from his fear. He would grip the armrest until his knuckles were white, even before takeoff.

Every time the memories of losing his parents came back, they were as dark and heavy as a midnight sea, drawing him down into their depths.

Royce grinned as he, Wes, and Emery raided his dad's liquor cabinet and sat in the den watching TV. His parents wouldn't get home until late tonight, and they could hide the empty bottle of Jack Daniel's long before then. They didn't talk about school. They talked about girls or sports or a hundred things that seemed so important at the time.

The phone rang, but he ignored it. Half an hour later the police arrived at his door. Two officers stepped out of their vehicles, caps in their hands, heads bowed.

"Are you Royce Devereaux?" one man asked.

He nodded and searched their faces, trying to figure out why cops would be here at all.

"There's been an accident. The plane carrying your parents missed the runway in the fog." The second officer swallowed thickly and continued. "I'm sorry, but there were no survivors."

The words seemed to make the air hum like a hive of bees deep in his skull. He couldn't escape the sound. He tried to speak, but no words came out. His eyes burned. His heart froze, unable to beat.

When Royce's legs gave out, it was his friends who caught him and held him up.

"Dr. Devereaux, do you want nuts?" The sweet, slightly husky voice jerked him out of the past.

Nuts? What the fuck?

Kenzie waved a bag of peanuts in front of him. "Peanuts. You want some?" The smile on her lips faltered, and he realized it was because he was glaring at her. He wiped the scowl from his face and took the shiny red packet from her. The flight attendant walked by, and Royce flagged her down. "One glass of scotch on the rocks, please."

The woman, who was no doubt barely older than Kenzie, smiled invitingly. Her eyes were warm and appreciative as she took him in. "Of course, sir. I'll bring that right away."

In another time and place, he would've taken the attendant into the nearest bathroom and punched another hole in his mile-high club card, but the thought wasn't as appealing as it used to be. He shot a look at Kenzie, who was focused on her laptop, which was already propped open on her tray table. Hans sat in the aisle seat in the row across from them, neck pillow behind his head, his eyes closed.

Smart man. I wish I could sleep on a plane like him.

Royce focused on Kenzie again, not missing that the small confines of the plane even in first class made their legs touch and their arms press together on the armrests. A soft floral scent teased his nose, and he leaned in a little, wanting to inhale the fragrance. He started to close his eyes again, but as he did so Kenzie started talking.

"I downloaded some information about Mongolia before we left. Do you want to read it?" she asked.

"Mongolia?" He was still focused on that sweet scent that was beckoning him.

"Yeah. Monte said the Russian guy, Vadym-whatever, was involved in fossil smuggling in Mongolia, remember? I figure it has to be about the Gobi Desert. That's the richest fossil location in the world."

Royce nodded. He had been in Mongolia before when he was younger. One of his first digs had been out on the steppes.

"Your drink, sir." The flight attendant set the scotch in his hands, and he didn't miss how her touch lingered on his hand a little too long. An invitation?

"Thanks. Do you want a drink, Little Mac?"

Kenzie glanced up from her screen, her cheeks pinkened. "I don't need anything."

"Rum and Coke for the lady," he told the attendant, who nodded and left.

"I don't think she wanted to get me a drink," Kenzie mused, a slightly puzzled look in her eyes.

"It's her job," Royce said. "Now show me some of the maps. It's been a while since I've been there."

Kenzie angled her computer his way. "What's the Gobi like? I've never been to a desert."

"It's colder than you'd think, this time of year. Plus, it's full of camels and yurts," Hans interrupted. Royce and Kenzie both stared at him. His eyes were still closed and he seemed to be asleep, but he'd been listening. *Crafty man*. Royce shook his head, trying not to laugh.

"Yurts?" Kenzie's nose wrinkled.

"Big circular enclosed tents. Can house about fifty people comfortably," Royce added.

"Comfortably?" Hans said, his eyes still closed. "Try packed like sardines."

Kenzie returned to her original question. "What's the desert like?"

Royce tried to think of a way to describe it. "It's bleak and harsh. A vast open land that's eerily silent. Sound carries across the dunes for miles. There's ice-filled canyons, and the dinosaur fossils in the steppes. Once you're out among the dunes, you can completely disappear. In a lot of ways." He sipped his scotch and noticed Kenzie was watching him with fascination.

This was one of the things he loved about her. Whenever they talked it was a genuine conversation, not just small talk. They listened to each other. Kenzie wasn't picturing her next shopping spree or wondering if her makeup looked okay. She had depth—she was *real*. She loved dinosaurs, just like him. They passionately argued about the conclusions of various new discoveries, conversed about the latest academic papers, and he enjoyed every minute of it. Being with her wasn't like being with the women at the Gilded Cuff. Those women were there for sexual release and physical satisfaction. Sometimes he went for hours without saying a word to his partners. With Kenzie he felt he could *talk* for hours or sit in silence without awkwardness. It was nice.

Kenzie lowered her voice. "So what's your plan for when we reach Moscow?"

"I have a friend, Lev Abramov. He's a professor of paleontology at Moscow State University. If there's anything going on in the fossil world on that continent, he will know about it. He'll most likely have classes during the day, so we could take in some of the sights. Hans will take care of reconnaissance on Vadym. We need to find out who he is and anything else we can about him."

Royce sipped the last of his scotch as Kenzie finished her rum and Coke. He waved the flight attendant over to collect the empty glasses. The cabin lights dimmed overhead, and a yawn escaped Kenzie's lips.

"You've barely had any sleep," he reminded her. "Not deep sleep, anyway. Why don't you rest? Use my shoulder if you need to." He shifted his body closer. His inner Dom growled in approval. She nodded, her eyes drooping a little as she leaned her head against him and settled into sleep. When it came time, he would have their chairs reclined into beds and make sure that she slept comfortably.

One of her hands came up and curled around his biceps, holding him close like she would a favorite stuffed animal. Her dark lashes fanned across her cheeks as she closed her eyes and sighed, soft and sweet, like a dream of flowers and sunshine. She deserved such dreams.

Royce settled into his seat. Moments later, he too was falling asleep. The feminine scent of Kenzie and the feel of her body tucked against him were a dream he wished he deserved, a dream he would cling to as the god Morpheus dragged him into the darkness of sleep.

Hans Brummer opened one eye and smiled as he saw the grad student cuddle up to her professor. Royce acted tough, and hell, he *was* tough, but he wasn't much older than Kenzie.

Kids today. They think they control themselves.

It was obvious to any fool that Royce was captivated by Kenzie. Hans was no stranger to Royce's lifestyle or the type of women he met at the Gilded Cuff. He'd seen more than his share of that following Emery Lockwood around for the last decade in the shadows of the Cuff, watching over him.

BDSM required trust. But Hans knew that Royce had not yet learned to trust himself, and until he did he would never be truly happy, but Kenzie had made him open up. That made Hans nervous. Love could be dangerous. If he loved someone, they could be used against him, and that could get him hurt. He hadn't wanted Kenzie to come, but he knew Royce. Once his mind was set, there was no changing it.

Hans peered out the window of the plane, watching the clouds far below turn turbulent and stormy.

MOSCOW WAS A STRANGE MIX OF THE PAST AND PRESENT. Kenzie stared at the sights from inside the private cab that took them from the airport to the hotel. The famous multi-colored onion domes of Saint Basil's Cathedral shimmered in the distance, accented like a castle in a foggy world, backlit by snowy skies. The streets were full of tourists and locals bustling along the icy streets, coats clutched tight with woolen scarves blowing in the wind.

Beside her, Royce leaned back in the cab, seemingly at ease, his gaze distant. He'd been silent for much of the long flight, and she was afraid that spending most the time cuddled against him asleep had been a mistake. What if he was regretting letting her come? What if he didn't want her here? That led to worse questions.

What if he doesn't want me at all?

When they'd been together in the shower, he'd come so close to kissing and then after he punished her, he'd said things that had given her hope. Not that she should hope. They couldn't go down that road together, not when it could destroy their careers.

She tried to start a conversation. "So...where are we staying?"

"The Lotte." Royce pulled his cell phone out of his pocket and focused on the screen, ignoring her.

Right. So he didn't want to talk. "Hans, what's the hotel like? Have you been there?"

"Once. Pretty good. They have an underground pool." He offered her a smile from where he sat in the front seat next to their driver.

"A pool?" She'd packed a swimsuit, thinking she might use a hotel pool if she had the chance. Swimming was one of the few ways she could truly find peace in the world around her.

I doubt we'll have time for swimming, though.

"Here we are," Hans said as the cab came to a stop.

Kenzie climbed out and gasped up at the glittering pair of buildings that formed the hotel. One was tall and the other short and wide. The words "Lotte Hotel" glowed in white over the shorter building.

Hans and Royce carried their bags into the lobby, where a bellhop rolled up with a cart and loaded the luggage onto it. Kenzie stuck close to Royce and Hans, following them deep into the lobby. The floors were a pale cream with alternating diamond patterns leading past lavishly decorated lounge areas. Crystal-encrusted chandeliers guided guests toward the check-in desk, illuminating the path on the floor. Everything around Kenzie was clean and glittering, with subtle hints of gold in the design. It was stunning.

"Man, I can't wait until dinner," Hans grumbled as they reached the front desk.

"Dinner?" Kenzie asked.

Hans patted his stomach. "The Lotte has a couple of good restaurants, with menus prepared by a Michelin-starred chef. Not too bad, eh?"

"Michelin?" She'd never eaten at a restaurant of such renown before.

"Yeah." Hans grinned and sighed dramatically.

Royce checked in, while Kenzie and Hans hung back. "Hans, is he mad about me coming with you?" she finally asked, dreading the answer.

Hans's smile faded. "It's not that he doesn't want you here. This shit is dangerous. If it was up to me, you'd be in a safehouse stateside. I think the only reason he let you come is he's worried that there's no real safe place right now, except maybe by his side. Until he's made certain that you're safe, he's going to be grumpy about it."

"Great, a grumpy professor. Nothing I haven't dealt with before, especially when it's time to grade finals."

"Well, I imagine angry, dangerous Russian mobsters are a bit worse than grading finals."

Finished at the desk, Royce came over holding a trio of room keys. He handed the first to Hans.

"You the suite connected to us." Hans nodded and plucked his card from Royce's hand.

"Us?" Kenzie's voice came out breathless, and she inwardly cursed.

"There's no way you're staying alone *anywhere* in the city. You're out of your depth here. Human trafficking is big in this part of the world. You would be like fucking catnip to the sick fucks who steal women off the street."

Kenzie's mood deflated. So she would be sharing a room

with him, but only because she was being protected. She took her keycard from Royce.

Be glad it's not about sex. Sleeping with him ends your career before it even starts. Remember?

Royce led them to an elevator bay, and they got off on the fifteenth floor. Kenzie sagged with relief against the wall as Royce activated the door with his key. Despite sleeping on the flight, she was suddenly dead tired and was worried she couldn't make it another step.

"Our luggage will be here soon. Why don't you rest for a bit?" Royce opened the door after a cursory check that the room was empty, and then he let her join him. As the lights came on, her jaw dropped. There was a massive king-size bed with a dark wood frame and a dozen fancy pillows resting on top. A tall wall between the bed and the sitting room had two couches and a large dining table that could seat at least six people. Kenzie headed for the window, her feet dragging a little, but she really wanted to check out the view. She wasn't sure how long she stood there, taking in the seemingly unending skyline of Moscow.

Wow, I really am in Russia.

Royce's voice drew her focus to him. "I'll take a shower first, if you prefer to crash." He put their luggage on a set of racks and slid off his leather motorcycle jacket. He tossed the coat onto the bed and headed for the distant bathroom near the door of the massive suite.

Kenzie eased down on the bed, listening for the sounds of Royce in the bathroom, the door closing, the running of the taps, and finally the shower. Then, after waiting a few minutes, Kenzie inched her fingers along the bed to grasp the leather jacket. She pulled it up to her nose, inhaling Royce's masculine scent that clung to the leather.

The emotional roller coaster of the last couple days seemed to suddenly form a pit in her stomach that soon filled with a black leaden knot. She had been attacked, chased, shot at, and almost killed. She'd explored Royce's private life, feeling like an intruder as she was exposed to his secrets, and the dark desires he had that mirrored her own. When he'd spanked her on the billiard table, something had changed. She couldn't go back, whatever she wanted to believe. The truth was that he'd owned part of her in that moment, and she had wanted him to.

If she ever had sex with him, it would obliterate her completely. He was a living, breathing force of nature, and she felt suddenly very small and foolish that she could even exist on the same level as him.

Kenzie laid his coat back down on the bed and stretched herself out near the headboard. She closed her eyes, but sleep was slow to come. The faces of the men who'd attacked her were there waiting for her, as was the light glinting off the barrel of the gun.

She jolted awake at the sound of distant voices. The door to the connecting suite was almost shut, but not quite. Kenzie slipped off the bed and approached the crack in the door, straining to hear the voices.

Hans's deep voice rumbled. "Are you sure about bringing the kid? We could still put her on plane and send her with Fenn to Colorado. That ranch is hard to find, even for the Russian Mafia."

"Yeah, I'm sure," said Royce. "We can't risk getting anyone else hurt. She's my problem, and I'm the one who should be responsible for her." His words cut through Kenzie's heart like a knife.

I'm a problem. A burden. She wasn't here to help; she was here so he could keep an eye on her. Tears burned at her eyes. She hated when someone made her feel insignificant and childish, especially when that person was someone she respected and admired like Royce. How stupid she'd been to think she would be able to help him somehow. Instead, she'd thrown a fit like a child and demanded that he take her along. Now she knew why he'd agreed.

Kenzie almost opened the door, but confronting Royce would do no good. What was she doing here? She wasn't trained to fight or shoot a gun. It wasn't like she knew more about dinosaurs than Royce. She'd never even been to a dig site outside of the US. What was she even doing here? Maybe he was right. Maybe this was a mistake.

She walked over to her bag on the luggage rack and started to pack. She was zipping it up when Royce opened the connecting door and came back into their room.

He froze when he saw her standing there with her backpack. "Kenzie, what's going on?"

"I...I'm going home. I'm just in the way and—"

Royce's face darkened, and he strode over to her, putting one hand flat on her suitcase.

"You're not going home. You're staying here."

"I'm only going to get in the way. You'll be splitting your time between Vadym and looking after me. I'm a *problem*." She threw his words back at him, feeling foolish, but she wanted him to know she'd heard what he said.

He cupped her chin, holding her still. Her body trembled in fear and excitement at the way his gaze burned through her. "You *are* problem, and I *do* have to look after you. Do you want me to say why? Because once I do, there's no going back. There's no happy endings with white picket fences. You get the truth from me. The hard fucking truth."

Her nerves skittered through her. She'd never seen him like this before—no, wait, she *had* when he'd been standing over the man who tried to kill her. This was the Royce who was capable of anything. He was fierce, he was frightening, and yet he didn't scare her.

She knew asking for the truth would be a mistake, but she had to know. "Why?"

"Because the moment you walked into my office that first day, I wanted to do *bad* things to you. I wanted to make you moan and scream. I wanted to take you into my world and own you like no one else can. But if we did..."

"It would ruin our careers," Kenzie finished.

"But that doesn't change how you make me feel. How I feel about you. What I want to *do* to you."

His fingers moved from her chin down her throat in a featherlight caress. She held very still, spellbound by his words. He wanted not only to be with her, but to possess her. And as bad as it was to admit it, she wanted that too.

"So now you get it," he growled softly. "Those pretty brown eyes are wide with fear and I hate that, but you wanted the truth. You've been to my club, you've seen what I need from a woman. I'm a Dom. When a woman I want is in danger, I break all the rules. *That's* why I let you come to Moscow."

His fingers curled around her throat in a gentle hold. "Because whether or not we both want to admit it, you're mine. Even if I can't have you the way I want, I'll take whatever I can get, even if I can only see you in my office every day and do nothing else." His eyes burned into her, flooding her with an arousal so hot she almost forgot to breathe. She wanted to be his more than was wise.

"You done scaring her?" Hans asked, standing in the doorway that joined their rooms. "We've got a weapons deal to worry about." He looked a bit like an intimidating overprotective father. If Kenzie hadn't been shaken by Royce's words, she would've laughed.

Royce backed away from her. "Stay in the room until we get back. Don't open the door for anyone but us, do you understand?"

"You really think it's that dangerous?" She'd been hoping to go down to the pool and have a quick swim before dinner.

"It could be. We can't take any chances." Royce looked to her bags and then back at her. "Go ahead and unpack. Give us half an hour, then order room service. We should be back before it arrives."

"What about the Michelin star restaurant?"

"Not tonight, I'm afraid. Not until we know what we're dealing with here. I've got some friends in the city, and I need them to tell me what kind of shitstorm we're facing with Vadym."

Kenzie made a show of sitting on the edge of the bed. "Okay. I'll stay here."

Royce nodded in approval. "We'll be back soon." For a moment she thought he might come over and kiss her, but instead he turned away, following Hans into the hallway.

Kenzie waited for a good fifteen minutes and then got up from the bed to find her swimsuit. She was going to swim.

I'm not as helpless as he likes to think. With two older brothers in the family and an overprotective dad, she had gotten good at slipping away unnoticed. There were certain skills little sisters had to hone in order to do what they wanted—otherwise, they never did anything.

She found her suit and goggles, changed, and grabbed a towel. She would be done with her swim before Royce got back. And he would be none the wiser.

8

"So, are we going to talk about it?" Hans asked as he and Royce climbed in the back of their hired SUV.

Royce leaned back, resting his head on the headrest as he stared straight ahead. "Talk about what?" Hans had the most amazing way of making him feel like he was a ten-year-old boy and not a man of thirty-three.

"About the fact that you basically told your grad student you want to fuck her brains out. Are you fraternizing with students now?"

"No. There's a fuck ton of paperwork involved, for one thing. And I would have to stop working with her. If it's handled wrong, it could damage the academic integrity of any research we did together."

"Jesus. Why didn't you send her somewhere safe if she's such a temptation to you?" Hans asked. "She would have been fine at Fenn's ranch in Colorado."

Royce watched the streets of Moscow blur as their driver sped up when the street cleared. He didn't want to admit it, but he'd told Kenzie the truth. As a Dom, he had a natural urge to protect his sub. It was hard to fight that kind of pull.

"It's my own fault. I was sure she wasn't going to agree to my terms."

Hans shook his head. "You wouldn't have given her terms at all unless part of you wanted her to say yes. You should have just told her to stay, end of story."

"Well, it's too late for that now. I can't have her out of my sight. Not until this is over."

"Fine, so we find out about these bastards, who they are, what they want from you, and then we take them out. With most enemies you could find a way to convince them to leave you alone, but mobsters don't think like that. It's you or them. No other choice." Hans's succinct solution made Royce grin. It was why he'd made such a good bodyguard for Emery all these years.

"Who are we meeting with for the...equipment?" Royce asked more quietly in case their driver was listening. Even though Moscow was a heavily populated city, he didn't want to make the mistake of assuming that the Russian mob didn't have eyes and ears everywhere, even hired cabdrivers.

"Wes thought we should call Dimitri Razin. He is well connected in the right places, and he will have some idea of where to start when we track down those bastards."

Royce stroked his chin. Dimitri was a Russian art lover and no friend to the current political regime. Wes said Razin's family had been a solid supporter of the Imperial family before they were killed in the early twentieth century. Razin was not a member of the mob and never would be. He had his own team of loyal men and women, and he somehow kept himself apart from the reaching fingers of the Mafia. In fact, they stayed well clear of him.

"Dimitri is a good call," Royce agreed.

"I checked with him before we left the hotel. He's bringing a weapons specialist with them, some man named Barinov."

Royce grinned again. If things went south they were going to need some decent firepower, and Razin's connections would be very helpful.

"Where's this meeting going to be?" Royce sat up in his seat as the SUV slowed to a stop against the curb.

Hans pointed to the building just outside. "The Sandunovsky Baths." It was a rather unremarkable structure, probably built in the late eighteen hundreds. Royce paid the driver as they left.

Inside the bathhouse, Royce was impressed by the ornate archway, heavily decorated with sculptures of nymphs on horseback. The nymphs were emerging from the sea and using Triton's shell trumpets. At least some beautiful things hadn't been destroyed when the Bolsheviks took over.

Hans whistled low in appreciation as he followed Royce inside. The interior was a flamboyant mix of baroque, Gothic, and Moorish styles. It looked like something out of a James Bond movie. All that was missing were a bunch of aging tattooed Russians with nothing but towels and smoking cigars.

Royce went to the reception desk and gave his name to the young woman monitoring the guest arrivals.

"Dr. Devereaux, your suite is this way." She waved for them to come with her. The red-and-white diamond floors bore an Iberian influence, but the baroque columns presented a sumptuous counterpoint design. Typical of Dimitri to pick a place like this, he thought. He was one selective bastard.

The woman paused at the door, slipping a brass key from her pocket into the keyhole. Royce marveled at the ornamental mystique of a place like this for a clandestine meeting. The attendant opened the door but didn't enter. She simply inclined her head with a smile.

"The changing rooms are just inside, and beyond that is your pool. The rest of your party is already waiting."

Royce entered into the room, taking a moment to study the dark mahogany lockers and the supply of shoeboxes and hangers. Hans waited until the door closed behind them before he started stripping. Royce followed suit. With towels wrapped around their waists, they followed the signs pointing toward the private pool.

The room here was simple in terms of decoration compared to the rest of the bathhouse. The water was clear, and the blue tiles at the bottom contrasted with the white pillars that loomed around the pool like Athenian sentries. The light from the chandeliers hanging above the pool area was soft and muted, letting the water glow. It looked as though Royce and Hans had stepped into the past, to a place of old-world opulence.

Two men stood at the far end of the pool, fully dressed. Dimitri Razin wore an expensive suit, looking intimidating as fuck. A man in a leather jacket with dark-brown hair had to be Razin's contact, Barinov. Royce was a little pissed that he and Hans were practically naked while the Russians weren't, but perhaps that was by design. He saw Hans's eyes dart between the shadows into the nooks and crannies behind the pillars.

"Devereaux," Dimitri said with a chuckle, his gaze moving between Royce and Hans. "A little underdressed for an arms deal, aren't we?"

Royce rolled his eyes. "You said to meet at the bathhouse. You didn't warn us not to strip naked." He waved at the towel.

Dimitri grinned. "When Russians ask you meet them at the bathhouse, never undress."

"Duly noted," Hans said, his voice dry with sarcasm. "Although I'm not totally naked. Got my Barretta."

Royce glanced at the bodyguard, unable to see where the man kept the gun. "Aside from the fact that I don't know how you got that through customs, I don't want to know where you're hiding it," he whispered.

Hans chuckled. "You're right. You don't."

"Let's get straight to business then, shall we?" Dimitri said. "This is Rurik Barinov, a friend of mine. He has a decent grasp on mob activities in the city. More importantly, he's brought you just the right amount of firepower to comfortably protect yourselves."

Rurik grinned, and Royce noticed a thin scar on his face that stretched from his forehead down to his cheek turned a pale white. He bent to retrieve two black briefcases and handed them over to Hans.

"This should take care of your little smuggler problem," Rurik said with a dark chuckle.

"Much obliged," the bodyguard replied.

Royce turned back to Dimitri. "So what's the word on Vadym? He's based in Moscow, but he sent his cronies after me all the way on Long Island. That's an awful lot of trouble for one guy."

Dimitri crossed his arms. "From what I know of him, he's looking for new lucrative money streams. Fossil smuggling and raiding archaeological sites is his latest hobby for cash. He's been trying to get fossils out of Mongolia, and he needs a paleontologist to authenticate them as Russian fossils instead of Mongolian."

"But he can't use a Russian paleontologist," Rurik added. "It would only raise suspicions later on."

Dimitri nodded. "Once he gets them cleared, he could sell them to American and European museums or private buyers for a vast amount of money."

"Fuck, it's simple, but it makes sense," said Royce. "Get someone like me to verify the country of origin on fossils, and it's hard to challenge later unless the original country knows about the thefts and can prove it." He suddenly felt bone-weary. This was the kind of shit he hated dealing with: people who used the unique and rare bits of Earth's history to pad their own pockets. It wasn't just fossils, either. Ancient Russian burial mounds had been bulldozed to get at the treasures inside, not only robbing the world of those items, but of any chance of understanding the history surrounding them. Usually the authorities were three steps behind them at every turn. There was a war going on in the shadows, one that few even knew existed.

"So the bastard picked Royce," Hans mused. "Because of his high profile, no doubt."

Dimitri nodded. "It seems so. I heard he's watching for you, and he knows you're in Moscow. You threw yourself into the belly of the beast, my friend."

Rurik chuckled as though his comment was amusing and not damning.

Royce knew it would be impossible to protect the Mongolian fossils. The best he could hope for would be for the man to look elsewhere for his paleontologist. "So what can I do to stop this guy and get him to leave me alone?"

Dimitri and Rurik exchanged a long glance before Dimitri spoke grimly.

"He knows you know about him and his plan. He won't let go, and he won't let you expose him." Dimitri's tone was soft and deadly. "There's only one way to put an end to this."

"You mean put an end to *him*," Royce said. He *wasn't* a killer—he didn't just take lives. He glanced at Hans. The bodyguard had killed men before to protect Royce's best friends, Emery and Fenn, but that had been in the heat of battle with bullets flying.

But you almost killed someone, the voice inside reminded him. *You stood over Monte and almost shot him to protect Kenzie. Would this be so different?*

"I can get you in the club he frequents and get you close. Then you can take him out," Dimitri said.

Royce shook his head, balking at the idea. "I can't shoot a man in the club." He stared at the ceiling and the mosaic pattern.

"I've already thought of that." Dimitri held out a small vial of a dark crushed substance. Royce took the vial, wondering what was inside.

"It's ricin. Get it in his drink and he's done." Dimitri's deathly calm voice chilled Royce to the bone.

"Ricin is what killed Georgi Markov, that Bulgarian dissident writer," Hans cut in in a soft voice. "That's dangerous stuff."

Royce almost handed the vial back to Dimitri.

"It is," Dimitri agreed. "But Vadym is a dangerous man. He doesn't just deal in fossils. He deals in people."

Royce glanced at Rurik. The man was flexing his hands and curled them into fists, a growl barely audible. Dimitri's words sank in, and Royce felt his stomach heave. His blood began to boil.

"You mean human trafficking."

Dimitri slipped his hands into his pockets. "Yes. He's one of the biggest traders in the flesh markets."

If there was one thing in the world that could change Royce's mind about killing a man in cold blood, it was sex trafficking. The monsters who did that to women, who stole their freedom, their bodies, their lives—it was a fate worse than death. It was hell. Royce stared down at the vial of ricin in his hands, and made his decision.

"Then he's a dead man," Royce said. He wasn't going to let someone like Vadym continue breathing if he had a say in the matter. It wouldn't stop human trafficking in general, but he was going to stop this bastard if he could.

Hans looked to Dimitri. "Guess that's that. Where can we find him? You mentioned the club he gets into?"

"It's called the Black Diamond Bar, but it's not a bar." Dimitri flashed a rueful smile. "It's a BDSM club."

"You ever go there?" Royce asked him. "We need someone who's familiar with the territory."

Dimitri stroked his chin. "A few times, but they tend to prefer sadists, and that's never been my thing."

"How can I get in?"

Dimitri reached into his back pocket and pulled out a wallet. He handed Royce a black card with a silver diamond symbol.

"That will get you in, but you'll need a sub. They don't let unattached Doms come to play, not unless you're shopping for a pet who isn't legal. The club gets used as an auction house for traffickers. When I found that out, I looked for membership elsewhere."

Royce tapped the black card against his palm. It looked like a fancy hotel card key. "You still have an active membership?"

"Yes. I kept it to help with an Interpol raid once. They didn't catch everyone, but it did slow the trafficking for a short time. I felt it might come in handy again someday."

Royce glanced at Hans. "Tomorrow night I'll go with Kenzie."

"Don't be an idiot," said Hans.

Dimitri's eyes sharpened. "Who's Kenzie?"

"The assistant I mentioned earlier." Royce met the Russian's eyes. "I brought her to Moscow with me."

"The assistant Vadym almost killed?" said Dimitri. "You brought her to Moscow, and now you plan to take her to a BDSM club to hunt and kill Vadym? My, Devereaux, you just throw all the rules out the window, don't you?" The Russians laughed, but Royce didn't. Nothing was funny about him bringing Kenzie to the club, but he wasn't going to take anyone else with him.

"You have someone Hans could take, right?" Royce asked Dimitri.

Hans looked at his hands. "That bondage stuff isn't my thing."

"But you can't get in otherwise," Royce reminded him. "It's just an act."

"Fine. But I'm not spanking or whipping anyone."

"I will hire someone for Mr. Brummer. One who will understand her purpose there," Dimitri assured Hans. "We will see you at the Black Diamond Bar tomorrow. It's south of the center of the city. Ask a driver to take you to the Soho Rooms. It's a tourist spot where the runway models and the Mafia meet for a night of fun."

"Thanks." Royce shook hands with Dimitri and Rurik before he and Hans picked up the weapons and headed back to the changing room.

"I kinda hoped we'd get to use the bathing pools," Royce muttered.

Hans laughed. "You really have been watching too many James Bond movies."

"You stripped naked before I did," Royce reminded him.

"Touché."

"We have to get back to Kenzie. There was a mischievous twinkle in her eye that I don't quite trust." Royce reached into his locker and began pulling out his clothes and dressing.

"Mischievous twinkle? She's not Tinkerbell." Hans was grinning as he slid his jeans on.

"No, she's not," he growled. "But I'm afraid she's not taking this as seriously as she should. She might be treating this like a game to avoid the trauma of the past couple days."

"Yeah, well, taking her to this club isn't going to help that delusion. It's all about roleplay there."

He wished Hans hadn't reminded him of that. He didn't want to think about all the things he wanted to do to her, bad things, dirty things, things he knew by her reaction to the Gilded Cuff that she would love.

Hans must have seen the look in his eyes because of the way he grunted. "So it looks like I'll be babysitting *both* of you tomorrow, because one of you or the other is going to lose your mind."

"I don't lose my mind," Royce said as he jerked his leather jacket on.

"Yeah, you do, *kid*." Hans carried the weapon cases to Royce, who was putting on his boots.

Royce looked up at Hans's reflection in the mirror. "I haven't been a kid in a long time." Not since he was eight, when Emery and Fenn had been kidnapped. Everything had changed after that. *Everything*.

No matter how carefully he'd tried to put his world back together, he just couldn't make the pieces fit. Masked gunmen kidnapping your best friends had a way of destroying a boy's innocence. The intangible bogeymen of his boyhood nightmares suddenly became real, and they wore black ski masks.

There was a part of him that would always be that child who spent one evening camping in the woods, sharing ghost stories with his friends, and the next night sitting on his father's lap in his home, shaking as a policeman asked questions about his missing friends.

Hans's voice softened. "You went through hell, I know. Trust me, I know. I remember all of it, every damn minute from the day the Lockwoods hired me to protect Emery. I wanted to protect all of you. Just like I am now."

Royce's throat tightened and he straightened his leather jacket, tugging it down slightly. Hans was in his fifties, but he'd been close to Kenzie's age when he started protecting

Emery. Half of his life had been spent watching one rich kid with a target on his back.

"You're a good man, you know?" Royce could barely get the words out, even though he meant it.

Hans nodded, saying nothing. "Let's get you back to your brown-eyed girl, eh?"

"My brown-eyed girl, huh? I like that." Kenzie, his sexy, tempting, and forbidden brown-eyed girl.

When they got back to the hotel, they'd been gone far longer than he'd expected, and he assumed Kenzie would have ordered room service and fallen asleep. But as he opened the door, he didn't see Kenzie. His brown-eyed girl was nowhere to be found. He opened the connecting door to Hans's room.

"Kenzie there?" He peered around the second suite of rooms. Hans was checking the guns in the cases, and he shook his head.

"She's gone?"

"Yeah."

"Maybe she went to the pool?"

"Alone?" Royce almost growled the word. If she'd gone against his orders, orders he'd given to protect her, she was going to be punished. That kind of behavior in this situation could get her killed or kidnapped.

He stormed back into his room. "I'm going to redden that ass of hers."

"I think you might be overreacting," said Hans.

"She disobeyed me. If she does that now, what about later at the club? I agreed to bring her along, but I'll be damned if I let her put both our lives at risk."

"Don't forget to take your swim trunks!" Hans's laughter followed him as he grabbed a swimsuit from his bag and stepped into the large bathroom to change.

9

One, two, three, four…

Kenzie fell into the cathartic pace of counting her strokes as she did laps in the massive underground pool of the Lotte Hotel. The square blue tiles along the pool bottom seemed to glow like neon from the underwater pool lights. She felt weightless, as if she were swimming in a distant galaxy of glowing stars rather than a pool in Moscow.

She swam until her arms burned. With each stroke she tried to banish the memories of the horrors she'd faced.

Monte gripping her throat, squeezing…wood splintering above her. Glass and splinters raining down on her…gunshots piercing the night, louder than she'd ever imagined they could be…bullets embedded in the wall where her head had been… broken glass glittering on the expensive stone floors like hundreds of diamonds.

She'd never been close to death. She'd never seen the ugliness of true violence or crime. She had lived a sheltered life full of love, happiness, and her textbooks. Dinosaur bones over human bones. She could never have imagined the lingering stain the violence she'd experienced had made in her mind. Dark and yet bright, flashing there so as never to be forgotten, always dragging harder and faster until she thought she'd burst right through her own skin, powerless to erase the images from her brain.

So Kenzie swam faster. Long, furious strokes up and down the heated pool until her limbs felt like lead and her whole body was exhausted. Maybe, if she pushed herself hard enough, she'd be able to sleep tonight. Find peace in the dreamless absence from consciousness.

She gripped the edge of the pool, catching her breath, her cheeks flushed and her body buzzing with warmth. The room was silent except for her heavy breathing, and yet she felt something in the air. She looked up. She saw bare feet, inches from her hands. She tore her goggles off only to see Royce's thunderous expression staring down at her.

"Little Mac, I *told* you to stay in the room."

The last time she'd seen that expression, he'd been mad that she was pushing him on finishing his edits for her thesis paper.

She pushed away from the side of the pool, swimming into the center away from him. Royce was wearing navy-blue swim trunks, and he was bare-chested. The sight of him made her tongue stick to the roof of her mouth. God, he looked perfect, with corded biceps and a six-pack that didn't even look real. More like chiseled by a master sculptor.

He crossed his arms over his chest, scowling.

Finally, she found her voice. "I had to clear my head. I called the front desk, and he said the pool area was keycard protected. I thought it would be safe enough."

"Safe enough? Safeenough? You think Vadym couldn't book a hotel room and get his own damn keycard? Because he would if he knew we were here. No place is safe." His voice deepened as he began to prowl around the edge of the pool until he reached the shallow end. He used the ladder to climb down into the pool, his movements slow and measured as he faced her, now chest-deep in the water. She treaded water, keeping a safe distance away. They both knew that since he'd spoken to her before he left that things had somehow *changed*. The barrier they liked to pretend was there between them—protecting them from crossing that dangerous, seductive line—was gone. Like an ancient wall that had crumbled to ruins, she could see him clearly across the destroyed barrier, mere feet away, within reach.

He's what you've always wanted. And now you can have him. The wicked whisper coiled like a serpent around her heart, blinding her to reason and rationality.

"You promised to obey my orders if I let you come, Little Mac. Orders are supposed to keep you safe. You owe me your submission."

"I thought I was safe," she said. "Nothing happened."

"Kenzie." His burning eyes held her still. "Just because nothing happened doesn't mean you're safe. This man, Vadym, he knows about you now. And he's one of the worst kind of men. These Mafia types—they don't have souls. If he gets his hands on you"—Royce closed his eyes briefly—"I will never be able to find you again. That is a fate neither of us could survive."

This time she didn't see anger in his eyes, but the bright flash of fear. He'd been afraid for her, not angry. She swam closer, so close that her body stirred the water and currents against him.

"I'm sorry," she said.

His gaze moved over her, and then he took one slow step , curling an arm around her waist and dragging her into his arms so that her body pressed flush to his. Their faces were almost touching, and the heat of his body against hers filled her with a delicious burning arousal.

"You'd better tell me to stop," he warned. His voice was silky and seductive, but there was an edge to it that sent her senses spinning and her body humming to life the way she dreamed about in her darkest fantasies.

"Stop what?"

"This."

He crushed her lips to his in a violent, raw claiming. It was punishing, overpowering, and she moaned helplessly, wondering how he could own her with only a kiss. But then, nothing about Royce had ever been simple. His playful professor side, his brooding tortured side, his hard-edged dominant side, and this man here in the pool who was more animal than anything else—she liked it all, liked every part of him. The complexity of his character shifted like the gems of a kaleidoscope, creating beautiful new mysteries each time they changed.

His tongue traced her lips, and she opened to him. Royce curled an arm around her neck, holding her captive, and she lifted her legs in the water, wrapping them around his waist. The hardness of his arousal rubbed against her, and flashes of white heat rolled through her, making her dizzy.

"Make me stop," he begged in a raspy whisper. "Make me, Little Mac, before I lose my fucking mind and take you here in this pool."

"I don't want you to stop."

"You should." He nuzzled her throat, kissing her, licking the drops of water from her skin. "Because I came down here to punish you, to spank your ass until my hand is bright red and you can't sit for a week, but now..." He gripped her ass, lifting her on his body so she rocked against him. "Now I just want to rip your suit to shreds and bury myself inside you over and over until you pass out with pleasure."

Kenzie curled her arms around his neck, his desire for her electrifying her entire body. The moment she met Royce

Devereaux, she'd known deep down that a part of her would always belong to him. Perhaps tonight he would finally take what was already his.

But he didn't. Instead he continued to kiss her, drinking of her lips like she was a bottle of fine scotch, savoring each second. Then he lifted his head. The gentleness that had softened the previously stern line of his mouth made her all the more hungry for him, but not just in a carnal way. She wanted to see him, see that expression all the time, as long as it was just for her.

"Little Mac, you're going to kill me." With great reluctance, he let her go. She slipped away from him in the water, and for a moment she almost went under because she was too busy drowning in his eyes to remember to tread water.

"Let's get you upstairs. I'm starving, and you didn't order any food yet."

Kenzie was a little too stunned to speak. She climbed out of the pool after him. He offered one of the fluffy white towels from a rack against the wall and collected her goggles from the side of the pool.

"Do you swim to chase your demons away?" Royce asked as they walked to the elevator doors.

She tilted her head. "Demons?"

"The way you were swimming, it was like something was chasing you."

"Oh." She flushed. "I just...I can't stop seeing that night in your house, like awful flashes from a horror movie. I wanted to exhaust myself so I could forget."

"Did it work?" Royce asked as he dried off with his own towel.

"A little bit," she admitted, but she couldn't tell him that kissing him had banished it almost completely. She wasn't sure what kind of reaction she would get from that. All she knew was that by kissing her professor, she'd crossed the line. A line she'd sworn she would never cross.

When they got back to the hotel room, the smell of food hit Kenzie's nose, and her stomach rumbled. Hans came out of his room through the connecting doorway and gave Royce a questioning look.

"Everyone have a nice swim?" he asked.

Kenzie smiled at him. "Yeah. Sorry I wasn't here when you got back." It was clear he was being protective. Hell, he probably figured Royce had gone down there to paddle her ass, but he hadn't.

"Good. I ordered dinner. Borscht, kulebiaka, and pelmeni." He nodded to the small coffee table in front of the massive TV.

Kenzie grabbed a change of clothes and then dashed in the bathroom, getting back into her jeans and sweater. She ran a comb through her wet hair and plaited it into a braid before she emerged from the bathroom. Royce was outside waiting, his own clothes in his arms. Their eyes met as they traded places, and she blushed as she let him pass.

Back in the living room, Hans lifted up a bowl of a red substance. "Borscht. Beetroot soup with a dollop of sour cream and dill."

He held it out and she took it, lifting it to inhale the scent. She'd heard of borscht before but not the others he'd mentioned. She peered at a plate that looked to be dumplings. "What are those?"

"Pelmeni. Basically meat-stuffed dumplings. Looks like they served it in a tomato sauce." Hans plucked a pelmeni out with a fork and ate it. "Yep, tomato sauce. Not too spicy." Then he pointed out a sort of puffy pastry-like food. "That's kulebiaka. Good stuff, puff pastry wrapped around fish, hard-boiled eggs, rice, onion, and chopped dill."

Kenzie wrinkled her nose. "You lost me at *pastry* and *fish*."

Hans's booming laugh was irresistible, and she giggled along with him.

Royce emerged from the bathroom wearing jeans and a black sweater. He pushed up the sleeves, baring his muscled forearms, and he grinned when he saw the food.

"Pelmenis!" The light on such a gorgeous, panty-dropping face was devastatingly attractive. Kenzie was certain if he ever reacted to her with that sexy, charming enthusiasm, she would die on the spot. She and Royce took seats on the couch, Hans in the chair, and they dug into the food.

"How did the gun thing go?" Kenzie asked after a minute.

"The 'gun thing' went well." Hans pointed to black heavy-duty hard plastic cases propped against the wall by the closet. "But if we're lucky, we won't need to use them."

"Did you find anything out about this Vadym guy?" she asked as she dipped her spoon into the borscht.

Hans and Royce exchanged meaningful looks, but neither spoke.

"Seriously, guys? Just tell me. I can handle it."

Royce set his plate down and leaned back, stretching one arm around the back of the sofa. "Vadym doesn't just smuggle fossils. He smuggles people too."

"And by smuggling, you mean..." She did want to say the words, too horrified if they were true.

"Human trafficking," Hans said.

Kenzie suddenly lost her appetite. "Oh God." She couldn't imagine the living hell those people suffered. And then she remembered that Vadym knew about her, knew where she lived—everything. It was just like Royce had said. She really was in danger.

"Kenzie." Royce spoke her name in a gentle whisper. "Breathe, babe. You're turning blue."

Her lips parted, and air rushed into her lungs. "Will he come after me?"

"No," Royce growled, his brown eyes glowing with fire. "He'll never touch you."

Despite the assurance in his voice, she saw a shadow in his eyes, a hint of something he was holding back.

"You're keeping something from me. What is it?"

"We know where he'll be tomorrow night. At a club, a BDSM club. Hans and I are going to go there and put a stop to all this."

"Okay..." Kenzie waited for whatever it was he still wasn't telling her.

"There is a catch. I need a submissive to enter the club. No unattached Doms allowed." Royce moved a hand behind her on the couch so his fingertips stroked the back of her neck soothingly. "I need a submissive to get in, and you want to help. Do you want to come with us?"

"What?" Was he asking her to go as his sub? Fear and excitement dueled inside her, and her heart pounded in her ears hard enough that she almost couldn't hear anyone over the roaring.

"Little Mac, you okay?" Royce was staring at her as though he feared she might collapse.

"I'm fine." The word escaped breathlessly as she pulled at the end of her braid, embracing the sting of the tug because it helped clear her mind.

"You'll be safe, I promise. Hans will be there too."

Sure, the idea of a crazed Russian mobster was scary, but that wasn't the only thing she was afraid of. She was afraid of becoming Royce's sub. The intimacy of a BDSM relationship, even if they were just pretending, could be overpowering and overwhelming. Things between her and Royce had changed so much already. Being his sub would cement that change forever. Neither of them would ever be able to deny or forget what would happen at this club.

"I think I should go and clean the guns," Hans muttered.

He set the empty plate down, got up from his chair, and took the two gun cases into the other room. Royce still hadn't taken his eyes off Kenzie, but he reached for a bottle of vodka and poured her a small shot.

"Drink this." He held it out and she downed it, wincing at the burn.

"Thanks, I needed that," she said, still unable to meet his gaze.

"Little Mac, look at me." He caught her chin to turn her head his way. She stared up at him, seeing those burning brown eyes, the hint of stubble that was like a sexy shadow on his jaw.

"You can do this. It's just like in class—I give you an order and you obey, no questions, no sass. The only difference is that you'll be in revealing clothes, probably cuffed, collared, and..."

"And...?" Kenzie had a sense she knew what was coming.

"And I might have to be intimate with you. Probably not full-on sex, but there might be something else required to prove our 'legitimacy' if it comes to that."

Something else? Like what? Her mind filled with an electric and erotic array of images of her on her knees, sucking on his cock, or him pleasing her with his mouth, using his hands on her, stroking, grinding, penetrating. There was an entire world of dark, erotic fantasies contained in those two simple words—*something else*.

"I wouldn't ask this of you, Little Mac, but..." His expression became even more sober. "You *respond* to that life. There's no point in denying it. I've seen it firsthand. You respond to that edge, that raw carnality. I think you could make the most exquisite sub if you were with a Dom you trusted."

Kenzie saw his eyes track her movements with an almost predatory fixation.

"What... What would I have to do? I've never really done anything like...what you do."

Royce stroked her chin, then his thumb slid up to her mouth, and he brushed the pad over her bottom lip.

"My subs call me *sir*. They ask no questions, but if you have one, you ask permission to speak, and I may deny or approve that request. I prefer my subs to sit at my feet or on my lap when I'm with other Doms."

Kenzie couldn't get the image out of her mind. Her kneeling at his feet, his hands in her hair, stroking her like a pet. It didn't seem all that degrading. Rather, it made her feel *hot*.

"What are you thinking about?" he asked softly.

"I..." Suddenly tongue-tied, she felt unable to confess her fantasies.

"You can't be shy. Not with me. It's part of the rules, Little Mac. A question is asked, and you must answer." He moved his hand to the back of her neck, holding her still as he gazed deep into her eyes. Her breath caught as he ran his eyes slowly over her body. "Fuck, I can't tell you how much I want this. How I want you to call me *sir* and be at my mercy." He seemed to be talking more to himself than anyone else.

"Dr. Devereaux..." She suddenly needed to put a barrier between them, even a small one.

"*Sir*," he corrected. "You'd better practice now."

"Sir," she amended, her heart skittering in her chest.

"You want to start small? Something you can handle?" he asked. She knew her body betrayed her when she nodded. His mouth kicked up in a grin.

"Then for the next few minutes, you submit to me with no resistance, or I deliver punishment like I did at the billiard table. Understand?"

"Yes, sir."

"Good. If I scare you, but you think you can continue,

remember to say *yellow*. *Red* means no. It's absolute and final, so you'd better mean it."

She remembered the rules.

"Got it...sir," she said.

He chuckled. "You don't have to say it every time, just when you address me with a question. You will know if you made a mistake." He let go of her neck and reached for her long braid, tugging gently on it. "Your first command—undo the braid. Thread your fingers through the strands. Do it slow."

He watched her, his hungry gaze making her body hum as she slipped the hair from the tie in her braid and began to undo the plait. Then she combed her fingers through the wet strands.

"In a D/s relationship, the partners care for each other always. That means you rely on me for food, for clothes, even to bathe if I wish, while the game is played." He retrieved a bowl of fruit that had come with the meal. He picked up a blueberry and held it to her lips. She knew instinctively what he wanted. She opened her mouth, and he slipped the berry inside. The sweet taste of it exploded on her tongue, and she couldn't resist sighing. He shifted on the couch as she made that single sound.

"Thank me when I give you food."

"Thank you, sir," she whispered, captivated by the intensity of his stare.

"Good," he praised, his voice silken. "Now straddle my lap and share the sweet taste of the blueberry with me."

She slid onto the couch, straddling him. Her knees bumped the back of the couch, and her pelvis pressed against his. She couldn't believe she was on Royce's lap, taking orders from him, but then, after she'd kissed him in the pool all of this seemed inevitable. She and Royce were like two neutron stars finally colliding after millennia of spinning around one another's orbits. The explosion, when it finally happened, would either destroy them both or turn everything into silver and gold.

"Share with me," he said in a low gruff voice, like a wolf close to biting her. "Kill me with your sweetness, Little Mac."

With a sudden sense of fear that she would lose out on even one minute of kissing him, she lowered her head to his. Her perilous attraction to him only pushed her onward.

These violent delights have violent ends. Isn't that how Romeo and Juliet *goes?*

10

She kissed him, unleashing everything she'd buried inside her. Everything she was ashamed of. All of the dark desires. The secret needs she'd hidden even from herself. All of it poured out of her and through her, infusing that kiss with the hot wave of her own inhibitions unbinding. For so long she'd held her life in perfect balance, keeping out of trouble and free from complications. But now she craved the danger she'd fed with her recklessness.

Royce was the one man who could upset her fine edge of discipline and send her world tumbling. She didn't care. Consequences be damned. The burning connection of their mouths consumed her until there was only this man, this glorious kiss.

A soft whisper of pain made her gasp as he fisted a hand in her hair and pulled her head back from his. Their eyes held like a key settling into a lock. Everything inside her went wondrously still. Kenzie clung to that feeling, digging her nails into his shoulders, afraid it would shatter this perfect feeling if he let go of her.

"I used to imagine closing my office door when we worked

late," he said, his voice low and throaty. "I wanted to shove everything off my desk and bend you over it." His words were ragged, as though he was barely in control. He tugged a little on her hair, punctuating the words *bend you over*, and her channel quivered in anticipation and arousal.

Kenzie's body burned as she joined him in that fantasy, spellbound.

"I can feel it all in my head, feel how good it would be to jerk your jeans down and fuck you on my desk. You would come so hard you would scream, and the sound would ricochet off the walls." The hard lines of his perfect jaw could've been cut from stone. She was caught up in the moment, melting from the inside as his words rendered her speechless.

"Every time you looked at me from your desk, it was there in your eyes, that *Fuck me Dr. Devereaux* look."

Oh. My. God. He knew. Somehow he'd always known.

Kenzie's arousal had been building ever since they'd kissed in the hotel pool. But now she was on fire inside. Her thighs clamped down around his hips, and she couldn't resist rocking against him. He shifted beneath her.

"Don't test me, babe." He groaned with frustration. "I'm not good at self-control, not when we're so far away from home."

"Why's that...sir?" she asked quietly, their gazes still locked.

"Because *here* there's no one to remind me to be good." He pressed her closer, his hands shaking as though he was on the verge of losing all control. "I could take you over and over, here where there aren't students to see us, no faculty watching our every move. It's just *us*. So you'd better say *red* before I lose my mind and break every goddamn promise I ever made to stay away from you." The edge to his tone warned her he meant every word.

Kenzie couldn't breathe. He wanted her as much she wanted him. So much that they were both losing their minds.

She was done being good, done pretending she had to deny herself what she wanted. She bit her bottom lip, holding his attention, and then she spoke the words that would send their stars colliding.

"Fuck me, Dr. Devereaux."

Royce's eyes widened and then narrowed, his breathing turned harsh, and before she could react he lifted her off the couch. With a squeak, she wrapped her legs around his waist as he carried them over to the bed. He dropped her on the bed and stood there, towering over her. He gripped the bottom of his black sweater, pulled it over his head, and tossed it to the floor. As he unbuttoned his jeans, he paused, breathing hard as he looked at her.

Finally, she was going to get the one thing she thought she could never have. Him. Joy, pure and bright, filled her like an exploding star. Her body hummed with a building desire that was unstoppable now that she'd made up her mind that she wanted to be with him.

"You want to stop? Now is your last chance, Little Mac. It's all or nothing."

She lifted her chin, challenging him. "I want it all."

The slow, wicked grin on his lips made her stomach flutter. He lunged for her, rolling her over onto her stomach. Shocked, she gasped as he pulled her hips up, unbuttoned her jeans, and pulled them down to her knees. She wore a pair of black panties underneath, and he groaned as he gripped them in his fist and yanked. The snap of breaking elastic stung her skin, causing another wave of heat through her core. Her folds grew wet from his rough handling. He gave her ass a hard smack and she hissed, burrowing her head in the bed, swallowing down the hungry moan that almost escaped.

"Ask me," he growled. "No, *beg* me." She looked at him

over her shoulder as excitement electrified her senses. He pulled the foil packet of a condom out of his jeans and tore it open with his teeth. She knew what he wanted to hear, and she wanted to say it too.

"Fuck me, Dr. Devereaux, show me how bad I've been."

"Jesus fucking Christ," he cursed, and jerked his jeans down. She had only an instant to see the thick length of his impressive cock jutting out before he sheathed a condom over it and then surged into her. He was too big, stretching her with the full sensation of his cock inside her. Pleasure pooled in her belly, and she arched her back with a hiss of pleasure. He wasn't gentle—he was a pounding, merciless god of sex. It felt like he was trying to kill her with overwhelming pleasure as he rammed into her over and over. His fingers dug at her hips, and she knew his hold would leave bruises, but it felt so good she didn't care.

He's marking your body. He's owning you. Just like you always wanted.

She knew she wasn't going to last another second. When the climax hit, it was like she'd fallen into a pit of firecrackers that were going off all around her. Explosions of pleasure, flashes of blinding light. She whimpered into the mattress as he leaned over her, slowing down his thrusts.

"You like that, babe?"

She nodded weakly.

He kissed the shell of her ear before he straightened and gripped her hips and began to ride her slower, making her feel each burning inch of him. Little aftershocks of pleasure still pulsed inside her channel as she clamped down on his shaft, squeezing tight.

"God, you feel like paradise. Like I died and went to heaven." His voice was low, almost guttural now.

"Royce, I can't—"

"Sir," he snapped, and his hand came down on her ass cheek.

"*Sir*," she echoed, blood pounding in her ears.

"Do you have any idea how fucking hot you are, Little Mac? That little ass up in the air, the way you clamp down on my cock—you're so fucking tight babe, so tight it's like no man's ever been inside you before."

His thrusts began to build in speed again. "I need to hear you scream it, shout it." His commands were followed by his body ratcheting up like a jackhammer. His hips slammed against her ass over and over, and the words came out of her mouth just like he wanted.

"*Fuck me*, Dr. Devereaux." Over and over again, she wasn't sure how many times she shouted those words. When she came a second time, everything went dark around her.

She came back to life a few seconds later, her mind fuzzy and her body limp. Every muscle was completely drained. And he was still inside her, fucking her hard. She groaned as he shoved deep, his cock filling her again and again, and he bellowed hard enough to make the walls shake. Then she felt him pull out, his harsh breath above her as she closed her eyes, still bent over the bed. Her legs sagged into the side of the mattress, but she had no strength to move.

That strange hot fuzziness seemed to deepen, like she was buried in a dozen thick blankets before a roaring fire.

"Little Mac, you okay?" Royce's voice was soft and gentle again, and yet she couldn't find the strength to speak.

"Hold on, babe, I got you." He pulled her jeans completely off her body, and she rolled over onto her back. He stripped her of her sweater and bra, then pulled her into his arms, carrying her into the bathroom. He set her inside the massive jetted bathtub in the corner. She wrapped her arms around her body as a chill set in.

Royce leaned over the tub and turned on the taps, testing

the water. She flinched as the cold water sprinkled her toes, and she tucked her knees up to her chin. He changed the taps, and the hot water crept up the tub's base toward her.

"Hang on," Royce said as he kissed her forehead and removed his briefs. She stared at his fully naked body, still lightheaded.

"Plenty of room for us both." He eased into the tub and then lifted her up and settled her on his lap. She curled into him, pressing her face into his throat, comforted by the dark piney scent that was uniquely his as the bath tub filled. She had no idea why she felt so strange, so muddled, but she could barely think, except to realize she felt safe in Royce's arms.

"You're okay, Kenzie," Royce said, one of his hands holding her back, pressing her close to him.

"Everything feels so..." She couldn't find the right words. "Cloudy," she finally said.

"Yeah, I know, babe. I know." He nuzzled the crown of her hair before he spoke again. "I think I sent you into subspace."

"What's that?"

"It's where a submissive is so overcome with her experiences that she fully lets go. It's sort of a sensual state of meditation. You go deep into your own head."

"Is that bad?" Kenzie didn't like the sound of subspace. She wasn't accustomed to feeling weak. Being weak meant she was vulnerable, and she never liked that under any circumstances.

"No, it's a good thing. For you to go into subspace while you're with me, it's nirvana to me. It means you trust me. You gave me all of yourself, and that total trust and openness exhausted your body. You'll be back to normal soon, I promise." He kissed her forehead, and she looked up at him.

"But the best part about subspace is that when you're with a good Dom, he will take care of you, spoil you. It's called aftercare, and this part is all about you, babe." He reached up to shut the water off, and she noticed the water had come up to her neck, heating her whole body. Royce's hands moved over her skin, stroking each limb, petting and caressing. It wasn't sensual exactly—rather it was soothing. The burning sexual tension that had moments before sent them catapulting off the edge of control was still there, but it was softened by a layer of comfort and familiarity between them. Her body belonged to herself once again, and she felt strangely new inside it, like an out-of-body experience in reverse. But as long as he held her, she felt good; she felt safe and grounded in the moment.

"Do you have any regrets?" he asked.

"Regrets? About what we did?" She shook her head. "I should regret everything, but..." But she couldn't. He'd just given her the most mind-blowing sex of her life, based on her darkest and most intimate fantasies, fantasies she now knew he shared. How could she ever regret that?

"Good. I never want you to regret anything while you're with me," he said.

She wouldn't regret any of this now, but it didn't stop her from worrying about what would happen later, when they returned to Long Island. They'd have to go back to normal, or at least pretend. She didn't know how to protect herself or him if this ever came to light. And she definitely didn't want to think about what the future held or what "together" meant for them. It was all too complicated, and right now complicated was not what she needed.

She shifted on his lap, feeling his thick shaft nudge her bottom. He was aroused again, which was understandable given they were sitting naked in a tub, but he didn't push himself on her, didn't make her do anything about his arousal.

He was simply content to hold her in his arms and let the hot water soak into their skin.

She couldn't help it. It was so relaxing that she began to drift off to sleep, clinging to him like her life depended on it.

Because in a way, it did.

"*Fuck me, Dr. Devereaux.*"

He'd never forget how those words sounded as they escaped her lips. He'd shared his dream, his ultimate fantasy, the one he'd jacked off to in the shower more times than he could count, and she'd given in and surrendered to him and his fantasy.

And it had been a thousand times better than anything his imagination had come up with. She'd managed to drift into subspace during their first time together. He'd never had that happen before with any woman. Not even the trained submissives at the Gilded Cuff were able to manage that.

He stared down at her, relishing how small and delicate she felt in his arms. So beautiful. He'd jumped on her like a rutting beast and hadn't even taken the time to enjoy exploring her.

We still have time for that. He would make sure of it. He had a thousand other fantasies he wanted to try out on her: tie her up, lick her folds until she cried out in pleasure...

And yet it had taken a fossil-smuggling ring and the Russian mob to get his grad student into his bed.

He held Kenzie for another fifteen minutes, listening to her soft, shallow breaths. She was asleep now. Something fuzzy and indescribable turned over in his chest. A strange sense of contentment began to fill him. He hadn't felt like this since... He closed his eyes, memories coming back, sharp and clear as the day they'd happened.

The firelight of the small campfire cast shadows against the tent. He sat between Fenn and Emery Lockwood, while Wes Thorne sat at the far end of their group. They laughed, holding sticks with gooey marshmallows over the small fire in front of their tent. There was joy. There was innocence.

This was the last night before his world changed, before his boyhood was ripped away, leaving him wounded inside and his throat raw from silent screams. Holding Kenzie now was like that final night before his childhood ended.

Grief was a funny thing. He'd spent twenty-five years mourning Fenn, thinking the men who'd kidnapped him had killed him when he was eight years old. But Fenn was alive. Fenn was okay. Yet the grief remained.

He had to stop mourning a ghost. Perhaps he was actually mourning the twenty-five years of a friendship he'd never gotten to have? Fenn's childhood was a loss that Royce was still coming to grips with, but the loss of his parents? That ran far deeper. When he'd lost Fenn, his parents had been his last refuge from the rest of the world. But then he'd lost them too, and he'd realized just how completely alone he was. That kind of grief could kill a man. But Kenzie not only eased the grief, she made it fade almost entirely. When he laughed with her, talked with her, shared his passion for fossils with her, it felt like they were partners in a way he was only just now starting to understand. She was a woman a man built a life with, and as much as he was convinced he wasn't the marrying kind, she was tempting him far more than he'd ever imagined anyone could.

Royce tightened his arms around her. He tried never to think of the past, especially those years when he'd spiraled close to the edge, trying to lose himself in sex, alcohol, fast cars, and loose women. But now he had everything to lose. Kenzie, their careers, maybe even their lives. Suddenly everything he'd thought didn't matter now mattered so much it scared the hell out of him.

Was this how Emery, Fenn, and Wes felt when they held their women in their arms? If it was, he would never give them any shit again about it. He might not love Kenzie, but he cared about her a hell of a lot, cared like crazy, and that was enough to make him pause and think.

He couldn't take her to Vadym's club, not when it would put her at so much risk. He'd been a fool to think he could take her there and keep her safe while he also tried to take out Vadym, but he hadn't wanted to leave her alone. He had to protect her at all costs. He could call Dimitri and get another sub for the club tomorrow night; that way Kenzie would stay at the hotel.

Carefully lifting her off him, he pulled the drain in the tub and then carried her out of the bath. He set her down on the floor and wrapped her in a fluffy white towel. She stirred and mumbled something he didn't quite hear.

"Time to get you into bed." He lifted her up again, loving how good she felt, how perfect she was. When he laid her down on the bed, she sighed and nuzzled her pillow. As much as he wanted to sleep next to her, skin to skin, he knew if he did he wouldn't be able to keep his hands off her.

He dug through her suitcase until he found an oversize red flannel shirt and another pair of black panties. He gave her shoulder a gentle shake. She blinked her eyes awake.

"Hey, Little Mac, help me get these on you. Then you can go back to sleep."

She sat up, a little dazed as she took the panties from him and slipped them on. Then she dropped the towel and pulled the shirt on. He turned his head away, not out of a sense of modesty, but for his own peace of mind. If he saw her breasts and her full hips, he might jump her all over again, and she needed rest. A lot of it. Opening up to him, going into subspace in their first encounter was still unbelievable.

Kenzie crawled between the covers of the massive king-size bed and drifted back to sleep. God, she was so damn trusting. He slipped on a pair pajama pants before he got under the covers and pulled her body toward him. She rolled over, her hair falling onto his chest. She smelled so good, like vanilla and a hint of flowers. No expensive cloying perfume from a bottle for his Little Mac. Just natural perfection.

He folded an arm behind his head and closed his eyes. That sense of peace was still there inside him. Being with Kenzie like this reminded him of his first dig in the Badlands.

He remembered standing amid the tall red-and-yellow rock formations, his boots crunching on cracked clay beds. The wind whistled across the stones, and the fierce sun bathed the world in blood-red and gold shades of color. He'd felt so at peace there. He could still close his eyes and feel the sandstone beneath his palms, smoothed by the wind and rain over thousands of years. The sun's heat was trapped within the earth, burning his fingers, and the scent of limestone was carried on the breeze that rustled through the tents of his fellow paleontologists.

The thin rock spires in the distance had been like unsteady obelisks in a haunted landscape. The land bore some of the most varied dinosaur fossils the world had ever seen. He remembered the rock wrens burrowing into holes in walls, and how he felt at home there in a way he couldn't explain. Perhaps it was because he was one of Earth's most recent creatures on a quest for some of Earth's most ancient.

Holding Kenzie in his arms now was just like that, an ancient quest for something he wasn't quite able to put a name on. A strange and wondrous connection was growing between the two of them, and it both scared the hell out of him and fascinated him.

I'm in deep shit.

What if he got too close? What if she died? What if they both fucked this up so bad that it destroyed their lives? He stroked a hand over her silky dark hair and sighed. It was going to be a long damn night.

In time he managed to drift into that place between awake and asleep, the place that held him helpless as he watched dreams play behind his eyelids.

He was on a plane, in a small but luxurious cabin peering out at the night and seeing the city below. The lights glittered like a thousand diamonds scattered across a swath of black velvet. Mist and fog crawled up from the edge of the sea, blurring the twinkle of city lights.

He held his breath, and his heart tightened in his chest as the runway came into view, the blinking signal lights whipping by too fast. The fog turned into a dark wind, coiling around the plane like a snake, choking it. Then the crash of metal and flash of fire engulfed everything in a deafening explosion.

The dream changed, the darkness softening to reveal a heavily wooded glen where emerald and amber points of light played upon the landscape of colors. The woods behind the Lockwood mansion. The lights, like errant will-o'-the-wisps, then became the flashlights of searchers. They shouted the names of two boys in the dark. Two boys who were lost. No, not lost—stolen.

With a sudden sense of terror, Royce gasped and bolted upright. For a second he couldn't remember where he was or who he was with until Kenzie stirred and spoke his name.

She sat up, combing her fingers through his hair. "Royce?"

He didn't respond. His heart was racing, and he felt dizzy. The nightmares always clung to him longer than he wished, while any good dreams slipped through his fingers like grains of sand. Royce leaned his head back against the black leather headboard.

"Royce, you're scaring me." Kenzie's use of his first name

seemed to ground him. He looked her way, and in the dimly lit room he could see her wide brown eyes were on him.

"Sorry, Little Mac." He lifted his hand, brushing it through her dark hair. "Bad dreams. Really bad dreams."

She shifted closer to him, resting her head on his shoulder. "Sometimes it helps to talk about them."

He chuckled dryly. "You get bad dreams?"

"Of course. Everyone does."

Not like mine. Mine are nightmares.

She seemed to sense his disbelief and continued. "I get these dreams where I'm running from something or someone, and I can't move fast enough. It's like time slows down, but only for me. You're vulnerable. Powerless. Helpless. You feel like the end is coming, and all you can do is be a spectator to it." She shivered and burrowed closer into his side and raised her head.

He looked down at her. There was an intimacy to this far greater than sex, and it scared him, but at the same time he didn't want to pull away.

"I have two dreams," he finally said. "Though they often follow one after the other. It starts off in a plane, flying over Manhattan. I can see the city lights, and the fog comes off the sea, swallowing everything below the plane. I know what's coming, but there's nothing I can do. I watch the runway disappear, and then it all ends in a fiery crash." His body seemed to shift to panic mode again, his heart racing, but he kept talking.

"Most of the time I don't wake up. Then I'm trapped in the woods behind the Lockwood mansion. I see searchlights, hear people calling out, but I can't make a sound. It's like I feel like I was Emery or Fenn when they were taken."

Kenzie was quiet a long moment. "You dream about the Lockwood kidnapping?"

Dark emotion seized his throat and threatened to strangle him. He nodded.

"I don't know much about what happened. I was only three." One of her hands lay flat on his chest, and he placed his hand over hers, holding her palm to his skin, needing that connection. It seemed to give him the strength to continue.

"They were kidnapped when we were only eight years old. We were just kids. I spent days at the police headquarters talking to child psychologists, social workers, FBI profilers, and none of them could help. My parents were there through it all, though, keeping me sane." He paused, pain lodged in his throat, and he swallowed past the lump in his throat.

"Three months later, Emery was found, but not Fenn. We didn't know it at the time, but he was taken by one of his kidnappers to Colorado and raised as his son. Twenty-five fucking years." He closed his eyes, seeing flashes of his nightmare. The beams of the flashlights swept the dark forest but never spotted them. "It's like I went into the woods that night with them, and part of me, just like a part of them, never came back."

Kenzie's nails dug into his chest. "Royce, that's awful. I'm so sorry."

He squeezed her hand. "It is what it is. I have lived with that missing part of myself for so long I don't know how to feel any other way." He knew what he was saying probably didn't make any sense. "And just when I thought I might be past it all, my parents died in a plane crash. I was nineteen."

"I knew about the crash," Kenzie admitted, rubbing her cheek against his shoulder. The tightness in his chest that always came whenever he talked about his parents eased a little.

"They were my world." He whispered the confession, and much to his relief she didn't laugh.

"I feel like that way about my parents, even my brothers."

"I forgot about your brothers." He chuckled.

"Yeah," she giggled. "And they would so kick your ass for what you did." She leaned in and sat up a little to kiss his startled lips.

"Babe, I'm sure your brothers are tough, but I can handle them." He cupped her cheek, and the smile on her mouth wilted at the corners, like flowers in the late fall.

"What is it?" he asked.

"Royce, what we're doing... It could ruin *everything*. It could end our careers."

He didn't blame her for worrying. He wasn't afraid of a lot of things, but losing his job at the university was a big one, and her career would be over before it even began.

"What do you want to do?" he asked. Whatever happened from this point on, it had to be her choice.

She bit her lip and gazed into his eyes. "I want this—I want *you*." She leaned into him, feathering her lips over his, relishing that she had this time to be with him, to have the right to kiss him whenever she wished without fear.

In that moment, she owned him in a way he hadn't thought possible. He kissed her back, cupping the back of her head and tasting her lips so sweetly that it brought tears to her eyes. She wanted him again, *needed* him in a way that was too strong for either of them to resist.

Kenzie reached for the buttons of her flannel nightshirt. "So..." She slowly revealed her body to him. The moonlight pouring in from the windows illuminated her breasts as she unwrapped herself like a Christmas present.

He knew just what he wanted to do. She sat on her knees next to him as she let the nightshirt fall away. He reached out, cupping one of her breasts, rubbing his thumb over one tight nipple. She arched her back, offering herself to him, and he groaned as he reached for her, gripping her by the waist and pulling her on top.

She settled onto his lap, straddling him. Her breasts were now close enough that he buried his face against them. He drew a nipple into his mouth and squeezed gently on her other breast. How could she taste so sweet? He let his hand slide down to her ass, tugging on the black panties. The urge to rip them again was almost overwhelming. Kenzie brought out a savage side in him. He always loved to be a bit rough, sure, but something about her made him feel like an animal, desperate to get at her.

"Wait," she said, hiking her hips up, giving him the chance to pull her panties down, but while she straddled him, he couldn't get them off. He grabbed her waist and pushed her gently so she landed on her back. Then he had the chance to slide the panties off her. He tossed them away and stared down at her.

"You're beautiful," he rasped, making it more than just praise for her body. The moonlight reflecting in her dark eyes. The way she spoke his name.

"*Royce*."

It made him weak-kneed.

"Go slow?" she asked timidly.

"Anything for you, Little Mac." He'd had her rough and dirty, and now he wanted her just like this, slow, agonizingly tender until it almost killed them both.

He slid back so he could part her knees with his hands. She was pink and wet, her core welcoming him, the patch of dark hair like an arrow pointing him to the most sensitive part of her. He needed to taste her, to feel her tremble and quake against his tongue. He kissed a path from her knee up to her inner thigh, and she wiggled, panting the closer he got. He was so used to tying a woman down to keep her immobile that he'd forgotten the pleasure of feeling a woman struggle to contain her building pleasure. He smiled as he pressed his lips to her clit. The swollen bud peeped out of its hood, and he latched on to it, sucking and swirling his tongue.

She hissed, her hips bucking, but he used his palms on her thighs to keep her legs spread open. He feasted upon her, licking at the sensitive folds, flicking his tongue at the most hidden part of her. He used his fingers with his mouth, bringing her to a panting, gasping orgasm.

She held in her scream, and her legs trembled around his shoulders. She was too weak to do much else but lie there, and that was exactly what he wanted. He slid up her body and freed his cock. He gripped his shaft, rubbing the tip of it over her wet slit. She moaned softly, arching her back. Kenzie was like a virgin sacrifice to a god, and he was so glad *he* was the one to own her. He took his time, sliding into her inch by precious inch. She reached up and gripped his shoulders as he fully seated himself inside her.

Royce leaned over, caging her with his body. She curled her arms around him, her nails scraping his neck in a way that sent shivers through him and made his cock even harder. When he took a woman, he liked it raw, hard, and dirty, and he rarely ever kissed them. But as he gently thrust into Kenzie, he felt the bone-deep need to kiss her, to feel her breath mixed with his as her body came apart at the same moment his did.

He slanted his mouth over hers. She kissed him back, and something inside him let go. He couldn't explain it, but the knot in his chest, the one that felt as heavy as lead, seemed to dissolve and finally disappear. He felt that pain and that darkness that had been inside of him since he was eight seem to ease. Kissing Kenzie and taking her body slowly in the darkness of this room made him feel like he'd been saved in a way he couldn't put into words. It was as if the flashlight beams swinging through the dark forest had finally found him.

His kiss became urgent, but he still rode her slowly,

keeping his thrusts gentle, and she responded in kind. Sweet agony flooded through him as he felt her climax. Her little gasp against his lips was so soft, and yet her coming apart seemed to rock though him to the very center of the world. His body seized, and he buried his face against her neck, kissing her as his own release exploded through him. Every part of his world shifted on its axis.

Long afterward, he continued to explore her mouth. It felt as though he'd never kissed a woman before. Her soft lips beneath his were heaven, and the playful dance of her tongue made him forget the dozens of women he'd been with. There was only this moment, only Kenzie for him.

He lifted his head to stare down at her. She was smiling drowsily. She didn't speak, but then he couldn't either as the lump in his throat made that impossible. Instead, he carefully lifted her up in his arms and tucked her beneath the sheets, curving his body around hers.

"Good night, Royce," she murmured against his chest, and her breathing slowly deepened. He held her close, his thoughts fractured as he tried to understand what had just happened to him. But deep down he knew. He'd always known. He was falling in love with her.

I'm so fucked.

11

Pale morning light roused Kenzie from one of the deepest sleeps she'd ever had. She opened her eyes, blinking slowly as she took in the elegant and lavish room around her.

This isn't home. This is...

She was bewildered for a long moment, wondering how she'd gotten here, in Russia with her professor and in his bed. Memories from last night hit her, and she winced as she shifted. Her inner legs were sore, and between her thighs hurt too. She bit her lip to hide a smile.

Dr. Devereaux sure knew how to make love, as they had stared into each other's eyes and he'd gone slow, it had rocked her to her very core. She hadn't been a virgin before, but that last time was what every girl dreamed her first time would be like.

She sat up in bed, still tender all over, and it felt *good.* She tucked her knees up to her chin and realized she was smiling. She couldn't seem to stop. That was when she heard it, the sound of the shower running and the voice of a man singing in deep tones. Normally, a man singing in the shower would have been cringeworthy, but not Royce. His voice called to her like a male siren luring a lady sailor to jump ship.

Kenzie slipped out of bed, wrapping the top sheet around her like a toga, and padded over to the bathroom. Beside the massive hot tub was a large marble shower. Royce had his back to her, the hot water pouring in rivulets over him from his head down to his muscled ass. All she could do was picture digging her nails in that ass when he thrust into her. Just like that, she was wet for him all over again.

She approached the shower, tilting her head to listen to him. He was singing the Metallica song "Nothing Else Matters" in a beautiful baritone. God, he could've been a rock star, not just a paleontologist.

"Dr. Devereaux?"

He froze, cutting off his song abruptly. He turned, revealing his cut body, the perfectly ripped muscles and abs too chiseled to be real, yet they were. She had stroked her hand over them last night.

"Little Mac," he replied, his eyes raking over her.

"Need some company?" She was so nervous asking, she thought she might die. What if he regretted last night? What if he'd had his fun and was done with her? She wasn't ready for this to end. Even though she knew this *would* end regardless when they returned to Long Island, she could pretend for a few more days that this wasn't going to be over.

"If I ever say no when you ask me..." He trailed off, shaking his head with a wry chuckle. He opened the shower door. "Get in here. Leave the sheet on the floor."

Laughing, she dropped the sheet and stepped inside, closing the shower door behind her. They stood there staring at each other, the water hitting his body before he placed her body in front of his, soaking her with the hot spray. She sighed and leaned back against him, feeling his cock press against her lower back. God, she loved that he was so much taller, like a dark-haired Viking. He reached up and massaged her shoulders.

"Want me to wash your hair?" She glanced at him in surprise. He shrugged. "What can I say? I give good *head*." He winked and she giggled, heat flooding her cheeks.

"I thought that was my line? You might have to give me a few pointers," she shot back.

He suddenly smacked her across the ass, giving a light sting and making her squeak in surprise.

"Sassy," he muttered, but the gleam of humor in his eyes pleased her. "Maybe you should prove your skills right now?" He rocked his hips, and she knew what he actually meant. Her heart raced madly as she turned to face him. She'd never really gone down on a man before and had been kidding with her comment, but the hungry look in his eyes made her want to give it a try.

"Okay..." She put a hand on his chest and shoved him back so he was pressed against the back of the shower.

Then she knelt down. His erect shaft, so close to her, was intimidating as hell. He was way too big for her mouth, but she could try. She placed one hand on his lower stomach, tracing the V indentation of his pelvis and hip while she reached up and gripped his cock with her other hand. She opened her mouth and took him inside. He groaned loud and low, his hips moving forward, as if he couldn't stop involuntarily thrusting.

"Fuck, Kenzie... Fuck." He moaned her name over and over.

She took him in. The slightly salty taste of his cock was different but not unpleasant. She took her time, listening to the sounds he made. She licked, sucked, squeezed with her hand, pumped him, and tried hollowing out her cheeks as she moved her mouth over his shaft. When he gripped her head and began to thrust hard, she couldn't help but moan at the tip of his cock on the back of her throat. He suddenly cursed, and she tasted *him* on her tongue.

He let go of her head and she swallowed, licking up every drop of him from her lips before she let him slide from her mouth with a pop. Her legs were so shaking hard from own arousal. That had been the hottest thing she'd ever done.

He lifted her to her feet and kissed her, his mouth moving over her like a ravenous beast. She moaned against his lips, and he smacked her ass again.

"You really are going to fucking kill me, Little Mac," he growled. They kissed for several minutes, their bodies pressed together until he was hard against her stomach.

"Again?" she teased before nibbling his bottom lip. His eyes almost rolled to the back of his head as he groaned in pleasure.

Before she could react, he lifted her up, pinning her against the side of the shower opposite the door and thrust up into her. He'd gotten hard again fast, and her channel was still sore from last night, yet he took her hard and furious and she loved every sharp, pleasurable second of it. Her breasts pressed to his chest, and she clung to him as he fucked her. Then she came and seconds later he did the same. He leaned against her, holding her up, still impaled on his cock. His forehead pressed to hers and he sighed, his eyes closed.

"You've got to slow me down, babe. Or else I'll just keep fucking you like there's no tomorrow."

She laughed. "That's not a bad thing. I'm just mad this is the kind of sex I've been missing out on. I'm making up for lost time."

"I've been missing out too. Being with you—" He paused, his eyes searching hers, and the sudden blossom of vulnerability she found in his eyes undid her. "It's like nothing else, like *no one* else."

Her heart pounded against her ribs. "It's the same for

me," she whispered back.

Neither of them spoke for a moment. The water sprayed on their backs, steam crawling up all around them. He finally withdrew from her and let her back down to her feet, but he didn't let go, didn't put any distance between them.

"Now, I think you said something about washing my hair?" she reminded him, loving that at least for now she could tease him. She could be herself. They weren't Ms. Martin and Dr. Devereaux—they were Kenzie and Royce. Someday she would look back on these precious moments and hold them close in her heart, no matter what happened after.

"I did, didn't I? All right. Turn around, babe." He twirled a finger in the air, and she obeyed, letting the water hit her skin before she dipped her hair beneath the spray. Once her hair was wet, she let him massage her scalp with shampoo. It felt like heaven having his strong hands rub her head. Lord, she would've done anything he wanted as long as he kept doing that.

"Better than sex," she moaned in delight as he finally let her rinse.

His low, rough chuckle made her shiver. "I'll have to do better next time I'm inside you. Can't let a little scalp massage show me up."

Kenzie grinned at him as she reached for the shower gel. She was too short to wash his hair, but she could still wash everything else. She put a dollop of gel in her palm and touched his chest, rubbing him in slow, steady caresses. She took her time, learning every slope, indent, and bulge of his muscled body. He became silent as she worked on cleaning him. She came across a small scar on his left arm, and she traced the ridge of it, raising questioning eyes to him.

"Motorcycle wreck," he said, watching her with dark, hot eyes.

She found another scar. "And this?"

"This?" He touched the mark on his rib. "Free-climbing a mountain. And this"—he lifted his arm and showed her a jagged scar on his lower torso—"tangled with a smuggler in China. The guy caught me with a knife."

"Jesus, you have a death wish," she joked, but he didn't laugh. "Royce." She spoke his name soberly, worried she might have upset him.

"You're not far off, Little Mac. For a long time, I had this need to risk *everything*."

She rinsed her hands and pressed herself against him, needing to hold him. He hugged her back, his voice becoming a whisper.

"I needed to feel something, something to pull me out of the grief I felt. For a long time I felt so fucked up, so dark in my head all the time. Doing stupid stuff somehow reminded me I was still here, that I hadn't lost myself."

She squeezed him tight, wishing she could banish the ghosts of his past and free him from the chains of his loss. "I'm so sorry."

"Don't be," he said. Her gaze met his, and she saw the real Royce. The young man who'd been forced to grow up far too soon into the man she had—

Kenzie blocked out the dangerous train of thought before it could fully manifest.

"Sometimes a man discovers who he really is when his soul is tested. Trials of fire, you might say. I've been tested many times, and it has made me one tough bastard."

She understood. She remembered Royce pinning down the man who'd dared to hurt her. A gun shoved in the man's face. The knowledge that he could have shot the man should have terrified her, but it didn't. He was Royce, and he was her safe harbor, always had been, even before she'd known she would someday need one.

She bit her lip and frowned. "I haven't been tested, not like you." Her calm, safe life hadn't given her anything. She wasn't tough, and she wasn't brave. How had she ever been foolish enough to think coming along as some kind of silly sidekick on this adventure was a good idea?

"Babe, I'm glad you had a happy life. Someone deserves it. But this?" He waved around them. "This situation is my fault. I nearly got you killed just because you were in my office when they came looking for me. And we're not even out of the woods yet. God, I wish none of this ever happened." He closed his eyes, and the momentary show of weakness was so unlike like him that she shuddered.

"We shouldn't be here, facing a fucking nightmare," Royce said. "The last thing I ever wanted to do was to put you in danger." He brushed a lock of wet hair back from her face and lowered his head to kiss her.

It was the kind of kiss she would never forget, the kind that seemed to shake her to her soul with the force of an earthquake. It was a life-changing kiss, one that was both tender and hungry, one that made her feel safe yet in danger of falling in love.

And that was what scared her like nothing else. She'd never been in love, and she *knew* that if she fell in love with Royce Devereaux she would never love anyone else. Some first loves are simply that, your *first*. But Royce? He was a man who would be the love of her life, the one that no other would ever compare to. There was no way she could love anyone else like this.

He's got my heart in his hands, and he doesn't even know it. She cleared her throat and mumbled something about needing to shave. They switched places as he washed his hair, and she used her razor to quickly take care of her legs and under her arms, trying not to let him see.

She hadn't thought any of this through when she'd snuck

into the bathroom with just her bedsheet. She finished shaving and turned to see him watching her.

"Nice view." He nodded at her and at her half-bent position.

Oh God, how mortifying.

"Never be ashamed to show me your ass, Little Mac." He chuckled and picked up his own razor and rubbed shaving cream over his face. She watched him shave, seeing his strong arms carefully move as he dragged the razor over his skin. Then he buried his face in the hot spray, and they both got one final rinse before Royce cranked the knob to the right, killing the water. He retrieved two towels, giving her one.

Hans's voice boomed from outside the bathroom door. "You two about ready to go? I want breakfast."

"Oh my God," Kenzie hissed. "He knows we—"

"Of course he knows. The man is a bodyguard. His job is to guard our bodies. I'm afraid that means he will know more than you want him to." Royce rubbed aftershave into his face and grinned before he swatted her ass through her towel. She squeaked and punched him in the arm.

He grabbed his arm, still smiling. "Yikes. Who taught you to hit like that?"

"My brothers. I have two of them, remember?"

"Right." He was still laughing. "Next time, I'll spank your ass when you're tied down. Then you can't punch me back."

"As if I'd let you." She returned his grin.

"Babe, I'm figuring out what makes you burn inside in the best way. In time, I'll get the chance to do all sorts of things to you. I promise you'll be thanking me long before I'm through."

She knew he was right, and damned if she didn't like the idea of all those things he would do to her.

"Hurry up, Little Mac. We're gonna meet an old friend of mine."

12

Vadym Andreikiv sat in his leather chair in his office, glaring at Jov Tomenko.

"You said they were in Moscow, but you lost track of them at the airport."

Jov was a burly brute born in Siberia. He was a man of few words, and he kept secrets well, but if he didn't start talking, then Vadym would replace him—permanently.

"They hired a private car service. Our hacker team checked all the major databases and the taxicabs. Electronic receipts are easy to track these days, but we couldn't get a lock on their location."

Vadym pulled a cigar cutter from his desk and stared at Jov as he sliced off the tip of the cigar with a menacing sound.

"Think carefully about your next words, Jov. You don't want to displease me."

Jov audibly swallowed.

"I'll find them. Or..."

"Or?"

"Well, you could *lure* him to you, couldn't you? Put the word out where you can be found. Make Devereaux come to us. Then I can deal with him." Jov clenched his hands together, his knuckles cracking.

Vadym considered the idea. That was certainly an option. Bring Devereaux to him, and then he would have that fucking American under his power, and the man would have to do what he wanted. Normally he'd bribe a man like Devereaux, but he knew enough to know Devereaux wouldn't take money and he wouldn't willingly lie about the origins of fossils. His reputation was beyond reproach. It was also what made him perfect for Vadym's plans.

"Put the word out, as you put it, that I'll be at the club tonight. He can come and meet my friends."

Jov grinned darkly. "And what about Dr. Abramov?"

"Tie up the loose ends."

Jov nodded and left Vadym's office. Vadym picked up his cell phone and dialed a number.

"Yes?" a gruff voice answered.

"Have the plane ready to fly to Kyakhta tomorrow. We will have guests."

"Of course."

He hung up and spun in his chair to stare up at the map of Russia and Mongolia that was pinned to the wall. He would make Dr. Devereaux accompany him to Ulaanbaatar, where his most recent acquisition of a complete velociraptor skeleton was being held securely. If he could get Dr. Devereaux to sign off on the papers and say the fossils came from just outside of Kyakhta, a Russian city on the edge of the Russian-Mongolian border, then he could sell the fossils to an American or European natural history museum for a few million dollars. Devereaux was an expert, one of the world's best on velociraptors. If any other museum claimed it, he would have been called in to verify the origins of the fossils, which mean Vadym had to have him and no other paleontologist sign off on the documents.

Vadym picked up a long, curved claw from a velociraptor and dragged its lethal tip along his palm, leaving a red mark. For so many years he'd never felt pain, never understood what made others feel anything. He'd scraped his way to power in Russia, to the point where even government officials tread lightly in his presence. They recognized that something was broken in him, something that made him dangerous. He would feed his own mother to stray dogs if he saw an advantage in it.

Devereaux had already robbed him of the sale of a complete nest of oviraptor eggs, which would have brought him millions. One more reason why Royce Devereaux had to be made to come to heel, and made to betray his principles. Vadym could not have someone like Devereaux stopping him from selling his fossils. Fossils were money, and money was power. Power was control. Vadym cared about nothing except the control of his own destiny.

It was harder and messier to trade in humans, and drugs were for fools. Weapons deals had no finesse. Fossils were a much better way to amass wealth. He ruled the sex trade because it amused him to see women and even some men lose their souls, die inside, and still be shells that breathed. That power over people, the ones he sold and the ones who came to him, desperate to buy—they were all under his control. But the sex trade needed funding, bribes for officials and law enforcement to keep quiet. It was costly, and Interpol had been breathing down his neck lately, looking for a way to bust him on charges, but so far he'd managed to hide his tracks and destroy all evidence when necessary. That meant Vadym needed to keep the fossil trade successful in order to afford his little hobby.

A hunger to hurt something rose up in him, and he stood and walked over to a bookshelf full of priceless Western literature first editions. Most were irreplaceable. He'd bought them because he loved to know he could destroy them at his leisure. He pulled one back halfway from its companions. There was a soft click as the shelf separated from the wall. Vadym pulled the bookshelf away from the wall, revealing a padlocked door. He removed a key from his pocket and unlocked it. When he opened it, the light from his office illuminated the dark confined space and the pathetic half-naked figure chained to a spike on the floor.

"Good afternoon, Elena," he said in English. The figure whimpered as he lifted a long black whip off the wall and flexed it in his hands. Her lovely green eyes were wide with terror. He felt it, that surge of something inside his empty chest. A flutter of joy? Pleasure? It was as close as he could get.

Such a sweet little creature, Elena. An American college student studying abroad in Moscow who had made the mistake of visiting the club with her friends. He'd had her abducted in the bathroom and taken to his private rooms. After he'd taken her, he'd basked in her screams and tears and decided he would keep her until she broke completely. Then he would toss her to his men. How long she would last after that, who was to say? His men were rough brutes, after all.

"Do you wish to play a game, Elena?" He caressed her name and she shuddered, but for a brief instant he saw a flash of fire in her eyes. It was that fire he had to destroy. He twisted the whip around his fists and reached her chain. She screamed, and Vadym laughed.

Yes, he would enjoy breaking this little bitch, and then he could relax. Jov would set the trap for Devereaux, and he would tie up all the loose ends. It was all coming together. His lips twisted in a cruel smile as he raised the whip.

ROYCE FACED MOSCOW STATE UNIVERSITY'S VAST CENTRAL building located on Sparrow Hills in the southwest part of the city. The building had been designed by Lev Vladimirovich Rudnev and was the tallest of Moscow's Seven Sisters, the high-rises built by Stalin's labor force. It was both grim and beautiful at the same time.

"Holy cow." Kenzie tilted her head back to look up at the center spire that reached toward the cloudless winter sky.

"One of the tallest buildings in the world, aside from the Sears Tower, until 1990," Hans said as he joined them. Royce and Kenzie both turned to stare at him.

"What?" He shrugged. "You guys didn't grab a brochure from the hotel lobby before we left?" He waved a small pamphlet.

Royce sighed and rubbed his eyes with his thumb and forefinger. He needed another hit of coffee. "This isn't a vacation, Hans."

"You say super-secret mission to stop a Russian mobster, I say vacation. To-ma-to, to-mah-toe." Kenzie giggled as Hans waggled his eyebrows teasingly.

"Let's just get inside. We need to find Dr. Abramov." He led the way. It was close to Christmas break here in Moscow, just like in the States, and the building was mostly deserted. There was a listing of professors, and Royce scanned the symbols, his familiarity with the Cyrillic alphabet strong enough to recognize Lev's name.

"Tenth floor." He nodded toward a set of gold elevator doors. "Let's go."

The tenth floor contained the offices for anthropology, geology, archaeology, and paleontology. Nearly all of the offices were closed, however, and the hall was dark except for the translucent glass of the windows on the professors' doors.

Lev's light was on, and his door was unlocked. Royce didn't bother knocking. He had known Lev since he was a grad student. They'd gone on groundbreaking digs in China, Mongolia, and the American Badlands. Lev was like an uncle to him—if that uncle had been a skinny old vodka-drinking Russian.

"Lev?" As they entered the office, Royce's feet trod upon broken glass. "What the—?"

He heard a soft gasp. Kenzie was covering her mouth with one hand and pointing at something behind the desk. He walked around the desk and froze. Lev Abramov was lying on the ground, his eyes open and blinking slowly, blood pooling beneath his lower back. A knife was shoved through the gray sweater he wore. His body drew in rapid breaths.

"Shit," Hans growled. "Knife's still in him. Royce, we interrupted the person who did this. He could still be here. You treat the wound, and I'll clear the halls." He rushed from the room, but all Royce saw was the blood and the wounds on his friend. The world spun a little, and he had to shake the fog out of his mind and regain control.

"Oh my God!" Kenzie gasped and rushed to Royce's side, gripping his arm.

"Stay back," he said as he checked on his friend. It looked bad. "Fuck." His heart sank as he knelt by Lev. There was too much blood. He knew that if he pulled the knife out the bleeding would only be faster. This wasn't a wound that could be treated.

"Royce..." The older man hissed out his name. His old friend's eyes were starting to turn glassy.

"What can I do?" Kenzie knelt by him, her face white as alabaster.

"Nothing, Little Mac, he's too far gone."

Lev lifted one hand, gripping Royce's arm. His brown eyes grew intense, as though what little life he had left was burning up fast. "Royce..."

"Lev, I'm sorry," Royce whispered.

The older man shook his head. "It is I...who am sorry." The man looked between Royce and Kenzie.

"Sorry? For what?"

"I betrayed you...to Vadym's men. They needed to fake fossil documents. They threatened my family."

"What?" Royce stared down at Lev, stunned.

"The oviraptor nest last year, the one you proved came from Mongolia—it was his. He was angry, and I told him where to find you." The sorrow and the pain in Lev's eyes made a lead knot form in Royce's stomach.

So that was how this bastard had found him. He'd kept his address and his information through the university concealed —even his picture wasn't available.

"Sorry, old friend." Lev's hand on his arm weakened.

"They did this? Vadym's men?" Royce asked, his voice breaking as he tried not to face the fact that his friend and mentor was bleeding out and there was nothing he could do to save him.

"Yes...wanted to—silence me. He knows you're here," Lev warned, but Royce already knew that.

The question was, did Vadym have a way of tracking or predicting his moves? He'd used independent cabs, paid with cash, and booked their rooms with fake identities. Even Kenzie had a fake passport. Hans's connection on Long Island had been thorough.

Royce stared at the man who'd been like family to him. "Lev..."

"Be brave...dig deep." The old paleontologist's eyes closed, and he exhaled one last time.

"Dig deep." Royce's chest tightened as he touched Lev's lifeless hand. He had lost yet another person in his life. He dropped his head, closing his eyes as he tried not to let panic race through him.

"Royce." Kenzie grabbed his other arm and pulled him up so he was standing. "Royce, I'm so sorry."

Royce nodded stiffly. The pain was locked inside his chest, like a demon trapped in an iron cage. It rattled and quaked, but the lock held it—for now.

"The police are coming. I called them, but we can't be seen here." Hans looked down at the body behind the desk.

Royce nodded. "What's the story?"

"The story is we have to go. *Now.* Wipe our prints off anything we touched. Take the stairs back down. We can't be seen, can't be interviewed. If Vadym is as powerful as you say he is, we won't last ten minutes if we end up being taken in by the police."

"Good point," Royce said. "Let's roll."

Hans waited for Royce and Kenzie to exit and he stayed behind, using a cloth to wipe down the handles of the door before he jogged to catch up with them as they reached the stairs.

"Royce, what was he saying about an oviraptor nest?" Kenzie kept pace with him as they raced down the stairs.

"A year ago I was called in to assess the country of origin for a rare find, a complete fossilized nest of oviraptor eggs that had been recovered after a smuggler raid. The ownership of the nest was in dispute. I happened to be in Mongolia on another dig and was called in to verify the origins. Mongolian authorities were unable to claim the nest, and the Russians firmly believed it was from their country near the border between Russia and Mongolia. When a dispute arises, they bring in an outside source—like me, someone who wouldn't benefit from the situation—to study the fossil specimen to determine the country of origin. I came in and ran soil samples and other examinations to conclude the nest was from the Bayanzag area of Mongolia."

Kenzie paused as they reached the landing to the seventh floor.

"Bayanzag?" Her eyes widened. "You mean the Flaming Cliffs? That's where Roy Chapman Andrews found the first discovery of dinosaurs in the Gobi Desert in the 1920s. It's illegal to remove fossils from there."

"Right. And that's exactly why the Russians need me. If I lie, it will carry a lot of weight. The Mongolians would be too afraid to challenge it, and someone like Vadym can claim it and sell the fossils as Russian finds. He has enough power, I imagine, to cut through any red tape that would stop most smugglers."

"So, the oviraptor?"

"It seems Vadym was the man behind the oviraptor nest sale. But because of me, the Mongolians were able to claim ownership of the nest. It's now in Ulaanbaatar, in a protected museum."

"So Vadym wants payback, right?" Hans suddenly chimed in, catching up to them. "That's what shitheads like him do. All these mobsters have serious control issues and what they think is pride, and you definitely wounded his. He wouldn't have forgotten. I bet he's been hurting to get you back."

"It sounds like it," Royce said. He'd put a target on his back, and he hadn't even known it. Now Kenzie was sharing that target, and it was all his fault.

As they reached the first floor, Hans poked his head out of the stairwell doorway into the corridor. "The police are waiting to catch the elevator. I told them what floor Abramov was on. If we act natural, we might get out without being questioned." He held up his hand, indicating for Royce and Kenzie to wait. Then he started walking into the hall, hands shoved into his coat pockets. He got past the elevators, the police still not looking his way. So he nodded at them with the barest lift of his head.

"Okay, let's go. Play along." Royce curled an arm around Kenzie's shoulders, pulling her close as they walked down the hall. The police officers glanced their way, their heads covered with furry hats that Royce had always thought was a stereotype rather than a reality, like Mounties wearing red uniforms all the time.

Royce nearly laughed. The entire situation was so damned awful, but he held it together and only glanced at the police officer as they passed. The man nodded in greeting at him as the elevator closed. Royce exhaled in relief as they slipped out into the chilly air, the police left far behind. They joined Hans, who was already farther down the sidewalk. He'd given them space to seem less suspicious, but the farther they got from the building, the more he let them catch up.

"That was fucking close."

"I shouldn't have called them," Hans growled. "I thought the professor might have been able to pull through."

Royce shook his head. "No, whoever attacked him knew the right spot to strike, even though we interrupted the attack. There was no way to stop the bleeding."

"We didn't know that at the time," Kenzie said. Royce tightened his arm around her. There was no chance he would let her go now. After everything they'd been through together, he didn't want her to pull away, to hide anything from him. She'd been shot at, chased, and had now witnessed a man bleed to death before her eyes. That wasn't the apple pie, sweet life she was used to.

And it's all my fault.

She stared up at him, her doe-like eyes as brown as chocolate and full of horrors a woman like her should never have to see.

"Let's get out of here, Hans. I need to buy some things for tonight."

"Things?" Kenzie asked.

"If I'm going to the club tonight, I'm going to need a few toys."

"I'm still going with you, right?" She came to a stop by the large lake near the university grounds.

"No chance. You're going to stay in the room. I'm not letting you get within a mile of Vadym."

Kenzie's lips thinned, and he saw that rebellious spirit he loved so much flare to life. She wasn't a brat, and she didn't fight him just for the sake of fighting, but she fought for what she believed in. It made him fucking hard as hell when he knew a battle with her was coming. Not because he would force her to agree, but because he loved how brave she was. Most TAs didn't argue with their professors because they felt it put their jobs at risk.

"I came here with you, I showed you I could obey commands. I showed you that I trusted you, and now you need to trust me. I know you think I'll be safer in the hotel room, but you're wrong. I'm safer with you and Hans. I agreed to come here knowing all the risks. These guys tried to kill me. I want to see Vadym face-to-face and..."

"Kenzie, you don't understand. You think we're like Batman and Robin, but you can't just tag along on this mission. It's clear we're at even more risk than I expected." Royce wanted to hug her, to pull her in his arms, but he had to keep his distance. He wasn't going to talk about cold-blooded murder while holding her. "When we go to the club tonight, we're taking him out. It's..." Royce struggled for words. "It's not going to be pretty. I don't want you to see me do what I have to do."

Kenzie's dark-brown lashes fell as she closed her eyes for a brief instant, and then she glared at him. There was a chill to her eyes, a resolve he'd never seen before.

"You said he's involved in human trafficking. It's not murder to put down a monster like that. We end him, and we try to save anyone we can. I have to help. I'd never forgive myself if I sat out of this fight." She drew the collar of her peacoat around her neck and continued to stare him down.

Royce glanced toward Hans. The bodyguard was studying Kenzie with an approving gaze. He shrugged when he noticed Royce looking his way.

"Your call," Hans said. "She's right about one thing, though—she might be safer with us than at the hotel. We have no idea how much Vadym knows about us right now."

Royce stroked his jaw, surprised by Little Mac's unflinching stare.

"Fine. But you must stay with me every minute. And if we tell you to get out of there, you do it, even if it means leaving us behind. Can you agree to that?"

He saw a flash of hesitation, but then she nodded.

"Good."

He only prayed that she wouldn't get hurt. He couldn't think of anything worse than losing her. His little grad student had wormed her way into his heart, one he'd protected like a fortress, yet there she was, buried deep inside, making him feel vulnerable and exposed.

13

Kenzie held her breath as she snapped the expensive black bra around her torso. The silky set was given to her by Royce earlier in the day, and they were definitely on the slightly too-tight side, making her feel restless and uncomfortable, even though the fabric was smooth and light against her skin.

As she adjusted the lingerie and looked herself over in the mirror, her thoughts turned from the elastic biting into her ass cheeks toward the things Royce would want to do to her once he saw her in the lingerie. She squeezed her thighs tight and slipped a shimmering knee-length gold sheath dress over the lingerie, then slipped on the black heels and finally a black coat with a fur collar.

She stepped out of the bathroom unnoticed by either Royce or Hans, who were caught up discussing their strategy for the night. Royce wore a black suit and a blue-gray shirt with a steel-gray tie. His wild, wavy dark hair had been tamed back a little, and he was leaning against the wall, arms crossed as he listened to what Hans was saying. He looked intimidating and gorgeous and too wonderful to be real. But he was real, and at least for a short time, he was hers.

Hans had cleaned up nicely as well, but he looked far less comfortable in his suit than Royce given the way he fidgeted and tugged at his collar.

She took another step into the room, and Royce turned, his eyes locking onto her and then sweeping over her dress. Her body responded the way it always did with him. Heat pooled low in her belly, and she fought off a shiver of need.

"So? Do I look okay?" she asked. She personally thought she looked pretty good. The gold dress hugged her curves, and the black heels made her legs look fantastic. She'd been able to get her hair to curl a little, and even her makeup wasn't too bad.

"You look—" Royce began, then cleared his throat and tried again. "You look good, kid."

Hans snorted. "He means you look fantastic. Forgive the boy for being tongue-tied around a pretty girl."

Royce shot the man a glare, and Kenzie couldn't help but giggle. Hans had a soft side, one that he only seemed to reveal around Royce. He probably wasn't aware of it, but she saw that look of fatherly approval on his face. From what Kenzie now knew about him, it didn't surprise her. The loyalty of the people in Royce's life was immense, and yet he seemed unaware of it at times.

He's too lost in the pain of the past to see what he has now.

Kenzie couldn't help but think of her own family. Her parents were so boring, so normal, but in the best possible way. Her brothers, Michael and John, were both attorneys in Manhattan. She had never known real fear or pain until she'd met Royce. But despite the danger, he made her feel alive, and she felt that being with him, even for just a little while, would change her. And she believed she was changing him too.

She closed her eyes, burning the sight of him looking at her like that into her memory. She was so close to falling in love, a feather could have knocked her over the edge. She'd be forever lost in his brown eyes, lost in his drugging kisses, and yet...not lost at all. He made her feel her own strength and sense of self.

She wasn't just someone's kid sister, a student with a promising future, or even a sex object to fill some need. From the moment they'd met, he had encouraged her to be the best version of herself. She was proud of her achievements, standing up for her theories and research and charting the course of her own career. That was the kind of man *any* woman would love.

"Ready to go?" Royce's deep voice pulled her from her thoughts.

"Ready as I can be." She laughed, trying to ignore the flutter of nerves inside her.

"It's going to be okay," he promised as he brushed a lock of hair behind her ear.

"Right." She gripped his wrist as he cupped her face, and they looked deep into one another's eyes.

"Come on, kids, time to go. Stop making googly eyes at each other. Plenty of time for that after we leave Moscow with one dead Mafia dickhead behind us."

That reminder of reality snapped them out of the spell. They stepped back from each other, and Royce waved for her to follow Hans into the hall. "Let's go."

A black SUV was waiting outside for them. Kenzie sat beside Royce in the back seat, while Hans took the seat next to the driver. The day had passed so quickly that Kenzie was shocked to see that night had fallen. It was nearly ten, the time when clubs and bars would be thriving throughout the city. She didn't see the street where they were when the car finally stopped. A crowd of people stood in the line by the front door.

"Did we get a confirmation from Dimitri that we can get in?" Hans asked Royce.

"Yeah. He just texted me. He's inside with your girl, Hans. He's got our names on the list. Vadym isn't there yet."

The bodyguard huffed something under his breath that sounded like, "I don't need a woman." Kenzie bit her lip to hide a smile. She couldn't picture the bodyguard indulging in BDSM. He was still very attractive, with a hint of silver in his dark hair and serious dark brown eyes, but he'd never once shown a hint of unprofessionalism around her except when he cracked jokes at Royce's expense.

Royce helped Kenzie out of the car and paid the driver in cash. She wasn't used to wearing heels, and the ones Royce had given her made her feel off balance. She just prayed she wouldn't have to run in them. If everything went as planned, they would deal with Vadym discreetly and leave. Just as they reached the steps leading up to the Black Diamond Bar, Royce pulled Kenzie close and slipped something into her hand.

"What—"

He kissed her hard. "Hide it under your dress," he growled against her mouth.

Kenzie kissed him back and slid the flat object up her dress, tucking it into the garter holding up her hose on her thighs. The object was slender but cold and heavy. Then Royce released her with a possessive smack on the bottom and led her to the club door, past the line of well-dressed men and women waiting to gain entrance.

"Jesus," Hans muttered. "Popular place, huh?"

"Guess so." Royce stepped in front of the doorman with a tablet in his hand.

"Robert Anderson and two guests," Royce said. It was a

fresh alias created just for the club. The man scrolled down the screen and said something to the larger man behind him, who was monitoring the door. Then they both stepped back and let Royce, Kenzie, and Hans go inside.

The hard rock music was so loud it shook the room. The bass seemed to try to change the beat of Kenzie's heart, and she had to focus on breathing. The darkness of the club shocked her the deeper she went, and she struggled to adjust to it. After a moment she saw lights near a bar and some dimly lit areas. The scents of sex and sweat filled the room, but unlike the Gilded Cuff, the air here was thick with it.

They passed by a young woman being flogged while strapped to a Saint Andrew's cross. A panicked shiver shot through Kenzie.

"You okay?" Royce leaned down to whisper in her ear.

"Yeah." She slipped her fingers through his, ready to stay connected to him as they moved more deeply into the club.

It was nothing like the club back on Long Island, which had been elegant, refined, and sensual. Even though people in the Cuff had been getting aroused at the various scene stations where Doms and subs performed agreed-upon scenes, it'd been beautiful and tasteful.

This place felt nothing like the Cuff. It was clear that many of the submissives weren't here willingly. The pleading eyes, tear-stained faces, the terror and screams coming from the scene stations—here was a hell like nothing Kenzie had ever seen.

"Royce..." She gripped his hand tighter, her heart racing.

"I know, babe. I know." The look of cold rage on his face told her he felt the same. They had entered Dante's Inferno. This was not BDSM. People who lived that lifestyle knew that activities between patrons had to be safe, sane, and most importantly, consensual. There was *none* of that here.

"Anderson?" The tall dark-haired man who called out to

them was gorgeous and, given his accent, Russian. He wore his suit the same way Royce did, like a second skin.

"Dimitri." Royce greeted the man quietly as they stood at an open spot near the bar.

"As promised, a woman for your man." Dimitri nodded toward the beautiful blonde next to him, who smiled politely at Hans. She wore a slinky black dress and killer heels. She was also older than Royce but younger than Hans, perhaps in her early forties. She winked at the bodyguard. Hans paled and nodded back at her.

The man called Dimitri grinned. "Tatiana, you will keep Mr. Brummer company tonight."

"Of course." The Russian beauty took Hans by the arm and led him a small distance away, placing a hand on his chest, speaking quietly.

"Tatiana?" Royce chuckled.

Dimitri grinned and leaned in to whisper in his ear. "She's actually Interpol. She'll behave, I promise. But she might make your Boy Scout blush a bit."

"A bit?" Royce's laugh deepened.

"So, who is your charming guest?" Dimitri asked, his eyes on Kenzie.

"This is Annabelle Gordon," he said with a nod. "Annabelle, this is Dimitri Razin."

Dimitri put her hand to his lips, and she flushed a little. He then raised his head to hers.

"Don't be afraid, Ms. Martin," he whispered against her ear. "I assure you, we are all here to keep you safe." Apparently he knew who she really was. She answered with a small nod. She couldn't deny that Dimitri was gorgeous. There was an intensity to him and a haunted look in his eyes that stole her breath. For a second her mind blanked of rationality as she imagined Dimitri kissing her...while Royce touched her. Two men, two hungers to match her own... The forbidden fantasy made her shiver, and she banished it quickly.

"Thank you, Mr. Razin."

"Now, shall we have a drink?" Dimitri offered.

"God, yes," Kenzie blurted out.

Dimitri smiled as he turned to the waiter and ordered two glasses of scotch and a bottle of water.

Kenzie frowned as she was handed the water bottle.

"Seriously?" she muttered. Right now she needed a real drink.

Royce slipped his arm around her waist. "Got to keep you safe and alert, babe. Nothing but water, not until we're far away from here. At these kinds of clubs, someone could slip a roofie in your drink."

"Right." Royce and Dimitri drank and talked quietly so as to not be overheard, even by her. It gave Kenzie time to survey the room. She noted the exits, the bar, and the various "play areas," but the more she looked, the more nervous she became. It was clear this club wasn't about mutual pleasure like the Gilded Cuff back on Long Island. The only people really enjoying themselves were the Doms.

"Little Mac?" Royce whispered in her ear. "You okay?"

"Yep." Her falsely cheerful reply earned a pinch on her bottom, and she gasped. "Hey!"

Dimitri laughed. "I think your sub needs reminding of her place. It may be a few hours before we need to properly focus. Why don't we take her up to a private room?" Dimitri offered.

Kenzie stared at the dark, handsome Russian. "*We?*"

Royce's head tilted to one side. "Tell me, Little Mac. What do you think of Dimitri?" Royce leaned in closer. "What do you think of him kissing you while I explore you with my mouth and hands?"

The sudden image of being shared between them should

have sent her running, but instead her body lit up like a supernova. Two guys at once. It was as if they'd glimpsed her inner thoughts, the fantasy she'd tried to bury only a moment ago. She didn't want to be in a long-term relationship with two men. But for one night? All of them into it?

Yes, please. The little voice of reason in her head seemed to lose the battle for control with the wild side of her, which was shouting at her to toss her coat off and run to the nearest bed.

Good God. It was crazy, but the way Royce and Dimitri were watching her? They wanted her, and that only made her want it even more. She nodded, just a little.

"I think I should find us a room." Dimitri walked toward a door with a sign in Russian that Kenzie couldn't read. She swallowed hard, her skin flushing. She knew they would see her full body blush soon. Her knees turned to jelly, and Royce's lips curved into a smile. He cupped her chin and tilted her face up to his.

"You okay with two of us, babe? Same rules apply. You can say no to anything you don't want to do. *Red* to stop and *yellow* to slow down and talk it through. Remember, you're in control."

She nodded slowly. "You're okay with me *being* with both of you? Won't that turn you off?" It was the one thing her fantasies never had to deal with - the reality that most people didn't like a three-way because jealousy got in the way.

"I would never share you long-term. If you were *mine*, Little Mac, truly *mine*, I'd be the only man in your life and in your bed, except perhaps for the occasional night when you want to test your limits. I don't have an attraction to men, so if I were to share you, it would always be about you. And I think the two of us will give you something else to focus on before Vadym arrives."

"It would definitely distract me," she said hastily, and pulled away from him so she could take a long drink of water.

"Come on." Royce pulled her past Hans and Tatiana, who were still deep in discussion. Hans was clearly fixated on the beautiful Interpol agent disguised as his submissive. The woman winked at Kenzie and stroked the silver collar she wore as they passed.

"Keep an eye on the door," said Royce. "If Vadym comes, knock three times." Hans gave a curt nod.

Kenzie was led into a room at the front of the hall. There was a massive bed with expensive furnishings. The restraints and the wall of toys were like the room Royce had taken her into in the Gilded Cuff, albeit a bit darker and less elegant. Dimitri was already there waiting, his coat off, his shirtsleeves rolled up. He walked along the wall of toys, examining each one. Kenzie halted a few feet inside the door when she saw him pick up a flogger.

"Oh God," she said. This two-man fantasy was fast becoming a reality—maybe too fast.

"No floggers. Not yet," Royce said as he closed and locked the door.

When she gulped and stared at him, he chuckled.

"It's to keep the bad men out, not you in."

"Right. Of course." She shrugged out of her coat and Royce took it, hanging it on a hook. Then he removed his own coat and rolled up his shirtsleeves. Both he and Dimitri were watching her, their eyes fixed on her every move.

"Not much training with this one?" Dimitri asked.

Royce shook his head "No training, actually, so be patient with her."

The Russian nodded, and a gentle but sexy smirk curved his lips.

"We won't bite, little one. Come here." Royce pointed to a spot near the bed closest to them. Kenzie walked toward him, her heart pounding and her body throbbing at the thought of what was to come. Royce pulled her into his arms, and the slow, burning kiss he gave her relaxed her instantly. She didn't even jump when she felt another set of hands, Dimitri's, massaging her shoulders, soothing away the tension that was coiled tight inside her at the thought of everything that was about to happen tonight.

This was about her pleasure. He was letting her explore a fantasy, and that made her dizzy with the thought of all the possibilities of what was to come. She moaned against his lips and barely noticed as her dress was unzipped from the back. She lowered her hands so the dress could puddle on the floor, then toed out of her high heels.

She gasped when Royce suddenly turned her around. Dimitri cupped her face and lowered his mouth to hers. The kiss burned, his mouth moving expertly, seductively over hers. She heard Royce's rough whisper in ear.

"How does he taste? Can you imagine him between your thighs? How he would lick you clean, so hard you'd be screaming. But I'd be swallowing those pretty cries with my mouth."

Kenzie's whole body reacted. There was no other word for it. One minute she was barely in control. The next it was like a pleasure bomb went off inside her. Her womb clenched as a mini climax shot through her, making her shake violently. She clutched at Dimitri, trying to stay on her feet. His husky laugh against her mouth only turned her on more.

"Let's play with her, Devereaux," Dimitri growled.

"Yes," she gasped hungrily. She wanted only one thing—to be taken and played with by both of them in the dark, forbidden world of this room. Tomorrow she'd feel embarrassed, but not tonight. *If we all survive.* The fatalistic thought only drove her hunger higher.

Dimitri released her, and Royce scooped her up to lay her

down on her back. He hooked her wrists into the cuffs held to the bedpost by a chain. She could move a little, but she couldn't do more than wiggle a few inches in either direction. If she rolled onto her stomach, the chains would tighten at the center and lock her wrists above her head, making her completely immobile. The thought made her hot as hell.

Royce and Dimitri stood at the foot of the bed, whispering. They glanced her way, dark smiles on both of their faces.

Oh crap.

"Remember your safe words?" Royce asked.

"*Yellow* to slow down, *red* to stop," she said.

"Good. But were going to make it a little more complicated." Royce held up a small bell. He gave it a good shake, and then he covered it with his hands, shaking it again. The first sound was clear, the second sound muffled.

"Close your fist and any muffled sound we hear we'll assume you're fine. If you need us to slow down, open your hand a little and shake it. We will hear the clearer sound. If you need us to stop, throw the bell on the floor. You'll have a chance to do it if you're scared. Got it?"

"Yes, but why can't I use the words?"

"Because he's going to gag you, little one." Dimitri handed Royce a strip of black cloth, and Royce walked over to her, wrapping the cloth around her face and tying it behind her head. It wasn't tight, but she couldn't speak with the gag filling her mouth.

"You all right, Little Mac?" Royce asked. He gazed into her eyes, searching for fear. She wasn't afraid, but she was nervous as hell. She answered with a shaky nod.

"Good girl." He stroked her cheek before he slipped the ball into her left palm. She gave it a test shake, sighing in relief when the bell chimed loudly.

"She's got the hang of it," Royce said as he turned back to the wall of toys. Dimitri came over to her, leaning over the bed so he could trail a fingertip down her breasts, toying with the lacy black cups of the bra.

"Who gets the first taste?" Dimitri asked as he brushed the pad of his thumb over her nipple beneath the cloth of her bra.

"I do." Royce came over to the bed and stood at the foot of it, watching Kenzie. She squirmed under the intensity of his hungry stare.

Dimitri climbed onto the bed beside her and cupped her face, turning her focus toward him as he traced her bottom lip.

"Then I shall feast upon her breasts." He moved his hand down again, this time with more force, enough to pull the bra down, letting her breasts spring free from their lacy black confinement. Kenzie jerked as he cupped her left breast.

"You have such lovely breasts, such pink nipples," the Russian growled and squeezed. He didn't hurt her; he seemed to know how to palm her, cup and knead her to make a low burning heat in her belly start up. He twirled his index finger around her nipple, which pebbled into a hard nub. He pinched it lightly, pulling on it a little.

Kenzie arched her back as a bolt of pleasure shot through her. She cried out, but the sound was muffled, the cloth pressing against her tongue. She threw her head back when she felt Dimitri's mouth close down on her breast, sucking the nipple hard. His other hand played with her other breast.

Then she felt her hips lifted and her panties pulled off. She tried to relax, knowing it was Royce, but even when she felt his shoulders between her knees she still tensed. The fan of his warm breath over the most sensitive parts of her was both thrilling and scary because she could not see him, not when Dimitri was sucking on her and blocking her view.

Royce's tongue flicked along her inner thighs, and she squeaked and jerked. Both men chuckled at her reaction but didn't relent. She gripped the bell tight, careful not to let it accidentally ring out. She whimpered as Royce moved his mouth to her slit. He licked with slow, deep strokes, his tongue playing the sensitive bud of her clit until he finally sucked it into his mouth. Dimitri switched breasts and began sucking on the other one while squeezing and pinching the sensitive peak his mouth had abandoned. The climax that hit her was so intense, it was like she'd jabbed a fork into a socket. Every part of her body became electrified.

"Fuck, babe," Royce groaned. "I'm not going to last." He sat up and spoke to Dimitri. "I'm going to take her from behind. You remove the gag and kiss her while I take her."

Dimitri growled his agreement, and Kenzie was suddenly lifted so she was on her knees facing the headboard. She gripped the top of the headboard. Dimitri knelt beside her and pulled the gag down, covering her mouth in a rough, punishing kiss. She whimpered as Royce moved into her from behind and rammed himself deep inside her. The angle he took seemed to stretch and fill her in the best possible way. She could barely breathe. The intense pleasure was too much, and she only clenched the bell tighter.

"That's it, babe, show him how well you kiss," Royce ordered while he pounded into her from behind.

Dimitri kissed her hot and hard, unrelenting, as though he wanted to fuck her entire mouth. One hand slid down her stomach between her thighs, finding her clit and rubbing it. He alternated between rubbing it, flicking it, and pinching it. Between his mouth, his hand, and Royce's cock slamming her from behind, it was...

The next orgasm hit, and she collapsed against the headboard. Dimitri curled his arm around her stomach, holding her upright until Royce released himself inside her. She could feel his release dripping down her thighs.

It was like every dark fantasy she'd ever had hitting her

all at once. He gave her ass a sharp smack, and she could only moan. Dimitri kissed her a long while, helping her come down from the haze. When Dimitri finally pulled away, she could see he was aroused, but he hadn't moved to touch her.

"Kenzie, babe, you okay?" Royce asked.

"Uh-huh." She still clutched the jingle bell. There had been no need to throw it, no need to shake it, but now she realized how selfish she'd been. She and Royce had their release, but not Dimitri.

"Should I...?" She looked down at the erection tenting his pants.

Dimitri smiled. "You are a very considerate sub, but I don't wish to come between you. If you were to have a taste of me, you would forget all about your professor." He tapped the tip of her nose and climbed off the bed. "I will return for you once Vadym arrives." Dimitri slipped off the bed, collected his jacket, and with a seductive smile, exited the room. Royce locked it behind him, shaking his head.

"Cocky Russian bastard," he muttered as he returned to Kenzie on the bed, releasing her wrists.

"Royce..."

"We're alone. The game is over for now." He rubbed her wrists, massaging them, but she was fine. The soft fur that lined the cuffs had felt good and hadn't pinched.

"Royce," she began again, but stopped as she began to digest what they had just done.

"Yes?"

"That was... I mean..." She couldn't tell him that he'd given her the best gift ever by letting her explore a two-man fantasy.

"You enjoyed it?" He removed the gag from where it hung loose around her throat.

"It was amazing. It's like you both knew my darkest fantasy." She looked down and realized she was naked and her breasts were pushed up by the bra cups still pulled below.

Royce noticed too. "I need to taste you, Little Mac. One more time," he said. She could never deny this man, especially when she knew it would end in him pleasing her even more. She dropped onto her back and he lay on top of her, his cock sliding back into the wet heat of her channel. He buried his face in her breasts, and when he kissed her, she was shocked at his tenderness.

"You really are bad," she whispered, and she clawed his shoulders through his white shirt while he slowly made love to her.

"You have no idea, babe. No idea." He nipped her bottom lip and rocked his hips against her until they both came in a sweet, building climax. They lay together on the large bed, limbs entwined, faces nuzzling as they caught their breath.

"Do you ever wonder if this is a dream?" Kenzie asked. "Like you slept in and didn't hear the buzz of your alarm, and you're just lost in this world instead?" She turned to look at him, watching the low light of the room affect his pupils, making his eyes appear all black.

"A dream? Yeah, sometimes. Then I feel your hand in mine and I forget about all the bad shit that's happened." He paused, his face growing somber. "And I remember that we can't do this forever. We have to find a way to go back, once we're home, or else..."

"Or else we'll both get burned," she added for him.

"Yeah."

"I know. We have both worked too hard to let sex destroy our careers, even great sex." Even as she said it, she didn't believe her own words. This thing between them, at least for her, was so much more than great sex.

"Let's just survive tonight, and then we can figure out what happens before we get home." He sat up and raked his hand through his hair, then rolled his shirtsleeves down and got off the bed, gathering his clothes as he went to the small bathroom and closed the door.

Kenzie heard the water running, and then she fixed her bra and grabbed her panties. By the time Royce was done, she was dressed. She traded places with him in the bathroom. She cleaned herself up and stared at herself in the mirror.

The woman who looked back at her was different. So different. The dark eyes, wavy brown hair, gold dress, and dark makeup—she'd just had sex with one man while kissing another, and it had been...*amazing*. The innocent girl from Rochester was gone. She'd grown up in ways she'd never expected. She touched the mirror, watching her fingers meet her mirror image.

"You're going to be okay," she said to the woman in the reflection. She just hoped it was true. Tonight was going to be more dangerous than she could truly imagine.

"You ready?" Royce called out. "Dimitri just gave us the signal. Vadym is here."

She lifted her chin and opened the door to face Royce. She gave him a nod. Her sweet, loving professor was gone, and in his place was a scary, dark-eyed man who was prepared to kill to protect her.

And if all went well, only one life would be taken tonight —and many others saved.

14

Royce felt the weight of the vial of ricin in his trousers.

It seemed to be burning through his pocket. Soon he would be slipping it into a drink and giving it to Vadym. Never in his life had he imagined he would be a man who would take a life like this. He'd always believed in being a hero, someone who would kill a bad guy in a glorious shootout, not this shady, spy-versus-spy, fucked-up shitstorm he was currently trapped in. Soon this nightmare would be over. He led Kenzie outside of the room and buried all thoughts of what they had just shared deep inside. He couldn't let his feelings get in the way of what had to be done.

He'd prefer to simply shoot the man in the midst of a fight. That would be fair, sure, but that was too dangerous. Innocents could get hurt in the process. They needed to be cold and calculated because they were putting more than just their own lives at risk.

While he had some qualms about using these means to kill someone, he certainly had none about the target. This man couldn't be more evil. He was destroying human lives and robbing nations of their history. There was *nothing* good about a man like this, yet Royce still felt a hesitation to take a human life.

I'm not a killer. It was true, he'd never killed in cold blood before, only in self-defense. But this was self-defense, after a fashion. It was clear the mob boss held a grudge and would not stop hunting Royce until he complied with his wishes. And when Vadym had no more use for him, he'd be disposed of.

He curled an arm around Kenzie and led her to the bar. Dimitri and Hans were already there.

"You okay to do this?" Hans whispered from beside him.

"I don't know," he muttered. "I'm not the kind of man who..." *Who murders people.*

Hans met his gaze, a solemn understanding between them. Then Hans held out his hand, and Royce wordlessly passed him the vial.

Fuck, he hoped this worked. They wouldn't know if their plan had succeeded for another thirty-six to seventy-two hours while the poison worked its way through Vadym's system.

"Which one is he?" Royce asked Dimitri.

"The man in the back. The one in the tall gold-and-black chair that looks like a fucking throne."

Royce finally saw the man who'd caused him so much pain, so much anger. Vadym sat in the chair, a damned throne like Hans said, with a cold smile as he gripped the chain of a collared woman who sat beside him on the floor. The woman's eyes were glassy with terror. She was definitely not there by choice. He could only pray he could find a way to help her. If Vadym died soon, they might be able to free the woman. The poison would take a few days.

Royce grabbed the arm of a waitress who was carrying

drinks toward Vadym that he'd already ordered, and while the waitress was distracted by Royce, Hans swapped out the glass of scotch on the tray for the one he'd dosed with ricin. Then the waitress continued toward Vadym and his men.

Everyone held their breath, waiting to see what would happen. Royce watched the waitress's progress out of the corner of his eye as she approached Vadym. Vadym took the glass and leaned forward as the waitress spoke to him. Then his gaze flicked to the girl Royce had pointed out. He raised the glass to his lips, and every muscle in Royce coiled tight. He was doing it, killing a man in cold blood, but the man was a monster.

Vadym lowered the glass from his lips untouched and slowly turned his head to Royce and smiled. He held the glass in the air in a salute and then lowered it toward the girl trapped on the floor at his side. Her haunted eyes fixed dully on the drink he offered.

A shout started to work its way through Royce's throat but not fast enough. Vadym had made them.

"No!" Kenzie's scream tore through the nightclub, and the girl who had just been forced to take the glass from Vadym dropped it. It hit the stone floor and shattered.

Royce turned to Hans, hoping for a plan B, but everything happened too fast. Men from every corner of the room pulled guns on them. All he could think was to get to Kenzie to protect her.

Hans and the others were just beyond the ring of armed men. Tatiana had a death grip on the bodyguard, whispering something to Hans, but the man didn't seem to be listening. He was going to break free and charge in. Royce gave a small shake of his head.

Stay there, don't expose yourself. He prayed Hans would understand. At least if he held back there was a chance the others could do something later.

But Vadym didn't move from his chair. He waited patiently while his men grabbed Royce by the arms and dragged him to their boss. He struggled, but more for show than actual effect. Then he was shoved in front of Vadym.

"Dr. Devereaux, thank you for the...drink. I thought perhaps it might not sit well, seeing as how you *prepared* it."

Royce eyed the glass shards and the young woman who'd almost died. She was looking at him, horror in her eyes. He'd almost gotten her killed.

"Well, Doctor?" Vadym sneered.

"Just returning the favor," Royce countered. "A present from Dr. Abramov."

The corner of Vadym's lip ticked up a little. "I see." He gave a short nod to the men behind Royce. One of the men who'd dragged Royce kicked him hard in the back, forcing him to his hands and knees.

"Royce?" Kenzie's cry startled him. He looked up and saw her being dragged into view by one of Vadym's goons as he spoke to Vadym in Russian.

"Dr. Devereaux, how thoughtful of you to bring *another* present. My current bitch is starting to displease me, and I could use another, one that has still some fight left in her." Vadym struck the chained woman, hard yet dismissively. She collapsed to the floor and lay motionless, but Royce saw she was still breathing.

"She isn't for you," Royce growled.

"I don't think you have a say in what happens to her."

"I think I do," Royce argued. "If you want me to help you falsify the country of origin on those Mongolian fossils, you will leave Kenzie unharmed and with me. If not, I won't cooperate."

Vadym shrugged. "I could torture her until you comply."

"You could." Royce sat back on his heels as he stared into the face of pure evil. "But you won't find anyone of my reputation to give you what you want, and if you harm her I won't do shit for you. And you won't have the pleasure of forcing me to lie, the man who robbed you of the oviraptor nest last year. I cost you fifteen million dollars, am I right?"

Royce chuckled, acting carefree, even though he was feeling anything but.

Vadym snarled. "You cost me much more than that, you American pig."

Royce *tsked*. "Now, now, Vadym. You don't want to get all Russian mob stereotype on me, now do you? Especially not in front of witnesses." He nodded at the crowd looking at them from beyond. Hans, Dimitri, and Tatiana were still there, but so far they had gone unnoticed.

"Witnesses? Please. I own the police," Vadym boasted.

"But I see at least one person in that crowd is filming you on their smartphone. When this shit goes viral on YouTube, you'll be screwed," Royce added. "It's better to keep me and my woman alive and unharmed."

Vadym was quiet for a long moment. Then he nodded at someone behind Royce, and pain exploded through his skull. He hit the ground, just inches from the poor woman Vadym had hit, and fell unconscious.

HANS COULD BARELY BREATHE. HANDS DUG INTO HIS ARMS, keeping him still as Royce and Kenzie were hauled away through the back door of the club.

I can't let that boy down. His eyes burned and his vision blurred with tears. *Am I fucking crying?*

"Brummer, everything will be fine. We'll go after them," Dimitri promised in a low tone only Hans and Tatiana could hear. The room was still full of armed men who were watching every move around them for signs that Royce and Kenzie had allies.

"He's right," said Tatiana, leaning into him by the bar. "If you tried to fight now, Vadym would only kill you. For now, Devereaux is safe and well, and if he's smart he can protect the girl."

But all Hans could picture was a tiny child, one who sat quietly beside another boy with bruises and cuts everywhere. Royce had been only eight years old when Emery had been rescued.

Hans hadn't been able to get the scene out of his head—Emery on one bed, knees tucked up to his chin, eyes wide and gaze distant and Royce sitting there with him, not speaking, offering his presence, the only thing he had to give. Hans had sworn to protect *all* of them with his life after that, Emery, Wes, and Royce. They were like his sons, and he wouldn't let anything happen to them.

Terror squeezed his heart until he could feel blood leaking out. *I've failed.* Royce was in the hands of a heartless monster, and Kenzie—God, sweet little Kenzie—she was at the mercy of a brutal human trafficker.

"*Hans.*" Dimitri's harsh tone pulled him abruptly out of the spinning pit his mind was falling into. "Finish your drink and we'll leave. Do you have a tracker on you? One of the Black Widows from Lockwood Industries?"

With a nod, Hans pulled the tracker—a tiny black dot in a clear bag—from his coat pocket. He slipped it out and handed it to Tatiana, and then he swept his gaze toward a guard with a gun as he was walking toward the door that Royce had been carried through.

Tatiana thrust out her chest and sauntered toward a guard, casually bumping into him. Hans watched as she apologized in slurred Russian and slipped her hand into the guard's pocket, seeming to grab his crotch. The guard lowered his gun, grinning as he copped a feel of her ass. Tatiana allowed it for a few seconds before she slowly withdrew her hand from his pocket, and with a drunken laugh, she slipped free of him and kept walking. She returned to Hans and Dimitri, brushed her hair back, and smiled.

"The tracker is planted on his phone."

Hans could have kissed the beautiful Russian bombshell, but there'd be time to celebrate once they had Royce and Kenzie safe. Hans pulled out his phone and dialed Emery's number. He answered on the second ring.

"Hans, how's Russia?" His happy voice filled Hans with some hope. At least one of his boys was safe. That calmed the raging beast inside him.

"Cold as fuck," he said with a chuckle. "I need you to run the location on the Black Widow I took from the stock before I left."

"Sure, hang on. Cody? You hear that?"

Cody Larson's voice could be heard in the background. "Yeah, I'm on it."

"How's Royce doing? And what's the deal with his TA? Did they ever...?" Emery trailed off, laughing.

"Royce is..." Hans couldn't tell Emery that he'd lost his childhood friend to an evil motherfucking Russian mobster. "Fine. He's fine. And yeah, he and Kenzie hooked up. She's good for him."

Emery sighed. "About time he settled down. He is the last one, you know. He was way too reckless."

"Yeah," Hans agreed, his eyes scanning the club as he saw the armed guard they'd bugged leaving the club out the back door. "Reckless."

"Found it. Who are we tracking?" Cody's voice was louder as Emery put them on speaker.

"A guard who works for Vadym. Cody, can you get any intel, legal or otherwise, on Vadym? Favorite haunts, favorite foods, mistresses, addresses of residences and businesses. Give me a whole damn dossier."

"Sure thing, man. What's up? You sound stressed."

Hans closed his eyes and rubbed them with his thumb and forefinger. "I made a mistake. Vadym got the upper hand. I've got to handle him."

"Hans," Emery cut in. "How bad is it?"

"Bad, but if you can link me to the tracker on my phone and get me that intel, I'll be fine."

"You sure?" Emery asked.

"Yeah." He made a silent vow to get Royce and Kenzie back safe or die trying.

"Your app has the new tracking info. I'll send everything I can find on Vadym ASAP," Cody promised.

"Thanks, kid," Hans said and hung up. Dimitri and Tatiana were still watching him as he opened the tracking app on his phone. The screen filled with the intimidating graphic of a black widow spider crawling across the screen, and then he was prompted for a password. Once he was in, he saw the tracking profile label, "Russian Bastard." No doubt Cody's idea. He tapped on the profile, and a map appeared. A red dot was slowly moving away from the club on a series of streets. Hans held up his phone.

"The tracker's up and running."

"Good," Dimitri said. "We watch and wait for them to stop moving, and then we can plan a rescue mission."

"If we're lucky, we could bust him for human trafficking." Tatiana's eyes were bright. "All I need is evidence of the victims being transported."

"Don't worry, we'll get your proof," Hans said. But he would much rather put a bullet between Vadym's eyes for taking Royce and Kenzie. Royce was too softhearted, using ricin. Fuckers like Vadym deserved a bullet, and Hans could be as cold-blooded as he needed to be when it came to killing monsters. Prison wasn't always enough. Men like Vadym could bribe their way out or control their empire from behind bars and still destroy lives. The only way to protect innocent lives from men like Vadym was by ending him.

I'm coming for you.

15

Kenzie was shoved into a black van outside the club, her hands bound in front of her. Two of Vadym's men tossed the poor unconscious woman onto the floor beside her, before they walked around to the front of the van and got in. Through the front windshield, Kenzie could see Royce being dragged to a black SUV parked in front of them.

When they'd knocked Royce out, Kenzie had nearly fainted. Her heart hadn't stopped pounding and she felt dizzy with terror, but she'd managed to stay in control. This was so much worse than Gary and Monte attacking her at Royce's office. Compared to this, that had been child's play.

Vadym had her in his clutches, and he'd made it clear he was going to use her to get what he wanted from Royce and then to hurt her after he disposed of this other poor woman. Kenzie crawled over to the woman and rolled her onto her back. The left side of her face was still red from Vadym's blow.

She pressed two fingers under the woman's jaw and felt the steady pulse of a heartbeat. Kenzie sat back, relieved, waiting, feeling the van's engine start, and then they pulled out into traffic. That's when she felt it. Something jarring into her hip under her dress. She'd completely forgotten that Royce had slipped her something when they'd first entered the club. She hiked up her dress and removed the object.

It was a slender old-fashioned pocketknife. The initials RD were engraved along with the Devereaux family crest. He'd given her his pocketknife, the one his father had given him when he turned sixteen. He said he never went anywhere without it.

But he gave it to me. Don't worry, Royce, I'll get out of this, I promise. Her resolve became like steel, as though her very soul had been forged and hardened into a blade. She knew in that instant that she could kill if it meant she could save Royce. All she needed was the right moment.

The girl beside her moaned. Her eyes fluttered open.

"Wha...What happened?" The girl struggled to sit up. Fortunately, she wasn't bound at her wrists like Kenzie.

"Hey, you okay?" Kenzie asked.

"I—" The girl shivered. "No." She leaned back against the other side of the van, her eyes looking off to a faraway place. "I haven't been okay in a long time."

"What's your name? I'm MacKenzie Martin. Everyone just calls me Kenzie."

The girl sniffed and wiped her tears. "I'm Elena Allen."

"It's nice to meet you, Elena. Everything's going to be okay. I promise."

Elena laughed bitterly and looked toward the front of the van, where a Plexiglas wall separated them from the drivers.

"You don't know these people," Elena said, her voice breaking. "I've been tortured, raped, and drugged for two months. Maybe longer. I'm not even sure what month it is. I don't think I can stand it. Not anymore. I—" Tears poured down her cheeks, and Kenzie was torn between horror and rage. She clenched her fists and carefully showed the girl the knife strapped to her garter.

"What's that?"

"A little friend." Kenzie tucked it back under her dress.

"You think a knife will help?" Elena sighed wearily. "These guys have guns. They're trained. They're sick. You think I haven't tried to get out of here? I have tried. Once they even let me think I had made it out of the building, only to find out it had been one of their twisted games. And each time the punishment was worse than the last."

Elena shifted, trying to pull her short black dress down her legs. Kenzie didn't miss the jagged scars on her thighs.

Oh God, what did Vadym do to her?

"You were alone, weren't you?" Kenzie asked.

Elena nodded. "Yeah."

"Well you aren't anymore. It isn't just me. Vadym pissed off my professor, Dr. Devereaux."

"The guy Vadym was talking to?"

Kenzie nodded.

"I don't think he's much help. No offense, but he wasn't exactly in a position to do anything."

Kenzie started to smile. "You don't know Royce. He's... he's a badass. Think of him like Indiana Jones. He's got more tricks up his sleeve. And we have outside help. They all want to bring Vadym down, and I think we will. They're probably tracking us right now." Kenzie prayed her words would fill Elena's heart with hope as well. They were not helpless.

"You really think we'll get out of this?" Elena asked.

She let her hands pat the pocketknife in its hidden spot. "Yeah, I do."

The van drove for nearly an hour before it stopped. Kenzie sat up and peered through the Plexiglas window. They were at an airport, one that looked private given the small number of expensive-looking planes and the low level of security.

"Vadym's private jet," Elena explained. "I've been on it a few times. He likes to drag me along when he travels." The SUV ahead of them stopped close to a plane. Kenzie saw Royce hauled out the back of the SUV, struggling. He managed to get his hands free and slam one man's head into the side of the door. He crumpled to the ground. Royce turned to face the other man, who quickly pulled out a gun. Royce froze.

Elena glanced from Royce to Kenzie, and Kenzie shrugged. "At least that's one less asshole to deal with."

"Right." Elena's lips pursed in a grim line. She was quite beautiful, with blonde hair and soft green eyes. But there was an intelligence and fire there that showed her inner strength. That was what Vadym was trying to kill.

But he won't get her again, not if I can help it. Royce may not think he needs a Robin to his Batman, but I can prove him wrong.

The two men from the front of the van exited, and Kenzie heard their voices as they came around the back.

"Just go with them, quietly," Elena said. "If you fight, they punch you—or worse. Trust me."

"Okay." Kenzie checked her knife once more, making doubly sure it was secure, and then she braced herself as the door opened and the two brutes waved her and Elena out.

"Go. Get out," one of them growled in stunted English.

Kenzie scooted along the floor of the van until she could stand, and then she hopped out of the van, Elena right behind her, sticking close.

"Get on plane," the other man snapped in heavily accented English.

Elena led the way, reaching behind her and taking Kenzie's bound hands. The connection brought her some comfort, and it seemed to give Elena a bit of courage as they climbed the steps and entered the aircraft. It was the most lavish plane Kenzie had ever seen, with pale-cream leather seats, a bedroom in the back, and a small bar near the middle.

So this was what wealth from smuggling and human trafficking bought? Kenzie swallowed down the bile that rose in her throat.

One of the men shoved her and Elena into the nearest seats, but there was no sign of Royce. She heard sounds of someone being pummeled and the grunts of pain coming from the back of the plane.

"Royce!" Kenzie jerked to her feet, but one of the men slapped her down hard. She saw stars as pain exploded through her face.

"Kenzie!" Elena grabbed her shoulders to steady her.

Kenzie choked back a cry. "I'm okay."

"Quiet!" the Russian snapped, and both women froze. He left them and walked to the back of the plane, where he opened the door. Kenzie leaned around the edge of the seat, trying to get a look. Royce was being held up by two men, and Vadym was standing in front of him, brass knuckles on his hand as he punched Royce over and over in the ribs and in the stomach, but not his face.

"Royce," Kenzie whispered to herself.

Royce's head was held high. He was smiling, but it was a jackal's smile, one of pain and death. He couldn't stand a beating like that forever. Kenzie tensed, trying to get out of her seat.

"No!" Elena hissed, dragging her back down. "He won't be killed. If what you said is true, you're the one who's expendable, so *you* have to keep yourself safe."

"But—"

"Trust me. I've suffered under Vadym for months. He'd kill you without a second thought if you're more trouble than you're worth. But if he has a use for Royce, then he'll hurt him, but he won't kill him."

It took every ounce of Kenzie's self-control not to scream Royce's name and run to him. She would have fought the devil himself to save him, but Elena was right. She'd only get killed, because she was expendable.

After another two blows, Vadym stepped back and slipped the bloody brass knuckles off his fingers, handing them to one of his men before he left the room. He smiled and wiped a speck of blood off his chin before he approached the women and took a seat across from them.

"It is a long flight. Ten hours to the private airport in Kyakhta. I suggest you find a way to amuse me." Vadym looked right at Kenzie. She was screwed if she couldn't find a way to distract him.

"What's the fossil in Mongolia that you're trying to transport?"

Vadym's gaze narrowed. "What do you know of fossils?"

"A lot," Kenzie said. She could feel Elena in the seat beside her, unmoving, terrified. "You didn't think I was sleeping with Dr. Devereaux, did you? He's a professor of paleontology, and I'm his teaching assistant. In five months, I'll be a professor of paleontology as well."

Her announcement caught Vadym by surprise. "You? You will be a doctor like him?" He looked back at the room where Royce lay on the floor, two goons hovering over him.

"Yes. I can assist Dr. Devereaux with his inspections of the fossils. There's more to it than signing a page of authenticity. He'll need to verify the time period the fossils came from, among other things. I can help him with that."

Vadym sat back, a smug smile on his face. "You will take Elena's place after the fossils are sold. I will make good use of you—in many ways."

Kenzie didn't rise to the bait. It was obvious that he liked a woman who would fight, and she wouldn't fight, not yet, not until it was her last option.

Vadym's phone rang. He rose with a scowl and walked to the other end of the plane to answer, speaking in a low tone. The engines began to whir, and Kenzie kept her gaze focused on the back door.

"You're paleontologist too?" Elena asked.

"Yeah."

"That's good. He'll keep you alive longer. You're lucky." There was a desperation in Elena's voice that tore Kenzie's focus away from the back of the plane. She gripped Elena's hands.

"It's going to be okay. I promise. We're going to get through this."

Elena smiled sadly. "I'm not the first girl he's had. He's taken, used, and disposed of dozens after keeping them only a few weeks. I lost hope a long time ago that I would survive this." Elena laid her head back in her seat and closed her eyes. "You should try to sleep while he's distracted."

Kenzie closed her eyes, trying to will herself to sleep. A short time later, she jerked awake as she sensed movement nearby. She saw Royce sliding into the seat across from her, one arm cradled against his chest. He winced.

"Hey, Little Mac," he groaned before he collapsed into his chair.

She leaned forward a little. "Oh my God, are you okay?"

She looked around the plane and found Vadym at the back with his slender laptop open and the phone still against his ear.

"He just used me as a personal punching bag. But I've been through worse."

"Worse? What could be worse?"

"This isn't my first rodeo. It's just my first Russian with brass knuckles." Royce's painful chuckle didn't reassure her.

"You've been through this before?" Kenzie was stunned. Royce had never mentioned anything like this.

"I've seen and done quite a bit of crazy shit in my day. These aren't the first fossil smugglers I've encountered, either. Usually they sneak up on a dig site and hold you up at gunpoint. Then you tussle a bit and render them harmless and call the authorities."

"These guys are anything but harmless," Kenzie muttered.

"You're right," Royce agreed more seriously. He reached across the small space between their seats and touched her bound hands. "You okay? They didn't hurt you, did they?"

"No," she replied.

He reached up to touch her chin and tilted her head to the side to get a better look. "Your face, it's red."

"One of those assholes slapped me, but I'm okay. I promise."

Royce frowned, a cloud of rage building in his eyes.

"We'll get through this, I promise. And they will pay for hurting you."

She nodded. Yeah, they would pay. She'd made a promise to herself never to be a victim. That meant getting payback on the jerk who'd hit her.

"Do you think Hans will be able to find us?" she asked.

Royce nodded. "I trust few things in this world, but one of them is that Hans always pulls through. I'm sure he has a plan to find us."

Kenzie couldn't ignore the knot in her stomach. Even assuming that Hans could figure out where they were headed, Vadym had a ten-hour head start.

"Come over here and rest. I need to hold you in my arms." Royce jerked his head to the seat next to him. Kenzie hesitated, not because she didn't want to feel his arms around her, but because she didn't want Elena to feel alone. Royce seemed to pick up on that, looking toward

Elena, who was fast asleep. "She'll be fine. I'll watch over her too."

Kenzie slipped into the seat beside him and rested her head on his shoulder. He winced as he put his arm around her shoulders, and she settled into him again. She wondered how much pain he was still in.

"Just sleep, Little Mac." Royce's lips pressed into the crown of her hair. For a moment, she pretended everything was okay, that they weren't facing death.

"Where do you think he'll take us after Kyakhta?" she asked, closing her eyes.

"My guess is we'll take a train to Ulaanbaatar from there."

"The Mongolian capital? Not the Gobi Desert or the Flaming Cliffs?" Royce's natural scent made her feel safe. If they just kept talking and she didn't open her eyes, she could lie there and pretend it was a dream, a nightmare she would wake up from.

"If he needs me, he's already had the fossils stashed somewhere. My guess is he's got some connections at the museum in Ulaanbaatar. He's probably got the fossils stored there, and for the right price he can have them conveniently go 'missing.' Most Mongolians want to preserve and protect their fossils and keep them in the rightful country, but there are always people who can be bought."

"But why fossils? There has to be easier ways to make money. Illegally, I mean."

"Fossils play to his pride. If he steals them from another country and some museum in the West buys them, not knowing they are helping his illegal operations, he enjoys knowing that sense of power and control it gives him. Men like him want nothing less than to be untouchable, and the deeper you work yourself into the legitimate world, the harder it is to weed you out. Take him down, and you risk ruining innocent lives with him. Even if he's exposed, it would be hard to find anyone willing to prosecute him. Human trafficking is another matter, though. That's his weak spot."

Kenzie yawned and burrowed deeper into his chest. She was relaxing, at least enough to sleep, but she didn't want to hear about human trafficking.

"Tell me about the Flaming Cliffs," she begged.

He chuckled, and she could feel his cheek pressing down on her head as she rested. "Sure, babe." He covered her hands with one of his as he began to speak in a low and hypnotic voice.

"Bayanzag means 'rich in shrubs,' but its nickname is the Flaming Cliffs, which Roy Chapman Andrews came up with during his expedition in 1922. Picture the land around the cliffs as a classic desert of rocks, red sand, scrub," Royce said in a reverent whisper. "You don't know what it's like. The emptiness is the most beautiful and peaceful thing you've ever seen. Every worry, every fear, every thought that clouds your mind just vanishes out there. There's only beautiful open emptiness."

Kenzie could picture it, almost like she was there. The quiet winds whistling on the sand, the open cloudless skies. It could drown her in its endless blue depths.

"If—*when* we get through this, I'll take you there. I'll show you how beautiful it is."

"I would like that." She sighed, and sleep soon welcomed her, her heart filled with hope. *He sees a future with me.* A future she wanted but had been so afraid to even dream about. Now she knew how much he really mattered to her. Seeing him get hurt and fearing for both their lives had made everything startlingly clear to her.

I want Royce—I want more than what we had. I want a future with him.

It wouldn't be easy, but where there was a will, there was a way. And she wasn't going to let fear take her, not anymore. And that meant she wasn't going to let Vadym have his way with them. Kenzie opened her palm so she could cradle Royce's hand between hers, and she gave him a squeeze.

"Hang in there, kid," he said.

"I will if you will."

16

Royce was watching out the window as the private jet landed on the airstrip outside of Kyakhta. Kenzie and Elena were still close to him. For some reason Vadym had left them alone after he'd given Royce one hell of a beating. Perhaps it was some kind of mind game, allowing him to sit and think about what he had to lose if he didn't cooperate.

But now that the plane had landed, Vadym would want his fossils. It went against everything Royce believed in to use his professional reputation to lie, but Royce wanted to live. More importantly, he wanted to protect Kenzie and Elena. The best way to do that was to play along with Vadym until a chance to fight presented itself or the cavalry showed up.

Vadym came up to Royce, a cold smile on his lips. "Now, Dr. Devereaux, this way." He jerked his head toward the plane door, indicating it was time to go.

Royce gritted his teeth but followed Vadym out of the plane. A truck of Russian officials was waiting for them.

"Royce?" Kenzie stuck close to him, worried as she watched Vadym's men speak to the guards.

"It's okay. Kyakhta isn't a city that allows foreigners to visit. I'm guessing Vadym will be bribing the officials to get us cleared. This is one situation where we don't want government officials to take us into custody. Trust me."

One of Vadym's men waved at them, and Royce and Kenzie and Elena were herded toward a pair of black SUVs.

"Where are we going?" Royce asked Vadym.

The Russian climbed in the front passenger seat before he looked back at Royce.

"I think you know. We will take the Trans-Siberian Railway to Ulaanbaatar. The fossils are being held in the city."

Royce buckled himself in. "The Central Museum of Mongolian Dinosaurs?"

Vadym's eyes narrowed. "I don't know what you're playing at, but I would suggest keeping your questions to a minimum. Remember, I only need you to authenticate the items."

Elena sat quietly to his left looking out the window, by all appearances tuning everything out. To his right, Kenzie sat still but her eyes were trained on Vadym. A shiver ran through him.

Despite the warning, Royce continued to act the part of being slightly clueless. "I just thought you might have kept them stored elsewhere, a warehouse or bank vault."

Vadym looked smug, as if he had overestimated Royce's intelligence. "What safer place is there than a museum? I have a contact there who will help to ensure that the find stays in good shape and will be ready for transport to Moscow."

Royce studied Vadym carefully, wondering what else he could get away with asking. The man had brutally beaten him on the plane, yet now Vadym seemed more relaxed, likely because his plans were going well.

"Any chance we could stop for food in Kyakhta before we

board the train? It's been nearly twelve hours since we've eaten."

"Dr. Devereaux, you are my guest. As you seem to be willing to cooperate, there is no need to continue with such rough treatment. I'll have my men stop at Letree Kafé, and you will eat on the train."

Royce settled back in the seat. Obviously Vadym assumed Royce wanted to stop at a restaurant in the hopes of an opportunity to escape. Kenzie leaned against him, and he kept his focus on her. His chest flooded with a cottony warmth, and he curled an arm around her shoulders.

By the time they arrived at the train, the central-Asian dishes in their to-go boxes they'd picked up between the airport and the train station were empty. Royce was relieved they'd had a chance to eat so he and Kenzie wouldn't be weak with hunger. Vadym hadn't allowed Elena to eat anything, and when Kenzie had tried to sneak her some food, one of the men had cuffed Kenzie hard on the temple.

"She doesn't eat unless I allow it. Isn't that right, Elena?" Vadym asked as he glanced at her from the front passenger seat.

"Yes." Elena's broken and complicit tone only stirred Royce's rage further, but he had to hide his emotions. He had to keep up the appearance of being cooperative until an opportunity presented itself.

As the SUVs pulled up in front of the railway station, Royce discreetly checked every avenue for escape. He couldn't see anything useful. For himself, perhaps. It would require a little gymnastics and a lot of luck. But what about Kenzie and Elena?

One of the Russian goons grabbed Elena by the back of the neck and dragged her toward the railway platforms.

"We can't leave her," Kenzie whispered as she followed them inside.

"I know," he sighed.

"You're fortunate, Dr. Devereaux. I had my men book you and Ms. Martin in a deluxe cabin right next to mine. You will travel in style and comfort."

"What's the catch?" Royce asked as he and Kenzie followed Vadym toward the waiting train.

"No catch. As I said, you are my guests. But guests must learn to behave, and you were *very* rude to me back at the club. You have learned your lesson, I hope, and from here we can start our relationship anew. Cooperate and things will go smoothly—you will eat well, travel well. But if you do not... Well..." Vadym didn't finish. But one of his men who stood behind him leered and dragged a finger across his neck as though cutting his throat. A couple of the other men chuckled. Vadym shot them a glare.

"Silence." He looked back to Royce. "The fact is, I may have further use for you, long after this task has ended. I could imagine more such adventures between the two of us. We could have you move to Moscow, set up in a penthouse befitting the lifestyle you are accustomed to. We could even move your job there. I understand there is an opening at Moscow State University."

Royce said nothing, but inside he seethed. He didn't know which fate would be worse, being killed after doing what Vadym asked or being kept on a short leash forever.

They boarded the beautiful blue car that belonged to the Golden Eagle, an upscale tourist train that ran along the Siberian railway. The attendant in the train car smiled as he took the tickets from Vadym.

"To the Imperial suites," he said.

The attendant nodded and led them down the corridor. He stopped and waved at the door next to him. "This cabin." He looked to Royce. "And the one farther down is yours."

Royce felt the nudge of a gun against his lower back as he

was shoved toward his cabin door. Once he and Kenzie were inside, Vadym stood there waiting, watching them from the doorway, one hand gripping Elena's arm.

"Have a pleasant evening, Dr. Devereaux. My men will be outside if you require any assistance." Vadym closed the door. Royce stared at the cabin door window and then pulled down the shade, no doubt to the irritation of the guard watching from the other side.

Kenzie sat back on the queen-size bed, still in shock. He came over and sat down beside her. She leaned into him, and he finally was able to free her bound wrists of the rope. He rubbed at the angry red welts on her skin, carefully massaging her wrists.

"Why don't you take a shower? These are the best cabins —Vadym was right about that." He wanted to keep her as calm as possible. The cabin was filled with an oddly muffled silence that cocooned them.

"Royce, I'm scared. I can barely breathe."

He lifted her chin with his fingers. Fear, stark and vivid, glittered in her eyes.

This is all my fault. If she hadn't worked late in my office that night, she never would've been pulled into any of this.

"Look at me, Little Mac. Put your hand over my heart." She lifted one hand and touched him. He felt the heat of her palm through his shirt.

"Feel my heart. Focus on the rhythm. You feel it? Now, breathe with me." Royce drew in a slow breath. Kenzie did too, shuddering at first, but soon she found his rhythm and they breathed in and out slowly together.

"That's it."

Her dark lashes dropped down across her cheeks. She was still too pale, but her breathing was normal again.

"You okay?" He brushed the backs of his fingers over her face, and she nodded.

"Yeah, thanks. I felt like I was going to lose it." She pulled back from him. "I think I will take that shower."

He watched her close the door and fell back flat on the bed, staring up at the gold-painted ceiling of the train cabin.

Fuck, I wish Hans were here with the cavalry.

KENZIE STRIPPED OUT OF HER CLOTHES AND STEPPED INTO the shower stall. The hot water eased the chill within her, but only a little. She felt numb, like her mind had turned everything off. How was she supposed to survive this?

She couldn't get Elena's face out of her mind, how tortured the woman had been. Vadym would kill Elena, and then Kenzie would be his next plaything. Bile rose in her throat. She gagged, doubled over, and spit in the shower, her stomach clenching. She smacked one palm on the shower wall, catching her breath.

I'm not alone. Royce is here. We are in this together. She winced as hot water hit her raw wrists. It was such a small thing to see the welts there when she'd suffered worse earlier, but... Tears welled up in her eyes, and her vision blurred.

I'm not weak—I'm not.

Yet she couldn't seem to stop crying. She turned the water off and got out of the shower, her legs starting to shake. She found a thick, expensive bathrobe on the counter and slipped it on. Then she leaned forward and wiped the condensation from the mirror. Haunted eyes stared back at her, and a slight bruise marred her cheek from where she'd been hit by one of Vadym's men.

Tears fell down her face, leaving streaks that shimmered white beneath the florescent lights.

I'll get through this. I will. I'm smart and levelheaded, and I can keep calm in a crisis, right? That's what Royce needs. Me levelheaded and calm.

She tightened the bathrobe belt around her waist and stepped back into the main cabin. She found Royce lying flat on his back on the bed. One of his hands rested on his stomach, his fingers tapping a little rhythm. The sight of him looking somewhat relaxed managed to calm her. When the bathroom door clicked shut behind her, he lifted his head, then bolted upright and opened his arms when he saw the look on her face.

"Little Mac," he said softly. She rushed into his embrace, fresh tears pouring from her eyes.

There was no stopping the sobs that followed. Royce held her throughout, absorbing every shake and tremble. Her heart stilled in her chest, and new trembling took over. This man, this beautiful man was the answer to questions she didn't even know she wanted to ask. There was no running from the truth, not now, not when the world was collapsing around them. She raised her head, facing him, their bodies caught in a warm embrace.

"Royce, I...I love you." The words slipped from her lips. She couldn't take them back. It reminded her of something her mother used to say about dreams: *Once you give them a voice, they are out in the world, alive.*

She never meant to dream about love, not like this. An all-consuming, overpowering love that was so scary she could barely breathe. But somehow it was there, *alive*. She could feel that love inside her, like an arrow shooting through her heart.

"You don't have to say anything. I just needed you to know," she said, ducking her head. Royce gave a cocky grin, one that made her momentarily forget the horrors that awaited them outside the cabin. For a moment, it was like he was flirting with her back at the university.

"I know you do. I'm irresistible," he announced with such authority she couldn't help but giggle.

"You're an ass, you know that?"

"But clearly a lovable one."

She shoved him and he fell back on the bed, pulling her down next to him. He curled one arm around her waist, kissing her forehead.

"Did I ever tell you about how I learned to pick locks? Hans and I broke into Wes's house..."

Kenzie settled more deeply into his arms, worries and fears for the moment banished. So she wasn't Robin to his Batman or Watson to his Holmes. She was just Kenzie, but she was finally seeing what she should have seen from the beginning. Royce had never needed a sidekick to follow him about. He needed a partner. There were a thousand reasons she loved this man, but right now this was the most important one. They would face trouble together, side by side.

17

The city of Ulaanbaatar was nothing like what Kenzie had expected. When Hans and Royce had spoken of mountains, lonely deserts, and yurts, they had been speaking of the countryside of Mongolia. But as the Trans-Siberian train pulled into the city, it left the valley hills with snowy pine trees far behind them. The horsemen who had darted alongside the train tracks like the Mongolian herdsmen of history vanished as the cityscape of Ulaanbaatar took over.

It was a curious mix of ancient temples, crumbling Soviet-era apartment blocks, and newer glass towers, along with derelict suburbs of yurts and brick houses. A mesh of wire, concrete, and metal piping all crashed together. But Kenzie was stunned by the energy and warmth of the people, which was so at odds with the city itself.

"Welcome to UB," Royce said. "The city's name means Red Hero." He coughed. "But honestly, they should call it Black Hero in the winter." He pointed at the hazy dark clouds that hovered above the city like an omen of doom.

"What is that?" Kenzie asked.

"Noxious smoke. It's only here in the winter because the families who live in the yurts in the ger district burn coal to fend off the extreme cold. It will hover over the city until March."

Now that he mentioned it, Kenzie could almost taste the coal in air, the acrid taste lingering on her tongue and in her nose. "Jesus."

One of Vadym's men opened their door abruptly. "Out. This way!"

"We're coming," Royce snapped, and he took Kenzie's hand as they followed the men from the train. Outside, several cars were already waiting for them.

"How the hell does Vadym have cars everywhere waiting for us?" Kenzie muttered.

"His Uber bill must be through the roof."

Kenzie almost laughed, but the knot of nerves in her stomach had returned. The cars drove through the city until they stopped in the parking lot of a massive gray-and-red building with gold designs. Over the front of the building, obscuring the words "Lenin Museum," its former name, hung a sign that read "Central Museum of Mongolian Dinosaurs," in English. A huge tyrannosaurus head jutted out of the exposed bricks, as though a dinosaur had come to life and was escaping the museum.

"I would love to have seen that as a kid," Royce said with a chuckle as they walked beneath the dinosaur and into the museum.

"This way, Dr. Devereaux." Vadym seemed almost cheerful as he led the way to a set of back doors that took them away from the visitor center.

He's happy because he's getting his way, Kenzie thought. *He thinks he's won. Good.*

A man rushed to meet them as they entered the lab beyond the offices. "Mr. Andreikiv!" His accent was clearly

Mongolian, but his excitement at seeing Vadym meant this had to be his inside man, the one who would help him rob this beautiful country of its birthright.

"Dr. Devereaux, this is Mr. Atlan Dorjsuren." Atlan held out his hand.

Royce shook Atlan's hand, though with little enthusiasm.

"Follow me," Atlan said. "On behalf of the museum, I'd like to offer our sincere regrets regarding the accidental acquisition of that which rightfully belongs to your country. It seems the dig site was on the Russian border, and the specimen was wrongfully extracted and transported here due to an error in the GPS devices. We have the specimen ready for shipment. We need only a few of the documents filled out and authorized."

Kenzie kept pace with Royce as they followed Atlan into a large warehouse. A large six-foot-by-five-foot box was carefully packed with bones tucked in straw. Each bone had a small tag with a diagram to show its location on the reconstructed skeleton.

"It's a velociraptor!" Kenzie exclaimed as she approached the box.

"Yes," Vadym said from behind her, making her jump. "The most complete one ever seen. It will bring in millions, once museums begin a bidding war." Vadym put a hand on her waist. Kenzie tensed and slid slowly out of Vadym's reach, moving closer to Royce. Her skin felt like ice where that man had touched her.

"Dr. Devereaux?" Atlan spoke up. "The papers are in my office. This way."

Royce reached for Kenzie's hand, but Vadym grabbed her and pulled her away.

"Sign the papers, Dr. Devereaux. When you come back, you can have her."

"Like hell," Royce growled, and his grip tightened on

Kenzie. Vadym smirked. The men on either side of Vadym pulled aside their coats, exposing their weapons. She couldn't let Royce get hurt trying to protect her. Without a plan, it was just pointless bravado.

"Go. I'm fine." Kenzie leaned against him, squeezing his arm to reassure him she would be okay. She tried to ignore the feel of Vadym's gaze on her, but it made her skin crawl.

"You could be most useful to me," he finally said. She didn't respond. "Aren't you interested in hearing my offer?"

"That depends," she finally replied. She couldn't keep running away from him, and she needed to buy more time. "Anything you offer better include Royce's safety and my own."

"If you come back to Moscow willingly and help me find fossils, warm *my bed*, then I won't kill Devereaux."

Kenzie froze, every part of her body tense. "You're planning to kill Royce? What about that talk about moving him to Moscow? I thought you needed him?"

"Useful, yes. Need? No." Vadym laughed softly, and the sound made her skin crawl. "This was always about control." He took his time in answering, seeming content to watch her dread increase. "Your lover defied me, robbed me of a huge auction prize. I couldn't let that stand. I had to make him come to heel." He let go of her arm and curled his hand into a fist, as though imagining crushing Royce in his palm. "But now that I have you, there's no more use for him. I should remind you that you will come either way, but willingly means you can spare his life."

"And what about Elena?"

Vadym's brow furrowed. "Who?"

"Elena. The girl."

Vadym acted as if her existence had completely slipped his mind. "What of her? She will not be needed."

"Would you let her live?"

Realization dawned on his face. “Oh, I see. If she matters so much to you, I’ll let you choose who lives.”

“*Both*.”

Vadym laughed. “You are in no position to bargain. But you have fire. That’s good. I will give you this one thing, before I take everything else. Both. *If* you agree to come with me.”

A devil’s bargain. But what choice was there? Royce would find a way to rescue her. She had to believe that.

“Fine. You have my willing participation,” she said softly, looking away from him.

Vadym’s smile turned her blood to ice. He cupped her chin, his fingers digging into her skin as he turned her toward him and slammed his mouth down on hers. She shoved him away as she heard Royce’s shout.

“Get away from her, Vadym! I signed your damn papers.”

Vadym let go of her, and she retreated. He laughed as he turned to Royce. “She has just agreed to come back to Moscow and serve me—in all ways.”

Royce’s face was pale as he looked between them. “Kenzie, what’s he talking about?”

“He said he’ll spare you and Elena if I do. Please, Royce, don’t cross him,” she pleaded with him, hoping he would read her thoughts. *It’s just for a short time, until you can save me from him.*

“You son of a bitch!” Royce moved fast, slamming his fist into Vadym’s face before his bodyguards could move in. The attack stunned everyone.

“Kenzie, run!” Royce shouted as he tackled Vadym to the ground. Kenzie turned and smacked hard into Jov Tomenko’s body. She hadn’t even known he was in the room. His heavy hand clamped around her arm, squeezing until she cried out. Vadym’s other guards grabbed Royce and dragged him off.

“Take them to the cars.”

"May I kill them?" Jov wrenched his hand down harder on Kenzie's arm. Her muscles seemed to tear beneath his hands, and she gasped in agony.

"Not here, you fool. Later you can do whatever you like."

Jov smiled darkly down at Kenzie. "He broke Elena before I had the chance to take over, but you? You still have fire in you. I will have such pleasure breaking you."

Vadym spat blood as he climbed off the floor. He waved Atlan away when the man tried to help him up. "See that the fossils are shipped tonight."

"Of course." Atlan rushed back to his office.

Royce was being held by two of Vadym's men. His mouth was bleeding from where one of the men had punched him. Jov dragged Kenzie toward the exit, along with Royce. Once they were back in the car, Elena was there waiting for them.

"You okay?" Elena whispered after they were shoved into their seats.

Kenzie nodded.

"Silence!" Jov snarled as he started the SUVs engine. Kenzie grasped Royce's hands in hers, squeezing it. Whatever happened next, at least they would be together now.

They were driving down a street called Peace Avenue when Jov paused, staring at the lights. He had to take a left turn, when the red light wouldn't let them go straight. Kenzie stared at the digital billboards above the car, unseeing as she tried not to think about what would happen to them. Then the billboard videos began to cut out, the picture disappearing and reappearing over and over again, like some kind of rapid power outage. That was odd. Royce leaned forward to look, and then his lips began to move and she could hear his faint whisper. "Ready—accident—Cody—ready —accident..."

"Accident?" she whispered back.

The car surged into the intersection, and half a second

later, Royce pushed her and Elena back against their seats in case the seat belts failed their jobs. A truck suddenly plowed into them from the left side, sending the car flying. The breath was knocked out of Kenzie's lungs. She couldn't breathe, couldn't scream, couldn't—

The vehicle rolled, and she, Royce, and Elena were bounced around like rag dolls. Metal screamed, glass shattered, and the blare of horns drilled into her skull. She couldn't move, couldn't think past the sweeping numbness inside her.

"Kenzie," Royce groaned as he struggled to sit up. Elena whimpered and twisted her legs as she tried to sit upright.

"Royce... What happened?" She felt like she was shouting. The ringing in her ears made her feel dizzy and nauseous.

"Morse code. Cody must've hacked the billboards somehow." Royce looked to the front of the car. The driver, Jov, wasn't moving. The other man in the passenger seat was awake, but blood dripped down his forehead. He was still trying to get his bearings.

"We have to move. Now." Royce opened the door beside him, half falling into the street. Kenzie followed, taking Elena's hand as she helped the other woman out of the car.

They found themselves in a world of chaos. Cars were jammed everywhere in the intersection. Smoke billowed up from the truck that had hit them.

"Oh God," Elena gasped. "Where's Vadym?"

Kenzie and Royce searched the crowd and saw his car ahead of them, pinned between two smaller cars. The red brake lights were on, and the car was jerking slowly out of its trapped position. Kenzie tugged on Royce's hand.

"We have to go. Jov will be coming for us."

"Not yet!" He was staring at the digital billboards, watching the way the images flashed as if pointing in a certain direction. "Embassy! Embassy!" Royce cried in triumph. "Come on! This way!" he shouted, jerking Kenzie along. The three of them sprinted through the wreckage and ran toward the American embassy in the distance.

Gunfire erupted behind them. Royce skidded to a stop behind a car and pulled Kenzie and Elena down as they covered their heads. In the distance, she could see the friendly wave of the American flag and the Marines standing at the gates as they tried to assess the cause of the gunfire.

"We can't make it!" Elena gasped. "The embassy is too far!"

"We *can* make it. Kenzie, you still have the knife I gave you?" Royce held out his palm. Kenzie handed him the knife, and he glanced around the taillights of the car.

"It's Jov. I'm going to lure him to me. You two crawl that way, toward the embassy. Use the cars as cover for long as you can, then run like hell when you're exposed. Shout that you're American. The Marines should let you in." He turned away.

Kenzie gripped his shoulder, dragging him back to face her. "What about you?"

"Trust me. I've got nine lives, kid. I'll be fine." He leaned in and cupped her cheek. "I fucking love you, Little Mac. Okay? This ain't no suicide run. I want to live every damn minute of our complicated lives together. So I'll survive, I promise."

He kissed her, hard, fast, and all too soon it ended.

"Now go!" he hissed, then crawled behind the taillights of the car. Then he stood up. "Jov, you fucking bastard. I'm over here!" Royce took off, running perpendicular to the route that led to the embassy. Jov raised his AK assault rifle and fired another volley, but he hit only cars.

Elena grabbed her arm. "Kenzie, we have to go!" They started crawling fast behind the cars toward the end of the street that led to the embassy.

Royce drew Jov's fire away from them, but it didn't lessen

the spike of fear that had a stranglehold on her throat. When the two of them broke the clearing of the cars, they ran and didn't look back. Everything seemed to slow down around her, the wind whipping her loose hair against her face, her harsh, labored breaths, the almost jellylike feeling to her legs, and the soldiers manning the gates, watching her and Elena with worry.

"We're American! Help us!" Kenzie screamed as she launched herself at the gate. The Marines rushed to open it, dragging her and Elena behind them.

"What's going on, ma'am? Who's firing out there?" a Marine demanded as he raised his rifle.

"It's Russians. They're attacking us. One of us is still out there. He's wearing black pants and a white dress shirt. His name is Dr. Royce Devereaux."

"Did you say Devereaux?"

"Yes."

One of the guards got on his radio. "Devereaux's here, outside the gates. Permission to engage if they reach the gates?"

"Permission granted!" came the reply over the radio. The Marines nearest Kenzie and Elena shouldered their guns and headed through the open fence so they were guarding the entrance to the embassy.

"Get inside, ladies!" one of the last guards shouted before he disappeared through the gates. Several other armed soldiers rushed out to meet them, escorting them toward the safety of the embassy's interior.

Kenzie held on to Elena, keeping the other girl on her feet as they reached the embassy doors. Medics rushed out to meet them. Kenzie pulled away as the medics took Elena inside. She turned, eyes searching the chaos in the street as several Marines opened the gates again and slipped just outside, waiting. A knot formed in her stomach. They couldn't save him, not unless he got closer to the gate. They couldn't risk starting an international incident.

Royce appeared through a gap in the abandoned cars, running, but limping. Blood streaked down his side, but he didn't stop. Jov was behind him, staggering, rifle still in hand. He fumbled as he changed the magazine, then raised his rifle, taking aim.

"No... No... No, no!" Kenzie sprinted back toward the gates, even though she was powerless to help.

"Weapon down! Now!" the Marines were shouting. Jov ignored them and pointed the rifle at Royce's back. Only twenty feet separated Royce and American soil. The soldiers couldn't do anything unless Jov aimed his rifle at them, but with the way Royce was running straight at the American soldiers, Jov would have to fire in their direction.

"Royce, get down!" Kenzie screamed. Royce dove without hesitation, sliding on the embassy lawn like a baseball player diving for home plate as Jov fired. The Marines fired back a second later in a deafening volley of shots.

Jov stumbled and the rifle dropped to the ground, and his body keeled over backward. Kenzie ran, landing next to Royce in the grass, covering his body with hers, hugging him.

"We need to get you inside!" a Marine shouted, and they were lifted up and rushed indoors.

The embassy was in turmoil, people running, speaking on phones, and arguing about what had to be done next. A fresh wave of medics took charge as they led Royce and Kenzie to an infirmary on the second floor. Kenzie was shaking hard, her hands clenching a paper cup of water someone had handed her.

"I'm so sorry!" she gasped and wrapped her hands together, unable to stop the tears. Royce lay on his back beside her, his breathing shallow, and he winced as they pulled his shirt up. The knife wound was deep, and the sight of blood made Kenzie woozy.

"Lie down, honey, you're turning green." A female doctor pressed on her shoulder, urging her to lie back. She all but collapsed, and then something sharp pinched her arm.

"Ow! What's that?"

"Just a little sedative, honey. You're in shock. Just close your eyes and rest."

Sedative? The world turned oddly fuzzy around her. Her eyelids became too heavy to hold up.

Royce... She slipped into darkness.

18

Royce came awake slowly, aware that he was in some sort of hospital, probably still at the embassy in Mongolia given the news station flashing on the TV in the corner of the room. Everything hurt like hell. Tubes were in his nose, and an IV bag hung on a pole nearby. His right hand was taped, keeping the IV needle in.

"Fuck," he groaned, his head falling back onto the pillow. Then he noticed a shape in a chair beside his hospital bed. *Kenzie*. She was curled up on the chair, her head pillowed by one arm and a jacket covering her. A man's jacket.

Not my jacket.

"Thank God," a deep voice said from the doorway. Hans Brummer stood there, a paper cup of coffee in his hand and a relieved look in his brown eyes.

"Give you a few new gray hairs, did I?" Royce's voice came out a croak.

Hans raked a hand through his scalp. "More than a few. I'll go full George Clooney in a month at this rate."

"How did you find us?"

Hans pulled a chair out and turned it around, not waking Kenzie. He sat on it backward with his arms on the backrest.

"Tatiana put a tracker on one of Vadym's men. Once we knew you'd boarded the Trans-Siberian Railway, we called Cody and he found your destination was here in Ulaanbaatar. Dimitri and I beat you here by just ten minutes. We couldn't try anything at the museum, but once you left, Cody said you were heading past the embassy. We knew we had to get you there. I didn't believe it, but fuck if you didn't make it." He chuckled and took a long sip of his coffee.

"Morse code on the billboards. The kid is a damn genius."

"And the pileup? He turned all the traffic lights green. Risky, but effective. It gave you time to get free. We weren't sure you'd get away if the driver of the car didn't wreck, but thank God it did." Hans turned toward Kenzie's sleeping form. Royce did the same.

"I..." Royce's voice broke a little. "I honestly didn't think we would make it. For the first time in all the crazy shit I've done..."

"And that's a lot of crazy shit," Hans noted.

"Yeah, but I never had...I've never needed to worry about..."

Hans gave a nod. "You had something to lose."

"Yeah. I had *everything* to lose. She's everything to me." The weight of those words in the past would've seemed like a curse, one more thing he needed to run away from. But now he saw what his friends had been saying for months. The love of a good woman was what a man really needed to live. And somehow, by a twist of fate, he'd found his woman when he wasn't even looking for her.

"This means you're finally going to settle down?" Hans asked as he sipped his coffee.

"I guess that depends on how you define settling down."

He grinned, but winked. "I'm in love, not dead. I won't stop traveling, teaching, or going on digs. But my days of recklessness are over. Being with Kenzie is the only real thrill I need."

"Thank God," Hans murmured. "Now maybe I can finally retire. You boys are all grown up, with lives of your own—kids will be next." Relief mixed with a hint of sorrow in Hans's eyes.

"You won't leave Long Island, though, will you?" The thought of the man who'd been like a father to him leaving left a void he didn't really want to think about.

"You don't want me to leave?" Hans's lips curved up in a grin.

"Of course not," Royce replied. "Maybe it's time you settle down too. Bring that sexy Russian Interpol agent over to visit."

Hans's face turned ruddy. He looked anywhere but at Royce, who winked.

"Maybe I'll do that," he finally said. "By the way, how the hell did you get knifed? The Marines said that Russian man chasing you had an AK assault rifle."

Royce grimaced. "I jumped him while he was loading up with weapons from the back of his car. He had a knife ready and got me, but I got a few punches in. Just didn't know I was bringing fists to a knife fight. When I saw his cache of weapons, I bolted, and that's when he started firing the rifle."

"Holy shit," Hans groaned. "Don't try to jump a Russian, kid. Didn't I teach you anything? You just run like hell for cover next time."

"Let's hope there isn't a next time."

"Agreed," Hans muttered, his disapproving frown so parental that Royce almost laughed.

"Why don't you rest? Knife wounds are bitch to heal. She needs you rested." He nodded to Kenzie.

"Yeah, good point. Did they catch Vadym?"

Hans shook his head. "No, but Cody has some ideas about how to track him down. Dimitri is keen to handle the matter back in Russia. I think Vadym pissed him off bad enough that he's ready to go against Vadym openly, and he's not nearly as nice as we are. He promised to let us know the moment Vadym is...taken care of."

"And Elena?"

Thunderclouds gathered in Hans's eyes. "Physically, she's okay, a little banged up. But emotionally? She'll never be the same. I was there when she gave her statement to the officials here at the embassy. He'd had his claws in her for months. Beaten, starved, raped... She's just a kid. Only twenty years old, for God's sake."

"What's going to happen to her?" Royce shifted in the bed, wincing as he felt stiches tug at his side, probably from the knife wound from Jov.

"She's going back to Moscow to get her possessions. Her university where she was studying abroad had her things in storage. Then I think she's coming home after that. Dimitri said he would make sure she was safe while she was in Moscow. He hasn't let her out of his sight since he got to the embassy."

Royce let out a sigh. He hoped Dimitri could handle Vadym. If he succeeded, Royce would owe that man his best bottle of scotch.

"Catch some sleep. The embassy is safe," Hans promised. "Hell, I don't even think I could break in here."

"Thanks." Royce laid his head back on the pillow and closed his eyes.

It must've been hours later when he opened them again because Kenzie was awake and watching him. She had a book in her lap, some romance novel with a couple embracing on the cover. She blushed and tucked the book in her chair.

"Hans found them in the embassy library for me. He must have seen me going crazy, and I needed a distraction. How do you feel?" She scooched her chair closer and carefully curled her fingers around his arm.

"I feel like I was hit by a truck and knifed by an angry Russian." He turned his hand over and wiggled his fingers in invitation. Kenzie smiled and placed her hand in his. A gentle heat blossomed at the simple contact. How had he been so blind? He'd loved her from the moment he'd spoken to her on the phone, before they'd even seen each other—he just hadn't realized that until now.

"You still love me?" he asked. He was teasing her, but a part of him feared she would think he was too dangerous, too damaged to settle down with.

She bit her lip, her brown eyes sparkling as she pinched her thumb and forefinger together. "I think I love you a little more than yesterday, and given how much I loved yesterday, I don't think my heart could love you any more than I already do." She squeezed his hand.

"That's a good thing, because we're going to need all that love to get through the mess we'll face when we get home."

"I know," she sighed. "What are we going to do?"

He tried to sit up, groaned, and lay back on the bed as he stared at her. "You'll have to file for a transfer to a new professor. People will talk about us, and it could get ugly."

"I think after everything we've been through, gossip is the least of my worries. Funny, it used to scare the hell out of me, but not now. Not after..." She didn't finish, but he knew she needed a distraction from the darkness of those thoughts.

"We'll still need to lay low so no one suspects we're dating. Maybe you can ask for Lionel Bigby as your new professor."

"No way! He's ancient!"

"Exactly. You won't fall in love with him when he makes you work late nights."

"Possessive much?"

"*Very*."

"I am not transferring to Bigby and losing all my research."

"Okay, But we'll have to wait until you graduate and your PhD's in the bag. That means no hot looks in the hall, no working late on the same nights, no public dates. Just secret clandestine meetings." He waggled his eyebrows and she giggled.

"I'll be good. Promise." She flashed him a sexy grin that made him doubt very much he could keep his hands off her. He'd have to, in public. But in private? Oh yeah, he'd be all over his Little Mac.

"Once you've gotten your PhD, then you move in with me."

"Move in?" Her breathless tone made his body harden.

"Yeah. Turns out I'm the marrying kind. You're it for me, Little Mac."

Her eyes misted, and he reached up to brush her cheek with the back of his hand as tears started to fall.

"You'll do it. The right way, right? On one knee, a ring, a call to my dad?" she asked.

"I'll do whatever you want as long as you know you're mine and I'm yours."

Her smile made him feel like he was standing on the edge of the Flaming Cliffs, the bright sun warming his face, as the wind whistled over the rocks. He knew, in the most ancient way a man could know anything, that they belonged together. The sea and the shore. The sun and the earth. What he felt went beyond soul-deep to someplace far stronger, far bigger than his own heart.

"Is that a yes?" he asked, his voice a little rough.

She nodded and leaned in to kiss him. It was an awkward kiss given that his body hurt all over, but it was the best damn kiss a man could ever have because he tasted her love for him in it.

So this was what it felt like to be loved, to love so much it hurt in the best way. A man could get used to this.

EPILOGUE

S*ix months later*

Kenzie held on to Royce's back as his motorcycle cruised down the private road toward their home—Devereaux House. She peered at the mansion through her helmet visor and sighed. She never got tired of looking at it. The gabled roofs and endless halls full of priceless paintings and lavish bedrooms and the study where Royce worked. It had all become a part of her life in the best possible way. He pulled up in front of the mansion and killed the engine. Kenzie let go of his hips and slid off. The sight of him astride the bike with his helmet, jacket, and jeans was utterly sinful.

He pulled the visor up. "What's up, babe? You're looking at me funny."

"I'm just picturing how much I want you to bend me over the pool table tonight."

He took off his helmet, leaving his hair playfully tousled, but his expression was hungry and serious.

"Are you asking me to fuck you, Dr. Martin?"

"Oh, most definitely, Dr. Devereaux."

He grinned. "That's too bad, Little Mac, because I have every intention of making love instead."

Kenzie tugged on a lock of her hair and tilted her head, as if considering the offer.

"Well, as long as you make it dirty..."

"Dirty?" He stepped off his bike and began to step toward her with playful menace. She retreated to the door, which opened behind her. Mr. Lansdown stood there waiting.

"Ah, Dr. Devereaux, Dr. Martin," the butler said.

"Lansdown, we'll be in the billiard room until dinner. Make sure we aren't disturbed."

"Of course." The butler tried to hide an indulgent smile.

Kenzie squealed as Royce tossed her over on his shoulder. He gave her ass a little smack, and she returned that with one of her own.

"You're a caveman, you know that?"

"Never said I wasn't, babe." He laughed as he carried her to the billiard room and set her down on the edge of the table. She spread her legs as he stepped closer, cupping her face in his hands. For a long moment he simply stared at her, and she was undone by the tenderness in his eyes.

"I love you, Little Mac," he said, and claimed her lips with his. It was a kiss that burned, a kiss that made her want to get his clothes off. Tear them off if she had to.

"You still—haven't—asked yet—" she said between feverish kisses.

"Haven't I?"

She shoved at his shoulders playfully. "No!"

"Well! My bad." He stole another kiss before he reached into his jacket pocket and pulled out a small box.

He slowly lowered down to one knee before her, looking too irresistible.

"I wish I had my mother's ring to give you, but this will have to do." He cleared his throat and opened the velvet box.

Inside was an elegant princess cut diamond with two small sapphires on either side.

"I chose this back in Mongolia before we came home. I thought it felt right."

She couldn't speak. She'd never had a thing for jewels, and she would have worn *anything* he gave her, but looking at the diamond and sapphires, knowing he'd brought the ring back from Mongolia, when they had almost died...

"MacKenzie Martin, would you do me the—"

Royce grunted as she tackled him to the ground, covering his face with kisses.

"Close enough! Yes, yes, yes!" That was the only word she'd ever want to say to this man, because they were destined for each other. Destined by forces set in motion millennia ago, when dinosaurs still walked the earth.

Their future wasn't written in the stars; rather, it had been held in the fossils within the bedrock deep inside the earth, waiting to be revealed.

DIMITRI RAZIN STUDIED THE CRIME SCENE PHOTOS showing Vadym lying dead, poisoned in a Moscow restaurant. The ricin had found its way into the bastard's food with a little help from a cook in Razin's employ. He should have killed the man a long time ago, but he'd been reluctant to start a turf war that would spill over into his private life. But after watching the hell Royce and Ms. Martin had been through, he owed it to them to deal with the problem.

He pulled up his email on his phone, and through an encrypted link he sent the photos to Royce. That would give the professor a bit of peace now that he was to be a married man and likely soon a father. Dimitri smiled a little, but there was an ache in his chest that he couldn't seem to fix. After being with Ms. Martin that night at the Black Diamond Bar, he'd glimpsed the way she'd looked at Royce, with so much love and hunger that Dimitri had been jealous. Not because he'd wanted to come between them—he hadn't. But he'd wanted what Royce had. That intense bond with another person. He'd likely never find it, not with the way he had dark desires pulsing in him. Finding the right woman, the one who would be submissive without fear in the bedroom, was a hard thing.

Movement ahead of him drew his focus away from his phone screen, and he glanced up. The Moscow airport was crowded, but he saw what he'd been watching for—a beautiful woman with blonde hair and green eyes making her way through the rows of seats next to the gate for the flight to Los Angeles.

Elena Allen clutched her purse to her chest like a shield. The clothes she wore were loose-fitting. Her eyes were still so full of fear that it made Dimitri growl. He'd learned all about her in the last few days. A young American college girl studying abroad, she'd been abducted in the Black Diamond Bar and kept for months as a sex slave by Vadym. After her rescue in Ulaanbaatar, she'd returned to Moscow to her university dorm, where her clothes and books had been stored after her disappearance. The Moscow police had checked her belongings and clothes when she first disappeared, but given that the case of her disappearance was still open, they hadn't allowed her clothing and belongings to go home to her parents. After picking up her things, she'd had her visa processed so she could leave. The US State Department had worked with the Russian government to see her safely and quietly home.

But it wasn't going to be enough. Dimitri knew she needed someone to watch over her, because the terror she'd suffered and the emotional and physical wounds she'd received wouldn't heal easily, if ever.

And I will be the one to watch over her. Protect her the way a good Dom should.

He could never claim this beautiful woman because she'd been through too much already, would likely never trust any man again after what had happened. But Dimitri felt compelled to be her silent shadow for as long as it took for her to find her way back to some kind of normalcy.

Elena eased down into a chair close to the gate, and Dimitri watched the way her hair tumbled over her shoulders as she dug around in the contents of her purse and pulled out a book to read.

Her gaze flicked up once, as though sensing she was being watched. Dimitri offered a pleasant smile and then casually glanced down at his phone as though more interested in emails than the passengers around him. She relaxed and resumed her reading. His lips twitched. She had good instincts, this one, but she needn't worry ever again. She was safe, and he would watch over her as long as it took for her to heal.

You're strong, malen'kaya roza. *Someday soon you will not need me to watch over you.*

The thought filled him with a strange sadness. Being her protective shadow had given him a sense of hope and purpose that he hadn't felt in years. She turned her head at the sound of a gate attendant making an announcement, and something about her face, the way she held it, reminded him of something—or rather, someone. The mystery of that moment drew him in. Who was Elena Allen? In that moment, he vowed that he would find out.

Thank you so much for reading *The Darkest Hour*! But wait, don't close the book!

Stay tuned for the next book *Dark Desire* coming soon! You'll read Dimitri and Elena's love story!

The best way to know when a new book is released is to do one or all of the following:

Join my Newsletter: http://laurensmithbooks.com/free-books-and-newsletter/

Follow Me on BookBub:
https://www.bookbub.com/authors/lauren-smith

Join my Facebook VIP Reader Group called Lauren Smith's League:
https://www.facebook.com/groups/400377546765661/

HAVE YOU READ THE FIRST BOOK STARING RECLUSIVE Emery Lockwood and investigative reporter Sophie Ryder as their passion for each other ignites during danger? Come on, you know you want to turn that page...

THE GILDED CUFF

CHAPTER 1

EMERY LOCKWOOD AND FENN LOCKWOOD, EIGHT-YEAR-OLD TWIN SONS OF ELLIOT AND MIRANDA LOCKWOOD, WERE ABDUCTED FROM THEIR FAMILY RESIDENCE ON LONG ISLAND BETWEEN SEVEN AND EIGHT P.M. THE KIDNAPPING OCCURRED DURING A SUMMER PARTY HOSTED BY THE LOCKWOODS.

—*New York Times,* June 10, 1990

Long Island, New York

This is absolutely the stupidest thing I've ever done.

Sophie Ryder tugged the hem of her short skirt down over her legs a few more inches. It was still way too high. But she couldn't have worn something modest, per her usual style. Not at an elite underground BDSM club on Long Island's Gold Coast. Sophie had never been to any club before, let alone one like this. She'd had to borrow the black mini-skirt and the red lace-up corset from her friend Hayden Thorne, who was a member of the club and knew what she should wear.

The Gilded Cuff. It was *the* place for those who enjoyed their kink and could afford to pay.

Sophie sighed. A journalist's salary wasn't enough to afford anything like what the people around her wore, and she was definitely feeling less sexy in her practical black flats with a bit of sparkle on the tips. Sensuality rippled off every person in the room as they brushed against her in their Armani suits and Dior gowns, and she was wary of getting too close. Their cultured voices echoed off the craggy gray stone walls as they chatted and gossiped. Although she was uneasy with the frank way the people around her touched and teased each other with looks and light caresses, even while patiently waiting in line, a stirring of nervousness skittered through her chest and her abdomen. Half of it had to do with the sexual chemistry of her surroundings, and the rest of it had to do with the story that would make her career, if she could only find who she was looking for and save his life in time. Her editor at the Kansas newspaper she wrote for had given her one week to break the story. What she didn't know was how long she had to save the life of a man who at this very moment was in the club somewhere. She swallowed hard and tried to focus her thoughts.

Following the crowd, she joined the line leading up to a single walnut wood desk with gilt edges. A woman in a tailored gray suit over a red silk blouse stood there checking names off a list with a feather pen. Sophie fought to restrain her frantic pulse and the flutter of rebellious butterflies in her stomach as she finally reached the desk.

"Name, please?" The woman peered over wide, black-rimmed glasses. She looked a cross between a sexy librarian and a no-nonsense lawyer.

A flicker of panic darted through Sophie. She hoped her inside source would come through. Not just anyone could get into the club. You had to be referred by an existing member as a guest.

"My name's Sophie Ryder. I'm Hayden Thorne's guest." At the mention of her new friend's name the other woman instantly smiled, warmth filling her gaze.

"Yes, of course. She called and mentioned you'd be coming. Welcome to the Gilded Cuff, Sophie." She reached for a small glossy pamphlet and handed it over. "These are the club rules. Read over them carefully before you go inside. Come to me if you have any questions. You can also go to anyone wearing a red armband. They are our club monitors. If you get in too deep and you get panicked, say the word "red" and that will make the game or the scene stop. It's the common safe word. Any Doms inside should respect that. If they don't, they face our monitors."

"Okay," Sophie sucked in a breath, trying not to think about what sort of scene would make her use a safe word. This really was the most stupid thing she'd ever done. Her heart drummed a staccato beat as a wave of dread swept through her. She should leave... No. She had to stay at least a few more minutes. A life could hang in the balance, a life she could save.

"There's just one more thing. I need to know if you are a domme or a sub." The woman trailed the feather tip end of her pen under the tip of her chin, considering Sophie, measuring her.

"A domme or sub?" Sophie knew the words. Dominant and submissive. Just another part of the BDSM world, a lifestyle she knew so little about. Sophie definitely wasn't a domme. Dommes were the feminine Dominants in a D/s relationship. She certainly had no urge to whip her bed partner.

She liked control, yes, but only when it came to her life and doing what she needed to do. In bed? Well...she'd always liked to think of an aggressive man as one who took what he wanted, gave her what she needed. Not that she'd ever had a man like that before. Until now, every bedroom encounter had been a stunning lesson in disappointment.

The woman suddenly smiled again, as though she'd been privy to Sophie's inner thoughts. "You're definitely not a domme." Amusement twitched the corners of her mouth. "I sense you would enjoy an *aggressive* partner."

How in the hell? Sophie quivered. The flash of a teasing image, a man pinning her to the mattress, ruthlessly pumping into her until she exploded with pleasure. Heat flooded her face.

"Ahh, there's the sub. Here, take these." The woman captured Sophie's wrists and clamped a pair of supple leather cuffs around each wrist. Sewn into the leather, a red satin ribbon ran the length of each cuff. The woman at the desk didn't secure Sophie's wrists together, but merely ensured she had cuffs ready to be cinched together should she find a partner inside. The feel of the cuffs around her wrists sent a ripple of excitement through her. How was it possible to feel already bound and trapped? They constrained her, but didn't cut off her circulation, like wearing a choker necklace. She wanted to tug at the cuffs the way she would a tight necklace, because she was unused to the restriction.

"These tell the doms inside that you're a sub, but you're unclaimed and new to the lifestyle. Other subs will be wearing cuffs; some won't. It depends on if they are currently connected with a particular Dom and whether that Dom wishes to show an ownership. Since you're not with anyone, the red ribbons tell everyone you're new and learning the lifestyle. They'll know to go easy on you and to ask permission before doing or trying anything with you. The monitors will keep a close eye on you."

Relief coursed through Sophie. Thank heavens. She was

only here to pursue a story. Part of the job was to get information however she could, do whatever it took. But she wasn't sure she would be ready to do the things she guessed went on behind the heavy oak doors. Still, for the story, she would probably have to do something out of her comfort zone. It was the nature of writing about criminal stories. Of course, tonight wasn't about a crime, but rather a victim—and this victim was the answer to everything she'd spent years hoping to learn. And she was positive he was in danger.

When she'd gone to the local police with her suspicions, they'd turned a blind eye and run her off with the usual assurances that they kept a close eye on their community. But they didn't see patterns like she did. They hadn't read thousands of articles about crimes and noticed what she did. Somewhere inside this club, a man's life was hanging by a thread and she would save him and get the story of the century.

"Cuffs please." A heavily muscled man reached for her wrists as she approached the door that led deeper into the club. He wore an expensive suit with a red armband on his bicep, but his sheer brawny power was actually accented, rather than hidden, by his attire. It surprised her. She'd expected men to be running around in black leather and women fully naked, surrounded by chains, whips, and the whole shebang.

The man looked at her wrists, then up at her face. "You know the safe word, little sub?"

"Red."

"Good girl. Go on in and have a good time." The man's mouth broke into a wide smile, but it vanished just as quickly. She smiled back, and bowed her head slightly in a nod as she passed by him.

She moved through the open door into another world. Instead of a dungeon with walls fitted with iron chains,

Sophie found the Gilded Cuff was the opposite of what she'd anticipated.

Music and darkness ruled the landscape of the club, engulfing her senses. She halted abruptly, her heart skittering in a brief flare of panic at not being able to see anything around her.

The dungeons and screams she'd expected weren't there. Was this typical for a BDSM atmosphere? Her initial research had clearly led her astray. It wasn't like her to be unprepared and The Gilded Cuff certainly surprised her. Every scenario she'd planned for in her head now seemed silly and ineffective. This place and these people weren't anything like what'd she'd imagined they would be and that frightened her more than the cuffs did. Being unprepared could get you killed. It was a lesson she'd learned the hard way and she had the scars to prove it. The club's rule pamphlet the woman at the desk had given her was still in her hands and a slight layer of sweat marked the glossy paper's surface.

I probably should have glanced at it. What if I break a rule by accident?

The last thing she needed to do was end up in trouble or worse, get kicked out and not have a chance to do what she'd come to do. It might be her *only* chance to save the man who'd become her obsession.

Sophie made her way through an expansive room bordered with roped-tied crimson velvet drapes that kept prying eyes away from the large beds beyond them when the curtains were untied. Only the sounds coming from behind the draperies hinted at what was happening there. Her body reacted to the sounds, and she became aroused despite her intention to remain aloof. Around here, people lounged on gothic-style, brocade-upholstered couches. Old portraits hung along the walls, imperious images of beautiful men and women from ages past watching coldly from their frames.

Sophie had the feeling that she'd stepped into another time and place entirely removed from the cozy streets of the small town of Weston, on the north shore of Long Island.

The slow pulse of a bass beat and a singer's husky crooning wrapped around Sophie like an erotic blanket. As if she were in a dark dream, moving shadows and music filled her, and she breathed deeply, teased by hints of sex and expensive perfume. Awareness of the world outside wavered, rippling in her mind like a mirage. Someone bumped into her from behind, trying to pass by her to go deeper into the club. The sudden movement jerked her back to herself and out of the club's dark spell.

"Sorry!" she gasped and stepped out of the way.

As her eyes adjusted to the dim light, bodies manifested in twisting shapes. The sounds of sexual exploration were an odd compliment to the song being played. A heavy blush flooded Sophie's cheeks, heating her entire face. Her own sexual experiences had been awkward and brief. The memories of those nights were unwanted, uncomfortable, and passionless. Merely reliving them in her mind made her feel like a stranger in her own skin. She raised her chin and focused on her goal again.

The cuffs on her wrists made her feel vulnerable. At any moment a dom could come and clip her wrists together and haul her into a dark corner to show her true passion at his hands. The idea made her body hum to life in a way she hadn't thought possible. Every cell in her seemed to yearn now toward an encounter with a stranger in this place of sins and secrets. She trailed her fingertips over the backs of velveteen couches and the slightly rough texture of the fabric made her wonder how it would feel against her bare skin as she was stretched out beneath a hard masculine body.

The oppressive sensual darkness that slithered around the edges of her own control was too much. There was a low-lit lamp not too far away, and Sophie headed for it, drawn by the promise of its comfort. Light was safe; you could see what was happening. It was the dark that set her on edge. If she couldn't see what was going on around her, she was vulnerable. There was barely enough light for her to see where she was headed. She needed to calm down, regain her composure and remind herself why she was here.

Her heart trampled a wild beat against her ribs as she realized it would be so easy for any one of the strong, muscular doms in the club to slide a hand inside her bodice and discover the thing she'd hidden there, an object that had become precious to her over the last few years.

Her hand came to rest on the copy of an old photograph. She knew taking it out would be a risk, but she couldn't fight the need to steal the quick glance the dim light would allow her.

Unfolding the picture gently, her lips pursed as she studied the face of the eight-year-old boy in the picture. This was the childhood photo of the man she'd come to meet tonight.

The black and white photo had been on the front page of the *New York Times* twenty-five years ago. The boy was dressed in rags, and bruises marred his angelic face; his haunted eyes gazed at the camera. A bloody cut traced the line of his jaw from chin to neck. Eyes wide, he clasped a thick woolen blanket to his body as a policeman held out a hand to him.

Emery Lockwood. The sole survivor of the most notorious child abduction in American history since that of the Lindbergh baby. And he was somewhere in the Gilded Cuff tonight.

Over the last year she'd become obsessed with the photo and had taken to looking at it when she needed reassurance. Its subject had been kidnapped but survived and escaped, when so many children like him over the years had not been so lucky. Sophie's throat constricted, and shards of invisible glass dug into her throat as she tried to shrug off her own awful memories. Her best friend Rachel, the playground, that man with the gray van...

The photo was creased in places and its edges were worn. The defiance in Emery's face compelled her in a way nothing else in her life had. Compelled with an intensity that scared her. She had to see him, had to talk to him and understand him and the tragedy he'd survived. She was afraid he might be the target of another attempt on his life and she had to warn him. It wouldn't be fair for him to die, not after everything he'd survived. She had to help him. But it wasn't just that. It was the only way she could ease the guilt she'd felt at not being able to help catch the man who'd taken her friend. She had to talk to Emery. Even though she knew it wouldn't bring Rachel back, something inside her felt like meeting him would bring closure.

With a forced shrug of her shoulders, she relaxed and focused on Emery's face. After years of studying kidnapping cases she'd noticed something crucial in a certain style of kidnappings, a tendency by the predators to repeat patterns of behavior. When she'd started digging through Emery's case and read the hundreds of articles and police reports, she'd sensed it. That prickling sensation at the back of her mind that warned her that what had been started twenty-five years ago wasn't over yet. She hadn't been able to save Rachel, but she would save Emery.

I have to. She owed it to Rachel, owed it to herself and to everyone who'd lost someone to the darkness, to evil. Guilt stained her deep inside but when she saw Emery's face in that photograph, it reminded her that not every stolen child died. A part of her, one she knowingly buried in her heart, was convinced that talking to him, hearing his story, would ease the old wounds from her own past that never seemed to heal. And in return, she might be the one to solve his kidnapping and rescue him from a threat she was convinced still existed.

She wasn't the boldest woman—at least not naturally—but the quest for truth always gave her that added level of bravery. Sometimes she felt, when in the grips of pursuing a story, that she became the person she ought to be, someone brave enough to fight the evil in the world. Not the tortured girl from Kansas who'd lost her best friend to a pedophile when she was seven years old.

Sophie would have preferred to conduct an interview somewhere less intimate, preferably wearing more clothing. But Emery was nearly impossible to reach—he avoided the press, apparently despising their efforts to get him to tell his story. She didn't blame him. Retelling his story could be traumatic for him, but she didn't have a choice. If what she suspected was true, she needed the details she was sure he'd kept from the police because they might be the keys to figuring out who'd kidnapped him and why.

She'd made calls to his company, but the front desk there had refused to transfer her to his line, probably because of his "no press" rule. Thanks to Hayden she knew Emery rarely left the Lockwood estate but he came to the Gilded Cuff a few times a month. This was the only opportunity she might have to reach him.

Emery ran his father's company from a vast mansion on the Lockwood estate, nestled in the thick woods of Long Island's Gold Coast. No visitors were permitted and he left the house only when in the company of private guards.

Sophie tucked the photo back into her corset and looked around, peering at the faces of the doms walking past her. More than once their gazes dropped to the cuffs on her wrists, possessively assessing her body. Her face scorched with an irremovable blush at their perusal. Whenever she made eye contact with a dom, he would frown and she'd instantly drop her gaze.

Respect; must remember to respect the doms and not make eye contact unless they command it. Otherwise she might end up bent over a spanking bench. Her corset seemed to shrink, making it hard to breathe, and heat flashed from her head to her toes.

Men and women—submissives judging by the cuffs they bore on their wrists—were wearing even less than she was as they walked around with drink trays, carrying glasses to doms on couches. Several doms had subs kneeling at their feet, heads bowed. A man sitting on a nearby love seat was watching her with hooded eyes. He had a sub at his feet, his hand stroking her long blond hair. The woman's eyes were half closed, cheeks flushed with pleasure. The dom's cobalt blue eyes measured her—not with sexual interest, but seemingly with mere curiosity—the way a sated mountain lion might watch a plump rabbit crossing its path.

Sophie pulled her eyes away from the red-headed dom and his ensnaring gaze. The club was almost too much to take in. Collars, leashes, the occasional pole with chains hanging from it, and a giant cross were all there, part of the fantasy world created amid the glitz and old world décor.

Sliding past entwined bodies and expensive furniture, she saw more that intrigued her. The club itself was this one large room with several halls splitting off the main room. Hayden had explained earlier that morning the layout of the club. She had pointed out that no matter which hall you went down you had to come back to the main room to exit the club. A handy safety feature. A little exhalation of relief escaped her lips. How deep did a man like Emery Lockwood live this lifestyle? Would she find him in one of the private rooms or would he be part of a public scene like the ones she was witnessing now?

She was nearly halfway across the room when a man caught her by her arm and spun her to face him. Her lips parted, ready to scream the word "red", but when she met his gaze she froze, the shout dying at the back of her throat. He raised her wrists, fingering the red ribbon around her leather cuffs. His gray eyes were as silver as moonlight, and openly interested. Sophie tried to jerk free of his hold. He held tight. The arousal that had been slowly building in her body flashed cold and sharp. She could use the safe word. She knew that. But after one deep breath, she forced herself to relax. Part of the job tonight was to blend in, to find Emery. She couldn't do that if she ran off and cried for help at the first contact. It would be smarter to let this play out a bit; maybe she could squeeze the dom for information about Emery later if she didn't find him soon. For Sophie, not being able to get to Emery was more frightening than anything this man might try to do to her.

"I see your cuffs, little sub. I'm not going to hurt you."

His russet hair fell across his eyes and he flicked his head: power, possession, dominance. He was raw masculinity. A natural dom. He was the sort of good-looking man that she would have mooned over when she was a teenager. Hell, even now at twenty-four she should have been melting into a puddle at this man's feet. His gaze bit into her. A stab of sudden apprehension made her stomach pitch, but she needed to find Emery and going along with this guy might be the best way to get information. He tugged her wrists, jerking her body against his as he regarded her hungrily. "I need an unclaimed sub for a contest. Tonight is your lucky night, sweetheart."

CHAPTER 2

Elliot and Miranda Lockwood were visible during the time the kidnapping is speculated to have occurred. The twins were last seen in the kitchen by their hired nanny Francesca Espina, age fifty-four years, who had summoned the boys to the kitchen for dinner.

—*New York Times*, June 10, 1990

Sophie barely had time to protest at the dom's tight hold on her wrist before he dragged her across the room to where a group of people circled a couch against the wall. She could have said "red" and stopped whatever game he'd intended to play so she could keep searching for Emery, but the word died on her lips. A large crowd of people all turned to face her, amusement flashing in their eyes. The crowd's focus on her was not comforting in the slightest. She was prey, for a so-called contest, in a BDSM club. Searching the faces for Emery's, she prayed she'd be lucky enough to find him. If not, she'd use her safe word and get free of the man and his "contest."

Holding her, he grinned darkly at the onlookers. "Found a newbie. She'll be perfect."

Sophie again jerked to get her wrist back and failed. She stifled a gasp as he promptly smacked her bottom with an open hand. Her gaze darted across the crowd, trying to seek out Emery's familiar face. He had to be here somewhere. Most of the club members had moved in to watch her and this dom.

"Stand still, bow your head," he commanded.

To her shock she obeyed instantly—not because she naturally bowed to anyone who shoved her around, but because something inside her responded to the commanding tone he'd just used on her. He seemed like a man who would enjoy punishing her, and she knew enough about this lifestyle to know she never wanted to end up over a spanking bench, even if the idea did make her insides flare to life.

"Bring her here, Royce." A cool, rich voice spoke, pouring over her skin like whisky—slightly rough, with an intoxicating bite to it. When this man spoke, the voices murmuring around her stopped and a hush fell over the area.

The crowd around her and the man, Royce, parted. Another man, sitting on the blue brocaded couch, watched them. His large hands rested on his thighs, fingers impatiently drumming a clipped beat. Royce shoved Sophie none too gently, sending her to her knees right at the man's feet. She reacted instinctively, throwing her hands out to balance herself, and her palms fell on his thighs and her chest collided with his knees.

Air rushed out of her lungs in a soft *whoosh*. For a few seconds she fought to regain her breath as she leaned against the stranger for support. The large muscles beneath his charcoal pants jumped and tensed beneath her hands, and she whipped her palms off him as though burned. She'd practically been in the man's lap, the heat of his body warming her, tempting her with his close proximity. Hastily she dropped her head and rested her hands on her own thighs, waiting. It took every ounce of her willpower to concentrate on breathing.

She still didn't look at his face, focusing instead on his expensive black shoes, the precision cuffs of his dark charcoal pants. Her eyes then tracked up his body, noting the crisp white shirt and thin, blood red tie he wore. It was loosened beneath the undone top button of his dress shirt. She had the sudden urge to crawl into his lap and trail kisses down his neck and taste him.

"Raise your eyes," the voice demanded.

Sophie drew a deep breath, letting air fill her, making her almost light-headed. And then she looked up.

Her heart leapt into her throat and her brain short-circuited.

Emery Lockwood, the object of her darkest fantasies, the ones she'd buried deep in her heart in the hours just before dawn, was looking down at her, predatory curiosity gleaming in his gaze. He trapped her with a magnetic pull, an air of mystery. She was caught in invisible strands of a spell woven around her body and soul.

The boy's soft angelic features were there, hidden beneath the surface of the man before her. He was the most devastatingly, sensual man she'd ever seen. His high cheekbones, full lips, and aquiline nose were all parts of the face of a man in his early thirties. But his eyes—the color of nutmeg and framed with long dark lashes any woman would kill to have—were the same as those of the wounded eight-year-old boy in her photo. Although she could see that they'd hardened with two decades of grief.

He was masculine perfection, except for the thin, almost

invisible scar that ran the length of his sharp jaw line. Even after twenty-five years, he still bore the marks of his suffering. She ached with every cell in her body to press her mouth to his, to steal fevered kisses from his lips. Her fingertips tingled with the need to stroke over the scar on his face, to smooth away the hurt he must have endured.

"Do you know the rules of our game?" Emery asked. As he spoke, his gaze still held her in place, like a butterfly caught beneath a pin and encased in glass. Hands trembling, she pursed her lips and tried to remain calm and collected. It was nearly impossible. The heat of his intense regard only increased as the corners of his mouth curved in a slow, wicked smile. Oh, the man knew just how he affected her!

Emery leaned forward, caught her chin in his palm, and tilted her face up to look at him. Her skin burned deliciously where his palm touched her. He pulled her, like the moon calling to the tides, demanding devotion and obedience with the promise of something great, something she couldn't understand. Her senses hummed with eagerness, ready to explore his touch, his taste. Like a minnow caught in a vast current, she was pulled out to deeper waters, helpless to resist. In any other situation, she wouldn't have been so off balance, and wouldn't be letting herself get sucked into this strange game she sensed she was about to play. But here in this dark fantasy of the Gilded Cuff, she didn't want to look away from him.

"The rules are as follows: I give you a command, you obey. I have to make you come in less than two minutes. I cannot do more than stroke any part of your body covered by cloth—no touching between your legs and no touching of your bare breasts. You are to look into my eyes and do whatever I say so long as my commands are within the rules. If you come, I win; if you don't, Royce wins."

Sophie struggled to think clearly. There was no way she

would have agreed to this anywhere else, but in the club, this was the sort of game the doms played... the sort of game Emery played, and he wanted to play with her. A shiver of desire shot through her, making her clit pulse. How could she refuse?

"Uh... permission to speak?"

"You will call me Sir, or Master Emery."

"Sir," Sophie corrected. She wanted to kick herself. She had read enough about this lifestyle that she should have remembered to address him formally, but in all honesty the way he was looking at her—like something he wanted to eat—she couldn't remain entirely rational.

"Permission to speak granted." Emery's voice dropped into a softer tone, approval warming his hazel eyes.

"What happens to me, Sir? Only one of you can win."

Royce shared a glance with Emery.

"She's a smart one, this little sub. Well, Emery? What do you think?"

Both men focused their intense gazes on her. It took everything in her not to look away.

"Punishment by the one who loses. But what form? Flogging?" Royce suggested.

Sophie flinched.

"No whips," Emery seemed to conclude, his eyes reading her tiniest reaction.

Emery ran a palm over his jaw, which was shadowed with night stubble. The look gave him a rugged edge, reminding her of the men back home in Kansas.

The tension in the crowd seemed to heighten as the subject of punishment continued. Emery continued to stare at her, his eyes seemingly unlocking the puzzle she presented. "She's new. Why not a spanking?" he murmured softly.

That caught her attention. Her clit thrummed to life, pulsing in a faint beat along with her heart. The twinge of uncomfortable pain in her knees was temporarily abated by this new distraction. Her eyes immediately settled on Emery's large, capable hands. She could practically feel the width of his palm striking her bottom.... Trouble. She was in so much trouble.

"Definitely spanking." Emery smiled. "My favorite form of punishment. It will be a disappointment when you come in my arms, and I shall have to allow Royce the pleasure of laying his palm to your flesh."

"Cocky bastard," Royce retorted. "She might resist you. I bet she's far less submissive than she looks, and given her clothes, far too self-conscious to come in front of people. When I win, you'll owe me your best case of bourbon."

Her knees were aching, pain flaring like sharp little needles through her skin and deep into her bones. She shifted on them, trying to favor one over the other, and then hastily switched, but it didn't help. There was no way she was going to make it much longer on her knees.

Emery's hazel eyes lit up with the challenge. "Like hell! When she comes, and she will, you'll owe me your best case of scotch."

As the men continued to posture and argue, Sophie sat back on her heels, her knees aching something fierce. Like metal rods were jabbing up between her knees into her nerves.

Screw this. I'm getting up. Surging to her feet, she breathed a sigh of relief as blood flow pumped through her legs.

The people gathered around her gasped. Both men stopped arguing and turned to face her, gazes dark with anger. It wasn't the lethal sort of anger she'd come across before, not like the murderers she'd interviewed for her crime stories. That anger was a terrifying anger, pure hatred. It rolled off those criminals in waves. The kind of anger that truly good people never felt, it was the sort of rage that consumed the soul and blackened the heart until only a killing machine was left its place.

With Royce and Emery, however, it was merely the anger of a parent or a mentor at a charge who'd clearly disobeyed a direct order. She knew the outcome. Punishment. She could read it on their faces, and it aroused them both. Hell, it aroused her.

"You weren't given permission to rise." Emery spoke slowly, as though trying to decide whether he would give her a chance to apologize or to just skip straight to the punishment.

Even as she opened her mouth she knew it was a bad idea.

"My knees hurt. This isn't carpet; it's rock. *Hard* rock."

Emery's jaw dropped. The people around them stepped back.

Royce was silent for a long moment, and then burst into long, hooting laughter. He doubled over, palms on his thighs, as he struggled to catch his breath. "Damn, this is going to be fun."

"Fun," Emery muttered and shook his head. "Back on your knees, until we decide what to do with you."

"Yeah...no thank you, Sir." Sophie challenged. "I'll stay on my feet until you're done."

He was up and on his feet and before she could react he had turned her to face the crowd and bent her over.

Whack! His palm landed on her butt. The impact stung, but it faded almost instantly to a warm, achy feeling. Her legs turned to jelly and she trembled helplessly against a shocking wave of pleasure that began to build inside her abdomen.

The glare she launched in Emery's direction had no effect. When he released her and took his seat again, she spun to face him. His narrowed eyes shot her pulse into overdrive.

"You have a safe word, little sub?" Royce asked.

She wracked her brain for one, knowing it had to be

something she could remember when she was panicking because it was the word that would get the doms to stop whatever they were doing if the interaction became too unbearable.

"Apricot," she decided. Being highly allergic to the fruit made it a word she wouldn't forget easily.

Her unusual choice of safe word had both men raising their brows. In that instant they could have been brothers. They mirrored each other the way only true friends could. A pang of envious longing cut through Sophie's heart and she sucked in a breath as she thought of Rachel.

"What's your name, little sub?"

"Sophie Ryder." When his brows lowered she hastily added, "Sir."

Emery patted his thigh with one palm. "Let us begin the contest. You will come and sit on my lap and I will command you."

Sophie's stomach pitched so deep it felt like it hit her toes. Emery leaned back, his arms rested on the back of the couch. He looked every bit a prince, a leader of a pride of lions, merely waiting for his conquest, his prey. His relaxed position only made her feel more helpless. She knew he could move fast, catch her in his arms and have her bent for punishment again in seconds if she dared to resist him. Her nipples pearled beneath the unforgiving leather of the corset, rubbing until they ached. She clenched her hands to stop them from shaking.

Here we go, you can do this. Sophie approached him and sat across his lap. She wriggled, trying to find a comfortable position, unable to ignore the feel of his muscular thighs beneath her.

He cocked one eyebrow imperiously, as though her restlessness had somehow offended him.

"Do not *squirm.*" He issued his first command.

She stilled instantly. Her only movement was her breasts rising and falling with her breaths.

"Look at my eyes, *only* my eyes." His tone softened, but the rough edge still scraped over her, making her hungry for the promise she found in his gaze. The voices around them faded and she slipped deeper and deeper into his dark spell.

He would be a rough lover; carnal, quiet. He wouldn't whisper sweet words, wouldn't utter harsh arousing statements. He'd simply take her, take her again and again, the grinding, the pounding. The soft silence punctuated by uneven breaths, the stroke of rough hands over her sensitive skin. Everything a sensible, modern woman shouldn't want from a man in bed. He'd be all animal in all the right ways.

She'd never been with someone like him before, might never be again, and the thought was an intoxicating one. To be at the mercy of such power, such electrifying sexual control and surrender it all to him... Her mouth was suddenly dry, her pulse tapping Morse code for help as she tried to maintain a semblance of calm. Would she be able to give in to him? To let him guide her through the dark lust that so often took hold of her when she had no way of releasing it? Yes... She could let go with him, and the uncertainty of what would happen when she did was half of the excitement that lit a fire in her veins.

His hands settled on her hips, fingers slowly stroking back and forth, teasing her skin beneath the leather mini-skirt. What would it be like to have his hands on her bare flesh? Fingers exploring between her legs.

"Tell me what you'd like, Sophie." Emery leaned his head down, his brow touching hers, eyes still locked on her face.

She gulped, her mouth dryer than the Gobi Desert.

"What would it take to make you lose control? Do you want a hard fuck? A desperate pounding? Or would you like to have your hands bound, lying face down on a large bed, softness against your belly and my hardness above you, in you?" His erotic whispers were so soft, so low that no one nearby could hear what he was saying to her. The images he painted were wild, vivid, yet blurry—like a strange combination between Van Gogh and Monet. Sweet and sensual, then dark, exotic and barely comprehendible. Emery was an artist in his own way, an erotic painter of words and pictures.

"I'd take you slow, so slow you'd lose all sense of time. You'd focus only on me, on my cock gliding between your thighs, possessing you." His words were slow and deliberate, as though he'd given them years of thought, but the slight breathless quality to the whisper made her realize she was not the only one affected.

The first quiver between her thighs was inevitable. She shifted, restless on his legs, despite his command not to move.

His breath fanned her lips. "Oh, god," she murmured.

He smiled, unblinking, and licked his lips. She wanted that tongue in her mouth, tangling with her own. She craved his hands on her bare flesh.

"Please..." she moaned. He moved his hands down from her hips, to her outer thighs, barely exerting any real pressure. That made it worse. The hint of his touch, the promise of the pressure she craved. Sophie wanted him digging his fingers into her skin, holding her legs apart as he slammed deep into her.

"Take a deep breath," he issued another command.

She obeyed. Her heartbeat seemed to expand outward from her chest until the pulse pounded through her entire body so hard she swore he could feel it beat through her skin wherever he touched her. The throb between her thighs nearly stung now—her need so great, his effect so potent.

"When I take you, no matter the position, you will like it. I'll bend you over a couch." He stroked one finger on her outer thigh, made circular patterns. "I'll push you up against a wall."

With little panting breaths she wriggled, trying to rock her hips against his lap, but he held her still. She nearly screamed in frustration at being denied what her body frantically needed.

The finger moved higher, past her hip, up to her ribcage. "Spread and bound open on my bed." His fingertip quested up past the laces of her corset. "You'll twist and writhe, unable to get free. At my mercy, Sophie, my mercy. You will beg and when I'm ready, I will grant your every desire, just as I take mine."

She couldn't breathe. The orgasm was so close. She could feel it, like a shadow inside her body, breathing, panting, waiting to be set free. She was ready; she wanted to climax in his arms, wanted to forge that connection which would tie her to him. Terrifying, shocking, intimate, but damn if she didn't want it more than anything in the world at that moment. Wanted it more than her story, more than the interview, more than easing her pain from the past. She needed pleasure. His pleasure.

The feathering touch of his fingers, Emery's erotic murmurs now incoherent with breathless anticipation against her neck as they both strained toward the great cliff, eagerly craving the fall back to earth. Why wouldn't he touch her where she needed it? The slightest pressure on her inner thighs, the rhythmic stroke of his hand against her clit, anything would do it if he could only...

"Time!" Royce's triumphant call shattered the glass bubble that had cocooned them for the last two minutes. Murmurs of shock from the surrounding crowd broke through.

"Damn." Emery's eyes darkened. Anger, but not at her, flared at the lines of his mouth. He bent to press his lips against her ear. "You were close, weren't you, darling? So close I almost had you." His body was trembling beneath hers, the little movements wracking his arms and chest. The press of his arousal beneath her bottom far too evident. He'd been there, right alongside her, dying to come. Together. And it hadn't happened for either of them; two minutes hadn't been enough time.

Sophie's legs shook as cold reality slashed through her. The climax her body had been prepared to give Emery faded away. In its wake little tremors reverberated along her limbs, made worse by the tension in her entire body that hadn't found release. She tried to breathe, to let her shoulders drop and her muscles relax. It was going to take a while to come down from this.

Almost had her? No. He definitely had her, practically wrapped up with a bow on top, totally and completely his. No question.

CHAPTER 3

THE KITCHEN IS NOW THE OFFICIAL CRIME SCENE WHERE THE ABDUCTION IS BELIEVED TO HAVE OCCURRED. THE CRIME SCENE WAS LITTERED WITH BROKEN COKE BOTTLES, BLOOD, AND HALF-EATEN SANDWICHES ON THE BOYS' PLATES.

—*New York Times*, June 10, 1990

"So, my best case of bourbon?" Emery raised his face to look at Royce, who stood in front of the couch.

"If you don't mind." Royce's eyes twinkled with devilish merriment, but he clapped a palm on Emery's shoulder with gentle camaraderie. "I'll be by the house later to pick it up."

"I'll have it ready for you," Emery assured him, and then turned his attention back to Sophie. "Now, little sub, let's see about that punishment."

A sensuous light flickered at the back of his eyes, like a lighthouse's beacon fighting to shine through the depths of a storm. Every emotion—a thousand of them—shuttered and then exploded behind his gaze. To Sophie it felt as if she was seeing the entire world captured in one rapid blink...and then it was gone. His eyes were heavy with desire and nothing else.

Oh dear. "I...uh..." How inadequate words were! What could she say to persuade him against punishing her?

Emery rose from the couch in a fluid movement with Sophie still clasped in his arms. She had only a moment to marvel that her weight didn't seem to bother him at all before he was carrying her through the group of people. There was a door ajar halfway down one of the halls that branched off the center room. He nudged it open with his foot. It was completely empty save for a thick rug spanning the entire room and a wooden piece of furniture that she knew from her research was a spanking bench.

At the sight of the bench Sophie went rigid; her limbs locked up, her hands balled into fists. Only a sliver of her panic came from fear. The rest of her wanted to know too badly how it felt to be bent over that, with his hand smacking her ass until she cried out. *That* scared her: how much she wanted to experience something so dark and sinful. Emery set her down and started to close the door. He left it open about an inch or two. Someone could come in, could get to her if she needed help. Still...Sophie shot a glance at the bench. There was no way in hell she was going to bend over that and...and...let herself go with him. She'd never been able to do that with anyone and she couldn't start with someone like him. He was tall, blond, and brooding. She'd make a fool of herself if she gave in to him. What would he think of her if she got aroused by a punishment? That she was just like any other woman in the club? The thought stopped her cold.

She didn't want to be just another woman to him. She wanted to be something more; she wanted him to trust her, to open up to her. Letting him spank the hell out of her might not be the best way to earn his trust....

Then again, maybe it would.

I wish I knew what I was doing. She cursed inwardly. With men, she was always awkward and unsure of herself, and now her typical failings seemed magnified because he affected her too strongly.

"Look, I'm sorry, but this whole scene just isn't for me. I shouldn't have come here." She edged toward the door. Maybe if she got far enough from the bench, he'd forget about punishing her and she could talk to him about the abduction. If he thought she was scared enough to leave, he might back off in his determination to spank her and she'd have her chance to speak.

Emery sidestepped, blocking her access to the exit. She saw the outline of well-defined muscles; he was much bigger and stronger than she was. To her sheer humiliation, something inside her started to purr with delight at the thought of that strength and size directed at her, for her protection and more importantly, her pleasure.

He placed a hand on the side of her neck where it connected to her shoulder. His thumb moved slowly back and forth against the base of her throat, as though questing for the frantic drum of her pulse. His lips moved, flirting at the tips with a smile.

She couldn't take much more of this. If she didn't get away, she'd let him take her over to that bench and she'd surrender to him. That couldn't happen.

"Please, let me leave." Her tone, thankfully, sounded stronger than the whimpering inside her which begged to stay, to let him bend her over the bench and do wicked things to her.

"If you want out, say your safe word." His sharp tone was edged with a challenge. Something deep inside her responded.

She knew enough of D/s relationships to know that subs weren't powerless; surrendering to a dom was their choice, one that had to be based on trust. Emery's challenge for her to surrender was tempting, too tempting if she was honest with herself. She'd never wanted to surrender to a man, but the idea of willingly letting one overpower her? Her thighs clenched together, her sensitive nerves inside jumping to life. Could she give in? Gain power by giving him power?

"I'm waiting for your answer."

When Sophie hesitated, Emery threaded his fingers through the black satin ribbons that laced the front of her corset. He tugged one bow's string with careless ease, so at odds with the cool, dispassionate expression on his face as he began to loosen the laces and peel her corset apart. A haze of heat settled over her skin and fogged her mind. Sophie prayed he'd keep going, would pull her corset open like they were in some torrid romance novel, and bend his head to her breasts to...

His fingers caressed the tip of the folded up photo. She jolted back, the memory of where she'd tucked his photo slamming into her. He couldn't see it; he'd never understand. Emery's hand shot out, caught her wrists, and lifted them above her head. In a move as smooth as the steps of a slow dance, he maneuvered her back against the wall by the door. One thick, muscled thigh pressed between hers, and he kept her wrists trapped above her. His other hand moved back to her corset, dipped between her breasts and retrieved the photo. His thumb and index finger deftly unfolded it and the wide-eyed interest of natural curiosity on his face morphed to an expression of narrowed suspicion.

He released her wrists, stepped back several feet and stared at the image in his hand. He was so still he could have been carved from marble — his eyes dark with horror, his tanned skin now alabaster white.

A long moment later he drew a deep measured breath and raised his eyes to hers.

"Where did you get this picture?" Each word seemed dragged out between his clenched teeth. He changed before her eyes, the prince transforming into a beast. Wounded rage filled his eyes, morphing with the promise of vengeance.

The pit of her stomach seemed to have dropped out. She felt as if she was falling, that awful sensation of losing control, of being seconds away from a sickening crash. This was what she'd come to talk about, come to warn him about, and she wasn't ready. It would hurt him to drag this out in the open again and she wasn't prepared, not after the way they'd been so close just seconds before. The truth was, she didn't want to lose him, not this sexy, addictive man. And she would lose him if she brought up the past. Like all victims he'd retreat into himself and pull away from her even as she tried to help him.

"The newspaper," Sophie replied breathlessly.

Emery continued to stare at her, his long elegant fingers curling around the photo, crumpling it. "Why do you have a picture of me from twenty-five years ago?" When Sophie opened her mouth he waved a hand at her. "Think carefully how you answer, Ms. Ryder. I'm not above lawsuits, and I have a very, very good lawyer."

Sophie bit her lip, tasted a drop of blood and licked at the sore spot before she replied. She'd only rehearsed this a thousand times yet now she didn't know where to begin.

"I wanted to be able to recognize you, because I wanted to interview you. I'm a freelance investigative journalist. I specialize in crime stories, primarily those about kidnappings." She knew she'd made a mistake the moment the words left her mouth. She felt incredibly small in that moment, like a mouse cornered in a lion's cage. Should she have started with the part where she thought his life was in danger? That would've made her sound crazy, and she needed his trust more than anything.

Emery's eyes turned dark as wood that had been consumed by flames and burnt to ash.

"You people are all the same." His tone was deadly calm. Quiet. The hand holding the photo started to shake. His fingers clenched so tightly that his knuckles whitened. The shaking spread outward; his shoulders visibly vibrated with his rage.

Sophie sucked in a breath. He wasn't withdrawing... He was going to lash out. The oppressive wave of guilt that cut off her air warred with a new, unexpected apprehension. This looked bad, she knew it. The sneaky reporter trying to get the scoop on a story that defined this man's worst moment in his life. God, she'd been an idiot to think she could waltz in here and start chatting about his kidnapping.

Goosebumps rippled along her bare arms and her muscles tensed. Despite the anger she could feel rolling off him in waves, he seemed to rein in that silken thread of self-control and loosened his fingers. The photo stayed crinkled in a tight ball, completely destroyed. When she swallowed, it felt like knives sliced her throat.

Emery spoke again, much to Sophie's dread. "Invade my life, my privacy. You know nothing of what I've endured or what happened to me and my..." the words faded but Sophie sensed he nearly said "brother."

Her eyes burned with a sudden rush of tears. His pain was so clear on his face, and it made her think of herself, of the way she felt when she thought of Rachel.

"Mr. Lockwood—" She had to explain, to show him she only wanted to help.

He threw the crumpled photo at her feet. He might as well have slapped her. Would he be more willing to listen if he knew she was here to save him? But how could she get him to listen long enough to explain everything?

Summoning her strength, she stepped toward him. "But

you survived. I think people want to know the truth, know how strong you are." Why couldn't he see what a miracle his escape was? He'd survived a horrific experience and was stronger, stronger than she was. Losing Rachel had destroyed her innocence and shattered her world.

A ruthless laugh broke from his lips. "Strong? Strong?" He shook his head from side to side, a wild smile splitting his face suddenly. "I'm strong now. I *wasn't* strong then. If I had been strong, Fenn would be here." When his eyes grew hollow Sophie realized how much that admission must have cost him. He blamed himself for whatever had happened to his brother, thought Fenn Lockwood's death was his fault. And she'd played right into reinforcing his delusion that an eight-year-old boy should have been able to stop kidnappers. That was ludicrous.

"At least you're here. You're alive and you have a good life." The words were hollow; Sophie didn't know what else to say so she repeated what her therapist had told her years ago, after Rachel was taken.

"It's a half-life, nothing more." Emery's soft utterance cut open her soul. He understood, felt the same way she did, if not more.

She'd poured her heart into what little life she felt she had left, but it wasn't enough to fill the empty space where Rachel should have been. She couldn't imagine what it must be like for Emery to have lost his twin. A sibling, a person he'd shared a womb with, had been raised alongside for eight years. Whatever had been between them had been destroyed, one life ended, the other haunted.

"I'm not going to agree to an interview. Your homework should've told you that. Now if you'll excuse me, I've had enough of the club tonight."

Sophie's heart cracked down the middle. She'd failed. But there was more to it—the loss of something else, something deeper and infinitely more important: his trust. She'd never met this man before today, didn't fully trust her, yet she hated that she'd let him down, abused what little trust he'd started to give her. It was like losing him, even though she sensed he'd never belong to anyone. He seemed so distant, buried beneath the past and that made him dangerous. A wildness emanated from him that made him seem like the sort of a man a woman couldn't own, couldn't claim, not matter how hard she wanted to or tried to. Her grandmother used to say you could never harness the wind.

Foolish woman that she was, Sophie just had to try. She waited a breathless moment that seemed to hang on the edge of forever. He needed her to submit to him; he needed the control between them. She could give it to him, right now, even if it was only temporary.

"Mr. Lockwood, please." Guided by some instinct, she grabbed his hand and fell to her knees at his feet, head bowed. "Please..." She knew the second his gaze shifted to her. The hairs on the back of her neck rose, her skin prickled, and arousal flooded through her, making her damp, and her breathing shallow. Even though he was upset with her, his focus heated her blood.

There was a long pause before he spoke. "Please, what?" Emery's voice was dom-like—cool, calm, commanding, not hard or biting like moments before. He shifted his feet, angling his body toward her—a few inches only, but it was enough to show she was getting through to him again. There might still be a chance.

She swallowed thickly. "Please, Sir."

"And what do you request of me?" He pulled the hand that she clutched free of her grasp, but moved it to the crown of her hair, stroking. His palm moved down to her neck, fingers threading and pulling tightly enough to make her arch her back to ease the pressure. It forced her face upward, and she had to look into his eyes. He stood over her now, his towering posture not threatening but completely dominating. She didn't cower but kept herself submissive, giving him what he needed.

No one understood. No one knew the agonizing grip of pain at losing someone you loved. But Emery did. And she wanted him to talk to her, to tell her how he'd survived with a broken heart. But when he turned to look at her, eyes so full of echoing pain, she came to a realization. He wasn't stronger, at least not in this. He was just as wounded as she. They were both lost. He without his brother, she without Rachel. Lives taken from them that could never come back. Memories tarnished by other men's evil, leaving them with nothing more than a child's fear of loss and death.

She didn't think he could give her the answers she needed. But he could give her the story, provide the details which might give her enough information to solve who was behind his kidnapping. She was so close to figuring it out. She could catch whoever was responsible and prevent them from harming Emery or anyone else ever again. It would have to be enough.

"I want your help to make the monster who did this to you pay. He's still out there. You know that." She paused, licking her lips. "And he could come after you again. It's why you've kept bodyguards and security high for the last twenty-five years," she guessed. Her reports always showed the same man shadowing Emery the few times he'd been photographed outside his home.

Emery's lips pursed into a thin line and his brows drew down over his eyes, which were more the color of chocolate-kissed honey now.

"You think you can catch a man who's eluded police and the FBI?"

Her heart jolted. He'd just admitted his captor had been a

man. The reports said three masked men, but he made it sound like only one man was involved. What had happened to the other two? More puzzle pieces shifted.

"I'm a skilled reporter. I've focused on criminal stories for years, Sir. If you let me, I can use whatever you tell me to solve the case. I *know* I can." She prayed he'd hear the sincerity and resolve in her tone. She meant every word. She'd protect him and catch the bastard who'd hurt him. As penance for Rachel. As penance for every child she couldn't save.

He seemed to consider her request.

"What would you do for me in return?" His eyes promised he meant something sexual. Something that might shatter her lonely world into pieces and leave her craving him for the rest of her life.

"D-do for you?" Sophie stuttered. That was becoming an irritating habit she needed to fix. The man had the ability to tie her in knots when he got her thinking of other things besides her job.

"I'm a dom, darling. Your needs should involve me, and your thoughts should be about what I need and want. If I am nice and give you what you need, you must give me something in return. And no... I'm not talking about money or anything so trivial as that. My story, as you call it, is worth something beyond money. I will need something just as important from you in return."

She hesitated. What could she give him? She had nothing to offer. Nothing but...herself. She could give herself to him. A scolding voice in her head warned her that it would be a devil's bargain. But she silenced the voice. Damn the consequences; her body wanted him. Never had she crossed a line before, never had she wanted to. She was tired of being the good girl, tired of playing it safe. The hint of danger and the thrill of dark passion in Emery's eyes was an escape, one she needed more than her next breath.

"I'll give you anything. Name it and it's yours. I came here knowing what to expect." She threw a glance around the room, eyes touching briefly on the spanking bench before settling back on him.

He chuckled and brushed the pad of one thumb over her lips. "That's a dangerous offer." His hand dropped to her neck, his fingers curling around her throat, the touch a warning, but he didn't hurt her.

"What if I demand you strip completely and I tie you to a St. Andrews cross and fuck you senseless? Or if I require you to walk through the main room and accept any intimate touch another dom wishes to give you? Would you agree to that? There are a thousand things I could ask of you that would not just push your limits but break them. You were spooked at the sight of one little bench, and that tells me everything I need to know. You may have studied domination and submission, but you haven't lived it. The importance of this particular lifestyle is that one must always be safe, sane and consensual. Your offer shows no consideration for any of those, and half the doms outside would do things you might not consent to. You have natural submissive tendencies. It's clear from the way you responded to my commands, but we aren't in a vanilla sex world, Sophie. While this life demands trust, it is a dark world, full of fire, passion, loss of control. Are you truly ready for that?" The bite to his tone made her arousal sharp; her womb clenched in eagerness, even as she felt a cold sweat dew on her body as trepidation set in.

Sophie breathed deeply. He'd warned her, hadn't just accepted her blanket offer. *Trust.* Even as scary as what he'd mentioned sounded, she also longed for a taste of that forbidden passion. She was hungry for it. But she needed to trust him in return.

"Would you really do those things?" She glanced away then forced her eyes back. He was watching her, the way a hawk at the tallest branches of a tree might survey a rabbit in the field below. Yet he was close, so incredibly close to her he could have kissed her.

With a sigh, Emery shook his head. "Absolutely, unless of course that fell within your hard limits. I'm not a saint, and I have only the semblance of being a gentleman, but I would respect your safe word. Sharing my bed would push you right to the edge of your limits. Lucky for you, I'm in no mood to bed a woman who inherently denies her submissive nature."

"You think I'm a real submissive?" Sophie could hear the shock in her own voice. Was she truly? More importantly, could she trust him to keep his word and respect her safe word if she needed to use it?

"You are submissive. To the right man, you are. When I held you in my arms and commanded you to focus only on me, you did it without hesitation, without question. You submitted to me and it was a beautiful thing to behold. You're too strong for most, but you still crave submission. Being a sub doesn't mean you're weak. It only means you need to surrender. Many weak people crave power, crave to hurt others, to take control, but they are still inherently weak individuals."

Sophie knew that was the truth. She had met killers and murderers—pathetic examples of humanity. They were too weak to stand up for themselves when it mattered, and the resulting loss of power or control turned them toward paths of violent retribution on innocents. Such behavior was more common than it should be.

A sudden thought struck her. "What if...I let you teach me how to surrender?"

Curiosity flitted shadowlike in his eyes, but his wariness was stronger.

"I'm not sure I come out on top in this bargain. You might prove to be too much trouble." Emery moved over to the spanking bench and sat down on the edge, seemingly unbothered by its real purpose. Sophie's face heated with a treacherous blush.

It should have surprised her how much she did want to please him. He seemed an intricate puzzle and knowing her behavior was a partial key; she couldn't help but wonder what doing his bidding would unlock.

He leaned back, crossing his legs at the ankles, and looked at her. She was still on her knees, hands clenched together, fingers knotted. Sophie studied him, traced the perfectly tailored suit that clung to his body like a second skin. He was every inch the rich recluse she'd heard him to be.

People spoke of him in sad whispers, their eyes full of pity. But when Sophie met Emery's gaze, she couldn't pity him. Sympathize? Yes. Pity? No. His expression of domination demanded obedience, respect, and not one second had passed where he'd let that expression falter, except when he'd stared at the picture from his past. Only then had she seen the other Emery, the one trapped in childhood memories. The one she had to save. For that was clear. Part of this man before her needed to be saved.

"I'm not sure bedding you is worth my tale of woe." His tone sounded almost taunting, rather like he was reciting Shakespeare. He was mocking her!

Embarrassment flooded her face with heat, but her pride was pricked. Without a second thought she slipped off one shoe and threw it at him.

Thunk! It bounced off the solid wall of his muscular chest and dropped to the floor. He didn't move an inch except to drop his eyes to the shoe, and then raise his gaze again. She could feel it passing over her body as he did so.

"You just threw a shoe at me." His eyes flashed fire, but his lips twitched.

"Yeah? Well, you just implied I'm not good in bed!" Muttering to herself, she bent to remove her second shoe, wanting nothing more than to chuck that one at him too. She was completely unprepared for his reaction.

One second she had her hand on her remaining shoe, the next he'd spun her around to face the wall, his body pressing tight against hers from behind. Both her wrists were caught in one of his hands at her lower back. He rolled his hips, rubbing against her bottom, grinding a very hard erection against her miniskirt. Emery put his free hand on her stomach, his large palm making her feel incredibly small.

"You have an unusual way of expressing your temper." His low growl summoned deep shivers from the base of her spine. "Some doms like to paddle that temper out of their subs, then they pound the sub into delicious submission until the sub is dying of pleasure." He punctuated this with a sharp arch of his hips again. Her clit throbbed and her breath quickened.

Images rose in her mind—him dragging her skirt up to her waist, tearing away underwear and taking her hard from behind. Sophie jerked when her knees smacked together and she wobbled. Emery held her upright, rubbing her stomach, the pressure arousing rather than soothing.

"Don't tell me I've struck you speechless." His husky laugh was rich as scotch and burned her to the core.

He nuzzled her ear, then nipped at it. An explosion went off somewhere below her waist and Sophie sucked in a breath. Her blood pounded in her ears, and a dark mist seemed to roll across her vision as she sank into him and his teasing kisses and touches.

"I'm having trouble...thinking," she admitted through the fog that seemed to curl around the logical part of her mind.

All she could focus on was his breath on her cheek, his tongue flicking inside her ear and the stinging jabs of arousal that spiked though her lower spine and zoomed straight to her clit. She was empty, needed something inside her, needed him. Her body actually hurt with the wild craving to have him. All it would take was his thrusting into her softness and giving it to her hard enough, and she'd die from the pleasure.

"You respond well to me. Perhaps you are worth a few nights." He licked a path up from her shoulder to a spot beneath her ear, and then feathered kisses before blowing softly on the now sensitive shell of her ear. Her hands shook violently in his hold.

Then he was gone. He'd released her and stepped back. Sophie fell forward a few inches, her body resting against the wall as she fought to regain her composure. The stone against her cheek was cool and slightly rough, like the craggy rocks of a castle's keep. It lent a dungeonlike atmosphere to their sparse surroundings, more than chains and whips and other objects might have. She was at his mercy, his to torture or to pleasure, or perhaps a combination. Her clit pulsed to life at the thought of both.

"Very well. Unlace your corset."

The command was so abrupt that Sophie balked instantly. There was no way she'd do that, and it didn't have anything to do with modesty.

"You can't obey a simple command?" One golden brow arched over his eye.

"It's not that I don't want to obey..."

"Are you plagued by modesty?" His lips tilted down, but a glimmer of amusement danced briefly across his face.

"I'm not plagued, I'm naturally modest. But that's not why I can't unlace the corset."

Emery sighed and crossed his arms. "I suppose I'll give you one easy out today. Tell me why you won't open your corset and I will release you of the command to actually unlace it. Can you do that without issue?"

"Just tell you?" She could do that, couldn't she?

"For now. Someday you will show me." He raised one hand to his hair, raking his fingers through it, mussing the blond waves. It made her ache to do the same. To lie beside him in bed and know that she mussed up his hair, that she had grasped the thick shimmering strands and tugged while in the midst of passion.

"I don't like delays, Sophie," he warned.

Swallowing a shivery breath, she nodded, more for herself than him. "I've got scars." There. It was out. No going back.

"What kind of scars?" Emery's voice was soft, velvety, like he wanted to soothe her.

His question confused her.

"Scars. There isn't any other kind."

Emery's eyes trained on her. "I mean, are they scars from abuse? From an accident?"

"No abuse. Surgery."

"What did you have surgery for?"

"Explaining that isn't part of the bargain," Sophie replied. She'd agreed to submit, not tell him her every secret.

Emery stood up and left the bench to come toward her. He moved so fast she had no time to react. He snatched her wrists and dragged her over to the bench, bending her over it and spreading her knees with one thigh. He pulled her wrists back behind her body and pinned them there with one of his hands. When he pushed his leg up against the apex of her thighs beneath the skirt she whimpered. The soft, expensive fabric of his suit rubbed erotically against the sensitive skin of her thighs.

"Lesson one: never lie to your dom, or any dom. Punishment is always the result, or worse, the dom severs the relationship and releases the sub. Now, let's try this again. What was the surgery for?"

"All right!" Sophie hissed. She was madder than a wet cat, but she knew he had her beat. Still, she jerked and jostled against the bench, testing his hold. Tight. No way to get out of this.

"Stop." His bark made her flinch and go slack. "Tell the truth. I have ways of making you talk if you think to keep quiet."

Did he mean he'd spank it out of her? She wish she knew, then again, maybe she didn't want to know. Her eyelashes fell against her cheeks and darkness captured her vision, thankfully making her feel alone enough to utter the truth. "I had an accident and got cut. The surgery was to sew the cuts back together. Is that a personal enough answer for you?" She flinched, waiting for a blow.

"I didn't want a personal answer, only a truthful one. And I don't *ever* beat answers of anyone, especially a sub who surrenders to my care." Although his words suggested a chastisement, he didn't seem angry, rather puzzled and hurt that she'd assumed he'd beat it out of her.

"How did you know I was afraid you would hit me?" she whispered.

"You flinched after you lashed out verbally. I've seen that before in other submissives. You expected me to spank you, but know this, I don't ever react with violence, only with erotic punishment. There is a difference and I will teach you."

Very slowly, he withdrew his leg from between her thighs and released her wrists. Sophie lay for a moment, unsure of what to do. But rather than standing, Emery sat on the floor and reached for her. He took her in his arms and laid her on the floor beside him. Sophie gasped as he settled over her. If she hadn't been so distracted by his close proximity she might have laughed. Emery Lockwood did not strike her as the type of man to prefer the missionary position.

But Sophie was distracted; he invaded her space, gently took hold of her wrists again and secured them to the floor above her head. He slid one hand down her ribs, over her belly and then between her knees, parting them so his hips could sink into the cradle of her legs. He rocked his pelvis forward, rubbing against her, showing her she couldn't shift, couldn't move unless he wished her to.

It had been ages since she'd been this close to a man, with every inch of their bodies touching except their lips, and his were so temptingly close. The last time hadn't affected her like this. Her universe was shrinking around this one single moment, to just the two of them. Their gazes locked.

"This is personal. My past is personal, Sophie. Everything you want from me and what I want from you is personal." His free hand slid up from her hip to rest on her lower ribcage. He toyed with the loose ribbon of her corset. She could feel him tug, tease, but not undo the laces any further. Still, he could if he wished; he could pry the corset open and see her scars, her ugliness.

Sophie's breath hitched, her breasts rising rapidly as she struggled to breathe.

Concern darkened his eyes. "You're like a frightened little sparrow, your chest heaving as you beat against the cat's paw holding you down. *Relax*, Sophie," he murmured. "Otherwise I might lose my already tenuous control. As a dom, I am aroused by your apprehension. I love bringing a woman to the fine edge between trust and fear. I'd never hurt you, but still I'm determined to push your boundaries, test your limits, and I know that scares you just as much as it arouses you." His once silky tone was now gruff and a little ragged.

The truth of his words was like a whip cracking in her

mind, more sharp and agonizing than anything she'd ever felt on her skin.

Sophie bucked her hips, trying to dislodge him. "Damn you!" His large erection dug into her, making her womb throb.

As though he could sense her rising need and frustration, Emery's eyes swirled with lust and hunger.

"So you have scars and they upset you," he observed.

She raised her chin, glowering at him. "Well, it's humiliating. Men don't like my...my..." To her own shame, her voice wavered.

"They don't like your breasts?" The sheer look of incredulity on his face startled her.

"Uh huh." Sophie shut her eyes, shame smashing her insides like a sledgehammer through fine china.

God, let this humiliation be over quickly. Every other man had left her alone after hearing this. Emery wouldn't be any different. He was too sexy, too gorgeous to ever settle for a scarred woman like her, not when he could have his pick.

Emery held still, didn't make a sound or move until she opened her eyes. When she did finally look up at him, he dropped his head a few inches, his nose touching hers, nuzzling her cheek.

"I'm not like other men, Sophie. Scars are a sign of strength, survival. Someday you'll be brave enough to show me, and I'll prove you have nothing to be ashamed of. Now, I am willing to accept the deal you proposed. Are you willing in return?"

She bit her lip. It had been her idea; she had to see it through. She wanted to see it through, even if it scared the living daylights out of her.

"Yes. I'll do it. Your story, my submission."

Want to find out what happens next? Grab Emery and Sophie's book HERE!

OTHER TITLES BY LAUREN SMITH

Historical

The League of Rogues Series

Wicked Designs

His Wicked Seduction

Her Wicked Proposal

Wicked Rivals

Her Wicked Longing

His Wicked Embrace

The Earl of Pembroke

His Wicked Secret

The Wicked Earls Club

The Earl of Pembroke

The Seduction Series

The Duelist's Seduction

The Rakehell's Seduction

The Rogue's Seduction

The Gentleman's Seduction

The Sins and Scandals Series

An Earl By Any Other Name

A Gentleman Never Surrenders
A Scottish Lord for Christmas

Standalone Stories

Tempted by A Rogue
Bewitching the Earl

Contemporary

Ever After Series

Legally Charming

The Surrender Series

The Gilded Cuff
The Gilded Cage
The Gilded Chain
The Darkest Hour

Her British Stepbrother

Forbidden: Her British Stepbrother
Seduction: Her British Stepbrother
Climax: Her British Stepbrother
Forever Be Mine (Coming soon)

Paranormal

Brothers of Ash and Fire

Grigori
Mikhail
Rurik
The Lost Barinov Dragon (coming soon)

Dark Seductions Series

The Shadows of Stormclyffe Hall

The Love Bites Series

The Bite of Winter

Brotherhood of the Blood Moon Series

Blood Moon on the Rise (coming soon)

Sci-Fi Romance

Cyborg Genesis Series

Across the Stars (coming soon)

ABOUT THE AUTHOR

USA TODAY Bestselling Author Lauren Smith is an Oklahoma attorney by day, who pens adventurous and edgy romance stories by the light of her smart phone flashlight app. She knew she was destined to be a romance writer when she attempted to re-write the entire *Titanic* movie just to save Jack from drowning. Connecting with readers by writing emotionally moving, realistic and sexy romances no matter what time period is her passion. She's won multiple awards in several romance subgenres including: New England Reader's Choice Awards, Greater Detroit Book-Seller's Best Awards, and a Semi-Finalist award for the Mary Wollstonecraft Shelley Award.

To connect with Lauren, visit her at:

www.laurensmithbooks.com
lauren@Laurensmithbooks.com

7948

CPSIA information can be obtained
at www.ICGtesting.com
Printed in the USA
LVHW110840011218
598389LV00001BA/41/P